# BLIND DATE WITH A BOOK

EMILY KERR

One More Chapter
a division of HarperCollins*Publishers* Ltd
1 London Bridge Street
London SE1 9GF
www.harpercollins.co.uk
HarperCollins*Publishers*
Macken House, 39/40 Mayor Street Upper,
Dublin 1, D01 C9W8, Ireland
This paperback edition 2026

1

First published in Great Britain in ebook format
by HarperCollins*Publishers* 2026
Copyright © Emily Kerr 2026
Emily Kerr asserts the moral right to be identified
as the author of this work
A catalogue record of this book is available from the British Library
ISBN: 978-0-00-878940-4

This novel is entirely a work of fiction. The names, characters and incidents portrayed in it are the work of the author's imagination. Any resemblance to actual persons, living or dead, events or localities is entirely coincidental.

Printed and bound in the UK using 100% Renewable Electricity by CPI Group (UK) Ltd

Emily Kerr has been scribbling stories on bits of paper ever since she learnt how to write. She studied Classics at the University of Oxford and loved her time living in the city of dreaming spires. As well as writing feel-good romances, she works as a journalist and is based in Yorkshire.

She can generally be found with her nose in a book or hunched up over her laptop typing away, although she has been known to venture outside every so often to take part in various running-based activities.

Her novel Take a Chance on Greece won the Jane Wenham-Jones Romantic Comedy Award at the Romantic Novelists' Association Awards in 2023.

www.emilykerrwrites.com

 instagram.com/emilykerrwrites
 facebook.com/emilykerrwrites

*To booksellers, the wonderful matchmakers who help readers find the right book at the right time.*

## Chapter One

'Oh my days, this place is the absolute cutest. It's like a doll house, but on water.'

I smiled proudly as the excitable tourist bounced around the shop, cooing at my hand-painted bookshelves and gazing in awe at the hundreds of volumes sitting on them.

'Let me know if you need any help,' I said, already itching to steer her towards the corner with the Jane Austen books. There was a brand-new edition of *Emma* which I had a strong feeling would be the perfect match for her, with its frustrating but ultimately endearing heroine. Call it my bookseller sixth sense, but somehow I had a knack for uniting the right book with the right person, and nothing gave me more of a thrill. When she next glanced in my direction, I'd make the recommendation, I decided, already picturing her expression of eager anticipation when she read the blurb and realised that this was the perfect novel for her current mood.

'Can you take my picture?' she asked instead, sending me crashing back to depressing reality.

'No problem,' I said, studiously polite. 'Are you ready? Say cheese.'

I sighed inwardly as she draped herself against a bookshelf in a practised pose. Yet another of *those* visitors who somehow never converted their love for the shop's aesthetics into becoming actual customers of its wares. They never failed to disappoint me.

'Hold on, I need a prop.'

Before I could respond, she'd grabbed a brand-new paperback at random from the central display. I winced as she audibly cracked its spine, then peeked coyly over the top of the open book and gestured impatiently for me to take the snap. Being an old hand at this kind of thing (unfortunately), I took half a dozen, zooming in for a couple, then passed the phone back. She discarded the paperback and scrolled through the pictures, frowning as she quickly added filters to her chosen image.

'Don't forget to tag the Oxford Bookship when you post it online,' I said, but it was already too late as she was out of the door and heading down the towpath without a backwards glance.

'Maybe I should pivot to being a professional photographer rather than a bookseller, what do you think, Hilda?' I pondered glumly as I tidied up the display, running my finger down the now-tarnished paperback and silently apologising to it for the way it had been mistreated. If the tourist had shown a genuine interest in the book's contents, I wouldn't have minded so much, but I couldn't forgive her casual carelessness all for the sake of the 'gram.

Hilda beat her tail sympathetically from her usual position sprawled out on the well deck, which set the boat gently rocking. If visitors to the Oxford Bookship didn't ask me to take pictures for their socials, they generally instead quizzed me about the wisdom of living on a narrowboat with an Irish wolfhound, one of the largest dog breeds in the world. Sadly, what they rarely did was actually purchase one of the books which filled my canal boat's main cabin.

When I first started trading just over a year ago, I'd rationalised the sluggish sales as being due to the newness of my boat bookshop venture, then as time wore on, the poor weather over autumn and winter had seemed like the obvious reason why would-be customers weren't wandering along the towpath to spend their wages on my lovingly curated stock. But Oxford was now basking in early summer, the streets thronging with visitors as well as the usual students and locals, and still my card machine spent more time gathering dust than processing payments.

I pushed the negative thought to the back of my mind, and went to join Hilda outside, taking a book with me. As she took up a good chunk of the deck area at the front of the boat, I clambered onto the roof instead and stretched out on a sun lounger next to my beautiful hand-painted Oxford Bookship sign to await more customers. Things would get better, I told myself fiercely, and I might as well enjoy the bookseller benefits of having a vast array of reading material at my fingertips.

'Ahoy there, Ms Bramble. Permission to come aboard.'

The voice dragged me away from Jane Eyre's bleak childhood experiences and back to reality. I blinked and gazed around in confusion, trying to pull myself out of the jet lag-like disconnect I always experienced when interrupted mid reading flow.

'Oh, hi, Eric, nice to see you,' I said, although in truth, I would much rather he hadn't turned up until I was at least at the end of a chapter. I was also slightly perturbed by his formal manner of address. Whenever he Ms Brambled me rather than using plain old Molly, it was usually followed by bad news. I sat up straighter and self-consciously tried to smooth my always unruly hair, aware that I'd been anxiously twirling it around my fingers as Jane endured the horrors of being locked in the Red Room by her cruel aunt. 'Do hop on. If Hilda's in the way, just give her a gentle shove. She won't mind,' I added.

Eric Sanderson, retired academic turned extremely diligent chairman of the Oxford Boating Association, adjusted the knot of his tie and shuffled awkwardly. Yep, the formal outfit confirmed it. He was definitely here on official business. Eric led the organisation, which made sure the Oxford Canal and all who used it were kept in order. The ducks couldn't even quack without Eric and his colleagues in the Association knowing about it or having an opinion on the acceptable decibel level they should be communicating at. My Nana Rose claimed that when Eric was off duty, he could be a right laugh, but the trouble was that since I'd opened the Bookship, I'd mostly encountered him in managing mode.

Eric tentatively picked his way over Hilda's limbs as she watched him benevolently. I hoped she was feeling too lazy today to sit up and sniff his crotch, which had been her mortifying trick last time he'd stopped by. She was normally impeccably polite with visitors, but her cheeky side had a tendency to emerge at the most inopportune moments, and generally with the most inappropriate of people. Thankfully on this occasion she restricted herself to a single twitch of the tail and a pointed yawn, before rolling over and going back to sleep.

I waited a moment or two for the subsequent Hilda-induced rocking to subside, then slid down from the roof and joined Eric in the cabin. Maybe I could distract him from whatever blow he was about to deliver by steering him towards the second-hand book I'd recently acquired on the history of time, which I reckoned would appeal to his love of order and precision.

'Trade good today?' he asked, nodding his head towards the jam-packed shelves. Space is at a premium on a narrowboat, so I made use of every available nook and cranny to display my stock. When Eric had first visited to check out my new venture, he'd raised an eyebrow and muttered about the 'chaotic atmosphere' which I knew was the complete antithesis of the ultra-modern hybrid narrowboat with sleek Scandi-inspired interiors he lived aboard during the summer months. But even he couldn't deny that the Oxford Bookship was a bibliophile's paradise, a treasure trove of volumes both new and second-hand stacked from floor to ceiling, every one of them carefully chosen, waiting to be united by me with their perfect reader.

If only more readers would turn up and actually make a purchase.

'Couldn't be better,' I lied cheerily, and tried not to think about the £21.73 which was the sum total of my takings so far today, a meagre figure which sadly wasn't an anomaly. The community on and around the Oxford Canal was a close-knit one, and news travelled fast along the towpath. I didn't want to run the risk of any of my business worries reaching Nana Rose in her care home. As far as she was concerned, I was living out my dreams and enjoying the perfect existence working on her old canal boat. And I was – I really was – as long as I managed to suppress the terrifying worries about my paltry turnover and the rapidly dwindling savings I barely scraped by on. I couldn't bear the thought of the Oxford Bookship, the embodiment of everything I'd ever hoped for, becoming the latest in my string of life failures, consequently proving my horrid ex right in his damning assessment that I was 'too wedded to made-up stuff in books' to be able to succeed in the real world.

'Excellent news, that's really good to hear,' said Eric. 'That makes me feel less concerned about delivering this.'

He took a crisp white envelope out of his jacket pocket and a pit opened in my stomach. I had a horrible feeling I knew exactly what that envelope contained, and I'd rather he put it straight back in his pocket and let me retreat to the safety of fictional jeopardy. Sadly, he held it out to me, and I had no choice but to take it.

I glanced down at the neatly typed label.

## Ms Molly Bramble
## The Oxford Bookship
## Oxford Canal

It was rare to see it written out like that. One of the quirks of living on water was that I didn't really have a proper address, and all of my post had to be sent to a PO box on land. Nana Rose had tried to persuade me to direct my mail to her care home when I moved on board, but when the final demand notices started arriving in the post as well as by email, I was relieved I hadn't succumbed. My beloved grandmother was still as feisty as she had always been, but there was no escaping the fragility of her limbs beneath the jewel-coloured outfits she loved, which were all slightly too big for her now. It was more important than ever to protect her from the fears which dominated my life.

'Thanks Eric,' I said, although gratitude was the last thing on my mind.

'The payment's due by September, as always. That work for you?' he asked politely, though we both knew it wasn't really a question.

'Absolutely,' I said, injecting as much enthusiasm into my tone as I could.

While living on water was undoubtedly less pricey than battling the rental market on land in Oxford, there were still some expenses which were unavoidable, mooring fees being one of them. And given the popularity of the waterways around Oxford, the mooring fees were high. I was in the extremely fortunate position of having a permanent berth for the Oxford Bookship, in a prime spot just a gentle stroll from the historic streets of Jericho. Before I took over the vessel, it had belonged to Nana Rose, and she'd negotiated a long-term contract for its mooring location, which had since been signed over to me. But it would only remain mine for as long as I could continue to pay for it. The fees were calculated upon the size of the boat, and what the Oxford Bookship lacked in width, she more than made up for in length. Sixty feet – or just over eighteen metres in modern money – of beautiful, traditional canal boat. When I started out last year, it was an expense I'd naively planned to cover through a combination of profits and savings. What I hadn't anticipated was how little I'd have of either at this point.

'Aren't you going to open it?' Eric asked, as if he'd handed me a birthday card rather than a bill.

'I guess so,' I said, although I'd actually been intending to file the envelope away safely under my laptop in the cabin and study its contents on another day when I was feeling braver. I glanced out of a porthole, hoping to see a crowd of customers heading down the towpath to give me the perfect excuse to get rid of my unwanted visitor and pretend this whole situation wasn't happening, but no such luck.

'Here goes,' I said. I got a papercut as I tore the envelope open, which seemed like a bad omen. Blood smeared on the thick letter paper as I unfolded it, and my immediate ridiculous response to seeing the figure written there was that no wonder the Oxford Boating Association could afford such luxurious stationery.

'It's had to go up a little,' said Eric, a note of apology in his voice.

I tried to swallow the boulder which had appeared in my throat. This innocuous, horrid piece of paper essentially signalled the death knell of my beloved business. 'A little? This is more than a little.' I quickly did the sums in my head, trying to stave off my rising panic. Surely this had to be a mistake. Even in my worst-case scenario imaginings I'd never thought it would be this bad. 'This is a 20 per cent increase. Even council tax doesn't go up by that much in a year.'

Eric nodded, as if he'd been expecting that response, then trotted out the party line.

'The Association has done its best to keep the fees down. We wrestled with the accounts long and hard to minimise the increase. But as an organisation we can only absorb so many costs, and with prices for everything going up...' His voice trailed off. 'Anyway, I'm glad that business is going well. So it won't be a problem, will it?'

He wanted me to reassure him. Pompous as he could be at times, underneath it all, Eric was a good man who genuinely cared about the canal and the people who lived and worked on it. Nana Rose had spent nearly eight decades as the heart of the boating community at this very mooring, and I knew Eric was delighted that I was continuing the Bramble family tradition. But being Nana Rose's granddaughter would only give me so many privileges. At the end of the day, the Oxford Boating Association had many miles of canal and towpaths to maintain, and they could only do that if everybody paid their way. If I didn't find the £4,500 fee by the end of the summer, the Oxford Boating Association would serve me with an eviction notice for my mooring, regardless of the chairman's soft spot for my grandmother. And that would be the end of the Oxford Bookship. Sure, I could change my boating licence to a continuous cruiser one and start travelling around the rest of the UK's waterways, but if trade was bad in a permanent location, it would be even worse in a scenario where I was having to move the boat to a different place every two weeks with zero chance of building up a regular clientele. Besides, it would break Nana Rose's heart to lose the long-held Bramble mooring. And it would break my heart to have to move away from her and the rest of the Oxford boating community who meant so much to me. This city had always been my home, and I desperately wanted it to remain so. I couldn't imagine myself living anywhere else.

'It'll be fine,' I said, doing my best to sound like the confident, successful business owner that I wished I was.

'Marvellous,' said Eric, looking relieved. I must have been a better actor than I thought I was. 'The bank transfer details are all on the letter. As I mentioned, the payment is due by September, but if you want to get it out of the way sooner, that's not a problem. Once you've made the transfer, you should receive an immediate automated response acknowledging that it's arrived safely, as per our usual system.'

'Sounds good.' There was definitely an edge of hysteria in my voice now, but Eric seemed oblivious to it.

'Excellent. See you around, Molly love.' Now business had been completed, he was back to calling me by my first name.

'See you.'

Eric walked towards the door, then stopped in his tracks by the small turquoise trolley which displayed my latest sales promotion, a collection of books artfully wrapped up in brown paper.

'What kind of books are you selling there? Nothing … inappropriate, I hope,' he said, looking all uncomfortable again.

I managed a smile as I realised where he was going with his misguided assumption. 'Don't worry, the erotic literature is at the other end of the cabin.' Eric's eyes widened in embarrassment, and I took pity on him. 'They're my Blind Date with a Book selection. Look, they've all got labels with clues on them indicating the genre and key themes, but readers don't get to find out the title or author until they've bought and unwrapped it.'

'Ah, that sounds fun,' said Eric, visibly relaxing. 'They do say you shouldn't judge a book by its cover after all.'

'Exactly. It's a good way of helping people to discover new authors, or books that they might have dismissed as being "not for them". The right book always has a way of finding the reader who needs it.'

Eric raised an eyebrow at what he no doubt considered to be whimsy, but he shuffled through the selection, pausing to peruse a couple of the labels I'd spent so much time and effort writing.

'A woman embarks on a mission to track down the "Awesome Andreas" whose name she's drunkenly had tattooed on her back after a wild night out in Greece,' he read out loud. 'Goodness me. I'm glad it says it's a romantic comedy. The situation sounds like a complete nightmare to me. I'll get it for my granddaughter; it might be the kind of thing she'll enjoy as a break from university finals revision. Hopefully it'll put her off getting a tattoo.'

I wasn't convinced it would have the effect he wanted.

Eric handed over a twenty-pound note, and I opened up my cash box to find the correct change, but he shook his head. 'Don't worry. You keep it. I'm delighted to have her birthday gift sorted and wrapped ready to go as well. You take care now, Molly.'

There was a hint of tenderness in his expression. Maybe I wasn't such a good actor after all. I didn't want to accept Eric's pity-inspired generosity, but I wasn't exactly in a position to refuse it.

'That's very kind of you,' I said.

He was nearly back on shore when I swallowed yet more of my pride and called after him.

'Is there any chance of a payment plan for the mooring fees?' If I could spread the cost out and trade improved, then maybe, just maybe I could make it work.

He softly patted Hilda's wiry head before he replied.

'I'm afraid the committee voted against offering payment plans several years ago. The decision is regularly reviewed, but unfortunately, I don't think our position is going to change by the time this year's fees are due. I'm sorry, Molly. I wish I could give you a different answer.'

His sympathetic grimace was nearly my undoing.

'That's fine, not a problem at all. Just thought I'd ask,' I said as cheerfully as I could manage. 'The money will be with you by September.'

Now I urgently needed to find a way to make that happen.

## Chapter Two

I tried to forget about the contents of the crisp white envelope as I carried on with the rest of my day, but terrifying words such as 'failure' kept leaping out from the pages of the book I was attempting to distract myself with, and even Hilda's tail seemed to be beating in rhythmic clusters of four and a half thuds reminding me I had to somehow find a thousand times that amount by the end of the summer. If only I were a pampered pooch whose biggest worry was how long it was until my next walk.

'Maybe I should set you up as a doggy influencer? The Hildabeast does Only Paws, what do you reckon?' I suggested to her. Her unimpressed response was to unleash a silent but deadly protest fart and go to stand staring pointedly at the door which led through to the private part of the boat.

'You're right. I should probably shut up shop. I reckon we've had our quota of business for the day, sadly. A watched-for customer never arrives and all that. Maybe that's where I've been going wrong.' Hilda made a low rumbling noise. 'Okay, okay, I know there are far more important things to consider at this moment in time, like sorting your dinner. Is that what you're after by any chance?'

Hilda blinked at me, doing her best impression of a mournful, deprived hound.

'I'll take that as a yes then. A much more sensible option than trying to pimp you out on the internet. I'm not going to lie, it would save me a fortune in dog food if we could get you a sponsorship deal. But I wouldn't be without you for the world.'

I rescued Hilda from a shelter eighteen months ago, although as many other pet parents have discovered, it was fair to say that in reality, she was the one to rescue me. I was stuck in yet another soul-destroying admin job, lacking direction and desperate to get off the treadmill of mundanity, but equal parts terrified and clueless about how to do it. Hilda's picture had popped up on one of my social media feeds, an underdog at the local rescue centre, constantly passed over because of her size. As someone who was six foot and gangling rather than gorgeous with it, I could empathise with her situation. I'd taken one look at her scruffy features and the description of her as a 'bundle of intelligence' and fallen in love. And when I first met her, miraculously, she'd seemed to feel the same way about me.

Hilda's expression of utterly devoted admiration as we'd finally walked away from the shelter together had made me feel invincible for the first time in my life. So when Nana Rose admitted a few weeks later that life afloat was becoming too hard and she might be forced to sell her beloved canal boat, bolstered by new-found confidence from the unquestioning faith of my four-legged best friend, I'd come up with a plan which would make my grandmother happy again and allow me to fulfil a dream I'd harboured ever since I could remember. I battled the banks to get every loan going and bought the boat from Nana Rose, so I could transform it into the cosy bookshop I'd always fantasised about opening. In my head, it would become a magnet for book lovers, the floating hub of Oxford's thriving literary scene, and I'd spend my days chatting about the stories I loved with fellow enthusiasts who would all leave the boat laden down with dozens of purchases apiece. Instead, I spent more time talking aloud to Hilda in lieu of the elusive customers, read more books than I sold and spent an inordinate number of hours staring helplessly at spreadsheets detailing my financial nightmare. It would have been much safer to stick to the daydreams. And now I had a deadline of September to turn it all around somehow or… No, I wasn't going to allow myself to think of the alternative. I had to make this work. Despite the stresses of running my own business, I couldn't imagine doing anything else now that I'd had a taste of being my own boss. And I definitely couldn't let Nana Rose down.

I took one last wistful look down the empty towpath, then went through the motions of bringing the Oxford Bookship sign in, locking up and checking through the day's accounts. It wasn't the worst day I'd ever had, but at this rate the only way I was going to be able to cover the mooring fees would be if I won the lottery, which wasn't going to happen as I never bought tickets, warned off by Nana Rose's declaration that it was a 'tax on hope'. Nevertheless, I could do with a bit of hope at the moment.

Hilda made another low grumbling noise, a gentle reminder that she was practically starving to death while I dawdled my way through closing up.

'Okay, you win. Work is officially over for the day, and it's dinner time for my bestest girl,' I said.

She shoved the door open with her nose, clattered through the boat's tiny bathroom and then let out a sonorous woof next to the cupboard in our living space where I stored her food. I pushed my way past her and prepared the meal under her close supervision. As soon as it was ready, she nudged open the rear door of the barge and leapt gracefully onto the towpath, doing a few celebratory spins in the little garden as I followed and set up her bowl on the raised platform I'd created out of an old packing crate so she didn't have to bend the significant distance down to the ground. She'd dropped a few hints about preferring to eat off the table in my galley-cum-living-room-cum-bedroom, but I had to maintain some standards.

While Hilda feasted on her luxury grain-free dog food specially formulated at great expense to suit her delicate stomach, I stared at the uninspiring contents of my tiny fridge. In the Oxford Bookship, the bulk of the food budget went on the four-legged resident, while I made do with whatever yellow-sticker items I could pick up. I really needed to do a shop at some point, although it would be better for my bank balance if I could delay it for as long as possible. On-the-turn cheese on toast it was. Again.

But on-the-turn cheese on toast prepared on board my very own canal boat was still better than any high-end landlocked version, I reminded myself. As I chomped my way through my meal, I considered the problem facing me. September was only three months away. That gave me approximately ninety days, which was over 2,100 hours. I forced myself to stop before my brain descended into the minutes and seconds calculations. The point to hang on to was that I had time, not a huge chunk of it, but time nevertheless. All I needed to do was apply myself to the problem and come up with a sensible and achievable plan of action to save my beloved boat bookshop. Simple. If only.

'We will not be defeated,' I said determinedly to Hilda who had returned on board to lounge at my feet and dream peacefully of her next meal. I looked around my modest living space and marvelled once again that I got to call it my home. From the wood-burning stove in the corner of the tiny kitchen area to the comfy sofa bench which transformed into my bed at night, every carefully chosen feature was a feat of clever design that made the most of each inch of space. As a small child I'd played house on board this boat during the school holidays when Nana Rose looked after me while my parents were at work, never thinking that one day it would actually become my home. The Oxford Bookship looked very different from when I was little, thanks to the months of renovation work I'd put in to transform the place from a boat that had barely changed since the mid-twentieth century when it was built, to the welcoming bookshop and snug home it was now. To keep the costs to a minimum, I'd learnt how to build bookshelves, strip down an engine and even fix a broken toilet pump-out system, thanks to a combination of trial and error, and YouTube tutorials. I was proud of what I had accomplished. Teachers at school and employers in the series of dead-end jobs I'd taken for most of my twenties had said I was too much of an impractical daydreamer to make a success of myself, but in establishing my business and setting up my canal boat home, I was determined to prove them all wrong. The gleaming Oxford Bookship was a floating representation of what I could achieve when I put my mind to it. And I was blowed if I was going to let the matter of expensive mooring fees bring my dreams to a premature end.

I stood up decisively. Instead of brooding for the rest of the night, I was going to carry on as normal. Solutions were more likely to present themselves if I wasn't bogged down in panic.

'Come on, Hilda, time for an evening stroll.'

Hilda was never one to say no to a walk. She made a token protest against putting her harness on, being, like me, a creature who preferred freedom, but we were soon strolling down the towpath away from Isis Lock and towards the streets of Jericho. It was peaceful alongside the canal at this time of the evening. The mooring next to the Oxford Bookship had lain empty ever since I moved in, and the owners of the berths closer to civilisation were still out at work, or busy below deck getting their tea on, judging by the variety of tantalising cooking smells wafting on the breeze.

A family of ducks swam casually past, having a final

outing before they retreated to their nests in the undergrowth. The sound of Oxford's ever-present traffic was more of a distant hum, fading into the background against the sweet trilling of the birds and the occasional splashes from the fish swimming to pick insects from the surface of the canal. It seemed extraordinary to believe that somewhere so serene could exist in a city inhabited by over a hundred and fifty thousand people.

A fellow dog walker hove into view, and we exchanged pleasantries as our canine companions carried out their sniff approvals of each other. In this corner of the city, strangers were happy to acknowledge each other, relaxed by the canal's presence into the assumption of friendliness more commonly seen in villages or small towns. She told me about some moorhen chicks that she'd seen playing near one of the old tumbledown boatsheds that the Oxford Boating Association was trying to sell, and I made a mental note to wander there without Hilda at some point. Hilda was always incredibly gentle around other animals, but we were both conscious that her size could be off-putting for those meeting her for the first time. I casually name-dropped the Oxford Bookship a few times, in the hope of recruiting another customer, then after a final nod (me) and wag of the tail (Hilda), we continued on our way.

'Fancy seeing the bright lights of the big city?' I asked Hilda, wanting to prolong our walk. I interpreted the twitch of her ears as assent, although the movement could equally have been provoked by the cackle of a mallard as it took off from the surface of the canal.

We climbed over the footbridge and dived among the

terraced houses which lined the streets of Jericho. Although the Victorian buildings were fairly uniform in architecture, they all asserted their own personalities, with a selection of brightly coloured front doors, rainbow rendering and chaotically verdant pots lined up on doorsteps. A couple of students whizzed past on their bikes, laughing loudly about a friend who'd fallen asleep in the middle of a lecture. Perhaps I should invest in textbooks to attract more of the academic market? I quickly dismissed the idea. I'd never be able to compete against the discounts which the land-based chains in the city could offer. Besides, I didn't have the capital to outlay on yet more products. I needed to find a way of increasing custom for the stock I already had.

Hilda and I turned another corner. Now businesses started to appear – independent coffee shops with their own roasteries, a pizza place where the chefs were skilfully throwing the dough at a central cooking station surrounded by their customers, and a pub from which the sounds of a microphone being tested echoed out through the welcoming open door.

'Check, check, one-two, one-two. Can anyone hear me?'

The gathering crowd responded with a chorus of good-natured heckling to the would-be compère. I paused, curious as to what had drawn such a large group of people on what was after all a pretty average Tuesday night at the end of May. Normally when Hilda and I walked past at this time on a weekday evening, it was deathly quiet in there.

'Ladies and gentlemen, welcome to the Boaters' Ale House. We're delighted you've all joined us for our quiz night.

It's great to see so many new faces, as well as welcoming back our lovely regulars. This week the theme for the quiz is everything Oxford, and then at the end of the evening, we'll be voting for next week's theme. Remember, if you buy a meal with us tonight, you get your quiz entry refunded.'

A couple of people cheered at this announcement. The presence of the enthusiastic crowd had got me wondering. It was only a kernel of an idea, but it was something. If a sleepy pub could create a hubbub by holding a Tuesday evening quiz, perhaps I could create a similar buzz by hosting some kind of event night at the Oxford Bookship. People could buy a ticket and then get the cost of it reimbursed if they bought a certain amount of books, which they'd probably do for the sake of a free ticket. After all, hadn't I fallen into the trap of topping up an online shopping basket for dog supplies just the other day in order to qualify for the free delivery service? But what kind of event could I hold that would make it stand out from all the other bookish events happening in the city? I needed a brainstorming session, and I knew exactly the person to have it with. I'd just have to be careful not to let slip the reason I was having to branch out from bookselling into hosting.

'Come on, Hilda, let's go and find Nana Rose.'

She picked up her pace immediately, delighted at the prospect of visiting her second-favourite person in the whole world. At least, I told myself it was that way round, although given that Nana Rose kept a stock of luxury treats for her great-grand-*dog*-ter, as she called Hilda, it could very well be that our positions in the love rankings were reversed.

Nana Rose was in her usual place, snuggled up on a window seat in the communal living room of her care home, munching on her favourite chocolate caramels and no doubt teasing the care assistants about their taste in TV viewing. I paused outside for a few moments, taking the opportunity to observe her unawares, trying to reassure myself that she was doing alright on land. I often worried that her life force depended on the canal, and that her increased weakness was because she no longer resided on its waters. I frowned as I spotted her wincing in pain as she moved position on the seat. She'd deny it if I said anything to her, but I wondered if I should have a quiet word with one of the staff members. I knew she'd be far too stubborn to listen if I suggested she should ask the doctor to review her medication for the debilitating arthritis which riddled her bones, but maybe she would pay more attention if someone outside the family spoke to her about it.

An urgent rapping on the window interrupted my thoughts. I waved back at Nana Rose, who was now beckoning me in with a huge smile on her face. Nothing escaped her notice for long.

'Let's go, Hilda,' I said, holding her lead more tightly now to keep me grounded. However friendly and welcoming the staff were, and however homely they'd made the place, it still felt like an institution, a world apart from life on the canal, and even though it was less than a mile away, I still wasn't used to seeing Nana Rose in such a different environment. But it had been Nana Rose's choice to move here, I reminded myself. And she had made new friends, enjoyed a packed routine of teaching craft classes to her fellow residents, and no longer had to worry about having to feed the log burner on cold days, or get up in the middle of the night to check the mooring ropes were still secure when the weather was bad. Her former neighbours on the canal were regular visitors and a couple of them were even members of staff at the home, plus I did my best to keep her appraised of most things that were happening on the water.

I checked in at the front desk, then walked into the super-heated lounge where Nana Rose was already on her feet and opening her arms.

'Molly, my darling girl,' she said, the joy in her musical voice making me wish I'd not left my visit to so late in the evening. 'And you've brought your emotional support dog too,' she added with a wink. 'What a delight to see you both.'

Technically only residents' pets were allowed at the Jericho Grange Care Home, but the staff were such big fans of Nana Rose that they turned a blind eye. Besides, Hilda with her knack for gentle empathy was a popular guest for even the most dog-phobic of residents.

I leaned down and kissed Nana Rose's soft cheek, the floral waft of her Chanel Chance perfume setting off an instant wave of nostalgic memories.

'How are you doing, oh Nana mine?' I asked, gently clasping her tiny hand, trying not to wince at her painfully swollen knuckles.

'All the better for seeing you, my darling.' She held me

at arm's length and looked me up and down, nodding with approval. I was pleased I was wearing one of the colourful patchwork skirts she'd made for me several years ago out of clothing which had been heading to the landfill. I'd always admired her ability to see the potential in overlooked things, even when it was very well hidden. That trait had seen her backing me on more than one occasion when everyone else, including myself, had despaired. I would never forget how Nana Rose had stood up for me when I'd devastated my parents by flunking my A-Levels. 'Molly has talents that exams are too blunt an instrument to detect,' she'd said. I'd struggled to believe her at the time, and a decade later, I feared I was going to prove her wrong all over again.

'You're looking very well,' said Nana Rose, blissfully ignorant of my internal torment. 'And what a pretty little star you have in. Somebody with exquisite taste must have bought you that delightful nose stud.'

'The best person I know,' I said.

Her eyes twinkled with pleasure. My best friend, Flick, always said that her grandma would have had a fit if she'd come home with a nose piercing, but my Nana Rose had taken me to have it done herself on my sixteenth birthday. 'You're from a long line of unconventional women, my darling girl,' she'd said, holding my hand as the piercer did his work. 'Never let anyone dull your shine or force you into society's identikit moulds.' It was a motto I tried my best to live by, although it felt increasingly hard to do so with the realities of my current situation.

'It must be my lucky day for visitors,' she said now.

'Come, sit down.' She lowered herself back onto the window seat and patted the space next to her. 'You two are definitely the best ones so far, fear not. Eric Sanderson stopped by a little earlier, full of all the latest dramas from the Boating Association's AGM. Those committee members are far too fond of the sound of their own voices, if you ask me. They spend too much time locked in meeting rooms rather than out on the water, and why Eric was bothering with wearing a suit and tie, I do not know. Totally impractical for any kind of boating activity, and the poor man was soon sweating in this place. They keep it hot because of all the old dears, you know. They weren't lucky enough to spend most of their lives without central heating, and I'm sure it's affected their temperature regulation. Anyway, I told Eric he must be having a hot flush, and he looked mortified.'

Her laugh was a gurgle of wicked delight.

'Nana, you really shouldn't tease him,' I said with a smile. 'You know how seriously he takes everything. He'll cancel my rubbish collections and escort me off the canal if you're too hard on him.'

Her expression suddenly turned grave, and I realised my error immediately. I'd opened the conversation into potentially dangerous territory.

'Is everything alright with you?' she asked, never one to miss a trick.

'I'm fine and dandy, as always,' I said, relieved that she hadn't specifically asked about how the Oxford Bookship was doing. I didn't want to have to lie to her, but it would be difficult to avoid answering a direct question about the health of my business without making it obvious. The last thing I wanted was for her to start worrying about me.

I could see that she was preparing for a follow up question, but thankfully one of the care assistants, who also happened to be a fellow canal dweller, arrived with a tray of tea and biscuits for us and a bowl of water for Hilda.

'Thanks, Bill, that's very kind of you.'

He cleared his throat and glanced around to check that no one else in the room was paying attention. 'Rozina heard that we had a special visitor and sent these through from the kitchen, if that's okay with you.'

He pulled a silver foil cover off one of the plates on the tray to reveal the sausages which his wife had prepared for Hilda.

'They're freshly cooked, so you might want to wait a few minutes for them to cool down. Or if Hilda's already had her meal quota for the day, feel free to wrap them up and take them back to the Bookship for tomorrow.'

I swear Hilda was following the conversation because she turned her rapt attention away from the sausages and looked pleadingly between me and Bill.

'Wrap them up rather than giving them to her now? If I do that, she'll be upping sticks and moving in with you two,' I joked.

Bill grinned. 'I'm not sure she'd fit given we've got a pair of hulking great teenagers taking up all the space. The sooner they go off to university the better.'

'You'll miss them when they're gone,' said Nana Rose. 'I always thank my lucky stars that Molly's dad stayed close to home for his studies, and this one here is as much a home bird as I ever was.'

'The advantage of being a home bird with a boat is that home is wherever you happen to moor up,' said Bill with a wink. 'I'll leave you two to it.'

'Nana, do you want to do the honours? Hilda's going to start drooling in a minute.' I quickly changed the subject away from all things mooring-related. I wasn't sure I agreed with Bill's sentiment. The Oxford Canal was inextricably linked with my sense of home.

'I'd be delighted.'

It cost her some effort to break the sausages into smaller pieces, but she laughed as Hilda delicately took each morsel from her fingers.

'She has better table manners than some humans I've known. In fact, most of the humans I've known,' she corrected herself.

'You bring out the best in her,' I replied. 'Her manners are less refined when she's eating by the towpath.'

'Grandmother's privilege. She's on her best behaviour because she knows it's my role in life to spoil my grandchildren, both the two- and the four-legged variety. I only want them to be happy. Speaking of which, perhaps you'd like to tell me what's on your mind, my darling?'

I should have known I couldn't get away with it that easily. For a second, I considered confessing the truth, sharing my business woes and letting her tell me everything would be alright, just like she used to when I was a little girl. But I knew it would be selfish to burden her with my worries, especially as she was frail enough already without adding emotional pain to the physical variety she endured.

I pasted on my cheeriest expression. 'Nothing gets past you, does it? I admit, I came here with a shameless ulterior motive. I need to pick your brains.'

Nana Rose sat up straighter, almost puffing out her chest with pride. 'They are considerable, my darling. How may I be of assistance?'

The rest of the evening flew by in a blur of laughter and scheming, the pair of us bouncing ideas for events back and forth, ideas which grew increasingly far-fetched, especially after Nana insisted on us enjoying a nightcap or two together. But despite the love and warmth of my grandmother's hospitality, I couldn't allow myself to fully relax, every moment of joy a painful reminder of what was at stake if my business went under.

## Chapter Three

The next day, I sat down at my laptop to start phase one of the plan Nana Rose had helped me come up with: send emails to every living author I could think of, inviting them to do a talk or even just a signing at the Oxford Bookship. I'd always intended to host author events but had been putting it off, afraid I wouldn't be able to replicate the lively literary salons I'd daydreamed about for so long. However, the time for allowing fear to hold me back was long past. Then I trawled through the online list of bookshops I admired elsewhere in the country to see what drew the crowds to their establishments. It was a dispiriting experience seeing shiny picture after shiny picture of bustling businesses and happy proprietors, and although I tried to remind myself that everyone presented the best versions of themselves on the internet, I couldn't help feeling like I must be the problem to be struggling in this way when everyone else appeared to be thriving.

When a visitor stepped on board and started browsing

the romance section, I welcomed the excuse to shut my laptop and bury my sense of inadequacy for a few minutes at least.

'That was quite the sigh of relief,' said the person I was hoping to convert into being an actual customer.

'I've spent far too long staring at a screen today,' I responded with a smile.

She pulled a face. 'Tell me about it. Real life sucks. You think you know where you stand and then… Give me a book any day. Or even better a book in the hands of one of those guys,' she added nodding her head towards the chiselled heroes who stared out from the covers.

'Now that would be the dream,' I said. 'At least there are plenty of fictional versions of decent guys to choose from in here.'

'You can say that again.' She glanced around the cabin, as if not quite believing what she saw in front of her. 'I've run past this boat a few times, but this is my first official trip on board. I had no idea you had such an amazing selection.'

'The Oxford Bookship is surprisingly Tardis-like. It's always great to meet new visitors. And if there's something in particular you're after, I can easily order it in. I'd only need a small deposit,' I added hastily.

'Perfect.'

She carried on browsing, but I soon started to think that she was looking in the wrong place. Maybe it was the short exchange we'd had, or maybe it was something I sensed from her slightly edgy body language, but I suspected she needed to read about someone like her, frustrated, maybe even trapped, by her circumstances but finding hope in an unexpected place. The book that would resonate with her couldn't be found on that shelf. I fought an internal battle about whether to say something, but in the end, I couldn't resist.

'Sorry to interrupt – I'm Molly by the way – can I make a recommendation…?'

'Natalia,' she handily filled in. 'And yes, that would be great, thanks.'

'Lovely to meet you, Natalia. There's a book I reckon you'll enjoy. If you're looking for a hot hero with depth, how do you feel about this one?'

I ran my finger along the bookshelf to the right of where she was standing and then pulled out a hardback with beautiful gold foil detailing.

'*Lady Chatterley's Lover,*' Natalia read the title out loud. 'Didn't it get banned or something?'

'There was an obscenity trial against the publisher. A sure-fire way to make a book super popular if you ask me. It's pretty spicy, although there's a lot more going on than just that – a woman taking control of her own destiny, female sensuality, class divides, all kinds of good stuff.'

She quickly scanned the blurb. 'Sounds right up my street.' She snorted. 'Sorry, a completely unintended innuendo there.'

I laughed. 'I'm sure the characters would have approved of it.'

As her gaze moved to the price, her face fell. 'Ah, that's a little more than I was planning to spend, I'm afraid.'

She still held on to the book, confirming my sense that this story would speak to her. If I was a better salesperson,

I would have pushed harder for her to buy that particular volume, knowing her desire for the novel had put her on the cusp of ignoring practical considerations. But as usual my conscience wouldn't allow me to, which was undoubtedly one of the reasons the shop was in the financial position it was.

'You're in luck. I know for a fact there's a copy in the second-hand section. Let me dig it out for you.' I hurried over and found it on the shelf. 'Here you are.'

'Two pound fifty? What a bargain. Thanks.' She fished the exact amount of change out of her purse. 'I can't wait to read it. And if you could hook me up with my perfect guy as easily as you've matched me with my next read, that would be great.'

She left the narrowboat looking considerably brighter than she had when she'd stepped on board. Meanwhile her parting statement had made me fizz with excitement. She might only have been joking, but her light-hearted comment was the spark of inspiration I needed for an event which was actually achievable. I liked to think of myself as a book matchmaker after all. Why not see if my skills would transfer to actual matchmaking? After my break-up I'd sworn off the heartless world of online dating, and my friends who still bothered with it spent half their time complaining about their nightmare app experiences. We couldn't be the only people feeling that way. Perhaps it was time to bring back IRL dating, and what better place for a meet-cute than the Oxford Bookship, which oozed romance from every porthole? I could hold a real-life Blind Date with a Book event, uniting people with their perfect book and hopefully their perfect date too. If matchmaking was good enough for Emma Woodhouse, it was good enough for me, although perhaps I'd better not think too hard about the trouble Jane Austen's heroine managed to get herself into with her schemes.

I picked up my notebook and set to work on my new money-making plan.

## Chapter Four

'Are you sure it's not going to rain? The sky looks rather ominous,' I said, peering out of a porthole for the millionth time. It was just over two weeks since I'd decided upon the Blind Date with a Book night, and May had turned to June, the new month bringing with it another batch of statements from the bank confirming that I needed to make the event happen sooner rather than later. Focusing on the weather was distracting me from the superstitious fear that deciding to hold it on the thirteenth of the month would doom it from the start.

'Stop fretting, there's absolutely zero chance of it raining,' said Flick, reaching across the table to take the sticky tape out of my hands before I ended up inadvertently binding my fingers together. She started measuring a length of brown paper for the next book to be wrapped in. 'Trust me, I've looked the forecast up on three different apps, plus I messaged that guy I matched with online who works at the Met Office.'

My nerves settled a little. 'Thanks. That was going above and beyond the call of friendship.'

She grinned. 'I didn't say I messaged him about the weather, but trust me when I say there was a warm front on the horizon by the end of our conversation.' Her exhale was practically a wolf whistle of appreciation. I rolled my eyes, pretending to disapprove of her distraction. 'Seriously though, it's going to be a great night. And if it does rain, who cares?' she said.

I forced a smile while my internal panic ratcheted up another level. If it rained, everyone would have to crowd into the cabin rather than mingling on deck or in the towpath garden as I'd planned, and they wouldn't have the space to enjoy a relaxing browsing experience, so they wouldn't buy any books which would completely defeat the object of the night.

'You've nothing to worry about,' Flick continued, blissfully ignorant of the concerns which weighed me down. We'd been best friends for as long as I could remember, but memories of her giddy delight when I'd told her that I was finally opening the bookshop after years rabbiting on to her about the idea, had stopped me from confiding in her about just how bad my situation was. Rationally I knew she'd be supportive and kind and would blame everyone but me for my problems, but I couldn't bear the thought of her disappointment and her sympathy at my failure. I so desperately wanted to be the successful person she and my Nana Rose believed I was. As far as they were both concerned, the Blind Date with a Book night was for a bit of fun, as opposed to the crucial fundraiser I needed it to be. I'd rather be isolated with my issues than feel the guilt of burdening my loved ones with them.

'Haven't you sold out anyway?' Flick asked.

I checked the online booking system again. 'There or thereabouts,' I said, still not quite believing it was true. For the first few days, it had looked like the Blind Date with a Book night was going to be just me and Hilda, but slowly and surely, after I'd put posters up around what felt like the entire city, the ticket sales had started to trickle in. And then I'd made a half-jokey, half-serious video for the socials playing up my bookish matchmaking credentials, complete with a cheesy soundtrack, and had been thrilled when a boating influencer with tens of thousands more followers than I could ever dream of having, reposted it, saying he was booking a ticket. The floodgates had opened and suddenly the Blind Date with a Book night was the hottest event in town.

'Please say you've arranged a way of rigging the blind dates so that your bestest friend in the whole entire world...'

'You mean Hilda?' I teased.

Flick playfully pretended to throw a book at me. 'So that your bestest *human* friend,' she corrected, 'can get the pick of the bunch?'

I frowned with mock severity at her. 'The bookish fates are in charge this evening, you know that. Besides, what about Met Office man?'

'He's fun to banter with, but I'm not sure there's much more going on than that. I'm merely keeping my options open,' she said with a pout. 'There has to be some advantage in me wrapping all these books up. Anyway, I refuse to believe that you aren't going to put your witchy powers to good use.'

I laughed, passing another book across for her to wrap. 'Being able to recommend books to people is hardly a supernatural talent,' I said, although, secretly, sometimes it felt like that. 'Much as I'd like to rig the system in your favour, there's only so much I can do.'

I'd decided to keep my matching process as simple as possible. I'd picked a selection of books from the shelves, more because I had two copies of each title, rather than for any other motivation. They were all being wrapped individually in brown paper, with carefully considered clues on the labels to help people deduce the title. Guests would choose a book from the pile, then I'd encourage them to mingle so they could help each other work out what they'd got and track down the person who had the identical book to them. Once they thought they'd found that person, they could unwrap their parcels together to find out if they were right. I was counting on them being so delighted at having acquired an excellent read *and* met their bookish perfect match that they'd decide to celebrate by buying dozens of extra books.

'You never know, *you* might meet the love of your life,' Flick said with a suggestive waggle of her eyebrows, dutifully rolling out another ream of brown paper. She was always on at me to put myself back out there again after my last relationship had ended in tears – mine, not his, sadly – but all my energy was going into my business. The thought of finishing a hard day's work then having to go and spend the evening making awkward small talk on a date was too much to contemplate. Curling up in my pyjamas with a good book and Hilda snoozing at my feet always seemed like a much better option.

'I will be in strictly bookseller mode tonight. I have no intention of taking part in the blind dating aspect of things. I'm perfectly content as one girl and her dog.'

'There's no harm in having a little fun while you're busy trying to make everyone else happy, as always. Did you know that at least one in ten people meet their partners in the workplace? I've been researching it for a feature.'

Flick's phone buzzed before I could respond. Hilda jumped up in surprise at the noise and knocked the stack of books onto the floor.

'It's alright, Hilda. It's only Aunty Flick being extremely popular and in demand.' I scratched her head reassuringly, and she soon settled back down.

Flick and I gathered up the fallen books, then she checked her phone screen and groaned. 'Balls. Sadly, the guy I'm most in demand from is boss man Neil, and I'm afraid that message from him is my cue to disappear for a bit. I've got to go and interview a woman about some bins. Such is the glamorous life of a journalist.' She pulled a face.

'You love it really. Judging by the latest newsletter from the Oxford Boating Association, there's nothing quite like rubbish to get people riled.'

'Yup, the holy trinity of local news – bins, potholes, and charity challenges. They all keep the *Oxford Gazette* going. Maybe one day the editor will let me branch out from the council fodder so I can do one of the many much more interesting stories I've suggested,' she said wistfully. 'Anyway, enough of my blethering.' She gave me a quick kiss on the cheek. 'Good luck, lovely, you've got this. I'll see you later. And if I'm not too distracted by all the hotties you've lined up for me, I'll take a few snaps and see if I can pitch a nice fluffy feature about the night to Neil. Local businesswoman does good kind of thing, he'll love it.'

'Thanks, matey, you're the best.'

After a final hug, Flick headed off to her interview, leaving me to my nervous preparations. I finished wrapping and labelling the last books, then carried them to the table I'd set up in my narrow garden by the towpath. I put out jugs of lemonade and some bowls of snacks, then stood back and surveyed the scene. It wasn't the most sophisticated of set-ups with the home-made bunting and basic refreshments, but hopefully the bookish would-be Romeos and Juliets would overlook that. I couldn't imagine a more romantic place to meet a life partner than here on the canal, but then again, I was biased.

I checked my watch. People should be arriving any moment now. As if on cue, the evening sun finally broke through the clouds, bathing the Oxford Bookship in soft, golden light, and I experienced a burst of pride. She'd never looked better, I told myself, trying not to stare too closely at the deck which, now that the light was shining on it, I realised was probably going to need revarnishing before winter. I mentally added it to my list of things to worry about once I'd paid the mooring fees. Boat maintenance was never ending, and that was something boaters like me had to accept. I snapped a couple of pictures for the socials and then stood nervously by the table waiting for the wannabe daters to arrive.

'Hello, am I too early for the Blind Date with a Book night?'

I jumped as a familiar-looking man clutching a camera appeared at my side, seemingly from nowhere. Hilda woofed in alarm. She seemed particularly jittery this evening, most likely picking up on my own nerves.

'Sorry, I didn't mean to startle you,' he said with a dazzling smile. He held his hand out. 'I'm Liam Crawford. I booked my ticket the other night.'

'Wow, you're Boaty Liam,' I said, astonished that a man whose content I'd watched pretty much from when he first started posting was now standing here in front of me shaking my hand.

'That's me. I'm flattered you recognised me.'

'No, it's me who's flattered that you reposted my video. Honestly, I don't think I would have sold half as many tickets if you hadn't. I'm thrilled you could make it,' I babbled like a starstruck teenager. He always came across as the approachable guy next door in his films, but what the camera had failed to convey was how incredibly blue his eyes were in real life.

'Molly, right?' he checked.

I nodded eagerly.

'Well, Molly, I couldn't resist the lure of books and good company. What an ideal combination. I'm moored up on Castle Mill Stream, and I've completely fallen in love with Oxford. And perhaps tonight I'll fall in love with one of its beautiful residents too. A bloke can dream, anyway.' He laughed.

'I have a good feeling that your love story is just waiting to be written,' I replied with a smile.

Liam took his phone out of his pocket and for a crazy moment, I wondered if he was about to ask for my number, but he quickly checked a message on the screen before turning his attention back to me.

'Could I ask you a massive favour? I was hoping to get some footage tonight. Would you mind? I won't film anyone without their consent, of course, and it'll mostly be me in shot.' He shrugged self-deprecatingly. 'For some reason my "day in the life" vlogs seem to do really well. It's a strange career chatting into camera all the time, but it keeps me afloat, and that's why I do it.'

I couldn't believe my luck. Boaty Liam's socials had five-figure followers, bordering on six. If all went well tonight and he posted about it, I might be able to sell out half a dozen Blind Date with a Book nights in the future.

I nodded vigorously. 'Of course, that sounds good to me.'

'You're a star, thank you. I really appreciate it.' The full force of his kind smile face to face rather than on screen was something else.

'As you're the first here, you get first dibs on book choice. Help yourself.' I quickly explained how the novel matching system worked.

'Sounds perfect.' He closed his eyes and reached towards the books. Although I'd promised myself I wouldn't do it, I pushed a particular volume towards him.

He made his pick, with a little help, then opened his eyes to examine the label (the clue read 'Ellis Bell's gothic take on moorland romance') and beamed. 'Oh, I definitely know what this one is.' He hummed a few bars of the Kate Bush song with the same title, playfully wafting his arms around to the tune. 'I have a very good feeling about who it might lead me to. This system seems much better than all that impersonal swiping on your phone. And given the literary location for the blind date, it's guaranteed everyone will have at least one thing in common. I wouldn't be surprised if you had a hit event on your hands.'

I grinned back at him, caught up in his optimism. 'I do hope so. And anyway, even if people don't want to date each other, they might find a new friend from the night, or even their next imaginary friends in the form of books.'

'Would you mind explaining it all again for the camera?' asked Liam. 'You'd be speaking to me rather than staring directly down the lens if that helps. My audience are going to love you.'

I hesitated. It was one thing doing silly videos for my own social media, but I wasn't sure I had the charisma necessary to appear on Liam's channel. 'Are you sure? I've always thought of myself as more of a behind the scenes kind of girl to be honest.' Besides, so much of my brain was occupied with worrying about how the night might go that I was concerned I'd struggle to construct a coherent sentence on camera.

'Same here. But guy rather than girl, I mean. However, it's a means to an end.' He smiled again, and I felt my resolve waver at his reassuring gawkiness. 'Why don't you give it a try? You might surprise yourself. It's all pre-recorded, and I'll let you see what clips I'm using before I put it out. Your enthusiasm for the venture is obvious. Who better to talk about the Oxford Bookship than the woman whose passion project it is?'

He put his hands together in a prayer position, and fluttered his eyelashes in a parody of pleading, as playful in real life as he always was in his videos.

'Go on then, I'll have a go. And you promise if I look like a muppet, you won't use it?'

'Scout's honour,' he said solemnly, then cracked another grin. 'In the spirit of full disclosure, I was never actually a member of the scouting movement, but I hope you'll appreciate the sentiment. You can trust me. If it helps, I've never met anyone less muppet-like.'

I cleared my throat to disguise my awkwardness at the compliment he'd paid me.

'Okay. Where do you want me? By the Oxford Bookship sign perhaps? Or does that look too obviously like product placement?'

'It's fine. And my rates for product placement are extremely reasonable,' said Liam, very serious all of a sudden.

'Oh, I hadn't—'

'Got you!' he said, clapping his hands together with glee. 'Don't worry, I was only teasing. By the sign would be perfect. And I wouldn't dream of charging you to appear in my videos. I know I'm the fortunate one to be allowed to film you. Right, give me a second to check it all looks good.'

I waited uneasily as he moved the camera around,

fighting the urge to smooth my hair down. The viewers would have to take me as they found me.

'Just quickly, can you introduce yourself so I can check the sound levels?' Liam struck his forehead with the palm of his hand. 'I'm a total idiot. I haven't even given you the mic. Do you mind?'

Before I could respond, he'd efficiently clipped something onto the collar of my cardigan. No chance of changing my mind now.

'Here we go. Who are you and what do you do?' he asked.

I tried to ignore the whirring sound which signalled that he was zooming in on my face.

I took a moment to compose myself, then waved awkwardly at the camera, instantly forgetting that I was meant to be talking to Liam rather than to the lens.

'Hi, I'm Molly Bramble and I'm the owner and proprietor of the Oxford Bookship, a proudly independent floating bookshop. And tonight, I'm helping Liam to find his perfect literary and romantic match through a Blind Date with a Book.' I quickly explained again how the evening was going to work, gradually relaxing into the flow of my theme.

When I'd finished speaking, Liam swung the camera round so he could film his own reaction to my statement. As soon as the lens was on him his expressions became even more enthusiastic.

'I'm very lucky to have the lovely Molly as my wing woman. What do you think, guys? Do you reckon I'm going to meet Miss Right tonight? Stay tuned to see how I get on.'

He gave a final thumbs up to the camera then pressed a button.

'All done. I've finished recording for now. Thanks for your help with that. I appreciate you.'

'No problem. And bang on cue. Your potential dates are arriving.'

I gestured at the eclectic collection of individuals making their way down the towpath who could only be heading for my shop. They certainly were a lot better dressed than the average dog walker, which was the usual type of person I saw wandering by the canal at this time of the evening. I braced myself and prepared to welcome my new customers, quickly assessing them as they walked towards me. Even though the motivation for this night was financial, I couldn't help but hope that Cupid fired a few arrows as well. What book lover doesn't like a happy ending, after all?

# Chapter Five

alf an hour into the event, and I told myself that things could be going much worse. Okay so the card machine was playing up, but on the plus side that was because it was getting more action than it had in weeks. I'd also been somewhat optimistic about what I reckoned would be a comfortable capacity. The Oxford Bookship was sitting rather lower in the water than usual, but the punters didn't seem to mind having to squeeze past each other to get to the bookshelves. Next time maybe it would be better to increase the price and sell slightly fewer tickets. If there was going to be a next time, that was.

'Sorry, sorry,' I apologised as I pushed my way through the crowd to take another stack of books through to my private quarters where I'd set up a station for people to leave their purchases so they didn't have to carry them for the rest of the evening. I'd figured it would encourage them to spend more, and so far, it seemed to be working.

'This is so fun. The place is buzzing,' I overheard one woman saying, making me feel a corresponding thrill of pride.

'Buzzing? Completely chaotic and full of *hoi polloi* more like,' replied a masculine voice with a deeply judgemental tone. 'I don't know who's in charge, but they must have their head in the clouds. This shambolic set-up couldn't be further from my idea of fun.'

My good mood instantly crashed. I tried to see who it was that had made such a damning assessment of all my hard work, but the voice could have come from any one of the half a dozen men milling around in the cabin. I told myself not to take the comments to heart, but they matched my own fears about the event and my organisation of it so exactly that I couldn't help but feel like this person had seen through my pretence and recognised me for the disaster I really was.

Feeling crushed, I retreated to the galley, shutting the door behind me so I could have a few minutes to gather myself.

'One man expressing an opinion does not make it true,' I recited in my head, but his words echoed those I'd heard over the years about me, first from teachers, then employers and exes. How could I doubt the accuracy in them? I'd put so much effort into making this evening a success, but it still wasn't good enough. That man had been rude enough to make his complaints out loud, but what if he was articulating what everyone else was thinking?

'Knock knock,' said Flick, sticking her head around the

door. 'Why are you hiding in here and missing out on all the fun?'

I pasted a smile on my face. 'I'm doing nothing of the sort. I was checking to see how much lemonade I've got left. I'm worried they're disappointed I can't offer them alcohol.'

'You worry too much. They don't care a jot about it because they're all high on lur-ve,' said Flick, waggling her eyebrows at me.

'Speaking of which, have you met your match yet?' I asked, keeping my voice casual.

She waved her still-wrapped book. 'I've been using my journalistic skills to interrogate a few potentials, but no luck so far.'

I smothered a smile. 'Maybe it was the interrogation side of things that they felt uncomfortable with,' I teased.

'If they can't cope with me when I'm barely in second gear conversationally, they'll never cope if I try fifth gear on them,' she pointed out.

'You are delightfully fearsome. Although I'm beginning to feel sorry for the guy I've sent your way.'

'Ha, I knew you wouldn't be able to resist getting involved,' said Flick, leaping on my admission with delight. 'Suddenly the whole evening is looking considerably more exciting. Are you going to give me any clues? Go on, point me in the right direction.'

I folded my arms and gave her a stern look. 'Where would the fun be in that?'

'Spoilsport. I'd better get back to the hunt. Do you need a hand carrying the refreshments out?' she asked as an afterthought.

'I'm fine. Go on, off you go,' I said. 'Enjoy.' She bounded enthusiastically back into the bookshop cabin in a manner uncannily like Hilda just before she's about to get her dinner.

I picked up the fresh jug of lemonade and went out via the rear deck to reach the towpath, telling myself that it was the quickest way of doing it, and that the presence of Mr Judgemental, as I'd termed him, hadn't influenced my choice not to go back through the bookshop one little bit. However, I didn't even get as far as the table in the towpath garden before people were swooping on me to get their glasses refilled.

'Are you having a good time?' I asked nervously. Everyone replied in the affirmative and they sounded genuine, so why wasn't I feeling happier about it? I had an irrational sense in the pit of my stomach that something was fundamentally wrong, that I'd messed up and it was only a matter of time until everyone here saw what the judgy guy had already recognised. At least, I hoped it was irrational. But as I set the now nearly empty jug down, I realised that my intuition had been speaking the truth to me. Because sitting there on the table in the towpath garden was a brown paper parcel, still waiting to be collected. I pulled my phone out and scanned the list of ticket holders, counting them off in my head, and cursed myself. I was a first-class idiot. Classic disorganised Molly. Why hadn't I realised there was an uneven number of guests signed up? That meant somebody was going to end up without a match. And that somebody was bound to be pretty disappointed at best, potentially very angry at worst. Mr Judgemental's disdain might look tame in comparison. If word got out – and this was an event which had sold out thanks to word of mouth on the socials – then nobody would want to come to a future Blind Date with a Book night. It could even taint the Oxford Bookship's reputation as a shop. What if my business ended up getting blacklisted?

With difficulty I forced my mind back to the practical and away from the negative panic spiral. It was too late to ring round my single friends and find a last-minute addition to the party. There was only one realistic solution to the problem. I would have to get involved myself. Without allowing myself too much time to think about it, I picked up the final book and quickly read the label.

'It is a truth universally acknowledged that first impressions shouldn't necessarily be trusted.'

I felt my anxiety settle a little. The fact that my favourite book had ended up in my hands had to be a good omen. I was pleased with the clue and the way I'd subtly incorporated *Pride and Prejudice*'s original title into it. The question was, had the other person who'd got this book worked it out yet and how pleased would they be when they eventually opened the parcel to see this stunning edition with its marbled blue sprayed edges and elegantly embossed cover? Hopefully their joy at their new book acquisition would compensate for the fact that I was most definitely not in the market for a blind date. Maybe I should have offered them a free ticket for the next event instead? But I was getting ahead of myself. I looked around at the chattering group. Quite a few were still to unwrap their books. I was going to have to mingle in order to track down my book's match.

I found myself gravitating towards Liam, even though unfortunately I knew our books weren't matches. If I hadn't been too busy trying to save my business to think about dating for real maybe I would have arranged things differently. But he was good company and this way I could steer him towards his actual match whose reaction I was keen to see.

'So you are playing the game,' he said, looking flatteringly pleased that I was approaching him with a book parcel under my arm.

'I'm a late addition.'

'And are you the Cathy to my Heathcliff? I'd like to point out that I'm much more even-tempered than my fictional counterpart and add that I hope our romance doesn't follow exactly the same lines theirs does.'

'Hmm, maybe I should have considered the storylines more when I was picking the books for the event,' I said. I showed him the label on my book, and he pulled a disappointed face.

'Shame. But that works. I can see you as an Eliza Bennet.'

I could feel my cheeks warming at his generous compliment. I was wondering how to respond when Flick joined us.

'Hello. You're far too cheerful-looking to be the hero from my book, but something tells me that you might just be my man anyway.' She gave me the ghost of a wink. 'If I'm Emily Brontë, that must make you…?'

'Ellis Bell,' Liam replied. 'Or plain old Liam if you'd like to know the real me.' He beamed at my best friend who practically melted in response, as I knew she would. He gently took the parcel from her outstretched hands and examined the label, before passing his across so she could check for herself. 'We're a match,' he said.

'I'm Felicity,' my friend stammered, caught up in the moment. 'But everyone who counts calls me Flick, which I hope you will.'

'I'd be honoured to,' said Liam.

'I'll leave you two to it,' I said, preparing to bow out gracefully as Flick mouthed, 'I owe you big time,' in my direction.

'Actually, before you head off, our Bookish Fairy Godmother, could I ask another huge favour?' said Liam. 'Would you mind filming us doing the big reveal? That is, if you're okay with that, Flick? I promised Molly I'd get some content from the evening for my YouTube channel.'

'Sure, why not?' said Flick, which confirmed that she must be really taken with him because she normally hated having her picture taken.

While Liam started getting his camera ready, I carefully tucked my own book parcel under my arm and stepped back to what I thought might be a better filming position.

'Ow,' said someone in a voice that I instantly recognised. Mr Judgemental himself.

I turned round and glared at the aristocratic-looking guy

dressed in casually chic linen whose toes I'd just trodden on.

'Is something the matter?' I asked, my tone icily polite. With anyone else I'd have been rushing to apologise, but the wicked side of me was glad that I'd been able to exact some kind of revenge for his earlier dismissive comments.

'That's the second time I've been trampled on this evening,' he said, each syllable clipped and annoyed. 'That horse masquerading as some kind of dog managed to get the other foot.'

He gestured towards Hilda who'd wandered over to say hello in her usual friendly manner. I bristled in indignation at the implied insult to my beloved pet. He was far from the first person to make the comparison, but this arrogant, brooding guy had already been rude about my event. I certainly wasn't going to let him be obnoxious about my beautiful girl as well.

'Hilda's not a horse; she's an Irish wolfhound. And it's her boat, so she has the right to put her paws wherever she wishes,' I told him.

I clicked my tongue, hoping Hilda would move obediently to my side, but instead she stayed put, staring up at the man.

'A horse who knows her own mind. When I signed up to this event, I expected my match to be human, rather than animal,' he said, the sarcasm dripping from every word.

I frowned. 'She's not a horse,' I repeated, even though I knew it was foolish to rise to his bait. 'Do you happen to have food in your pocket? Because that's probably what she's fixating on, rather than your oh-so-magnetic personality.'

His hand brushed past Hilda's ears, and she pressed her head towards his palm to prompt him to scratch her.

Instead of doing what any decent human being would have done and stroking the dog, he made a great show of checking his pockets and waving his expensive-looking leather wallet around. 'No food in here. Just a collection of random cards I'm afraid.'

*Alright Richie Rich, no need to show off,* I thought.

'Maybe you walked in something smelly on your way here,' was my disappointingly childish retort.

'I think not,' he said, lifting one foot, then the other to show off the pristine soles of his designer deck shoes.

'Good for you. I'd best be off. It's been lovely to have found the time to chat despite the complete chaos and the presence of the "hoi polloi".' I managed to get the dig in, but he showed no shame at having his rude words echoed back to him.

'It's actually just "hoi polloi",' he corrected me instead. '"Hoi" means "the" in ancient Greek, so if you say, "the hoi polloi", you're really saying "the the masses" which of course is tautology and more to the point, doesn't make any sense.' He smiled in a manner I could only describe as smug.

For a few seconds I was speechless, outraged at his arrogance in correcting my turn of phrase, and livid with myself for allowing him to make me feel foolish by getting it wrong in the first place.

'Great, next time I have a conversation in ancient Greek

I'll be sure to remember that supremely useful fact,' I said, knowing I would wake up in the middle of the night with a much better retort and kick myself for not having used it. However, he seemed completely unaffected by my sarcasm, his smile growing wider.

'If you'll excuse me, I have a big reveal to film,' I said, preparing to sweep off with what little of my dignity I could scrape together.

His expression turned grumpy again. 'Nothing screams true romance like documenting it for social media. I suppose I'll see if I can battle my way through the hordes below deck again. With my four-legged date.'

He could have injected a bit more enthusiasm into his voice at the prospect of book shopping. Much to my disappointment, Hilda trailed after him into the cabin. Maybe she could make up for her betrayal by trapping him in there until he bought half my stock, although I disliked the man so much, I'd happily forgo his business.

I turned round to find that Liam and Flick had disappeared off at some point during that exchange. My best friend wasn't wasting any time there. Hoping that Liam didn't get so distracted that he forgot to get the footage for the video he'd promised to make, I returned to my station by the refreshments table. Whoever was my book match would have to come and find me here. As long as Mr Judgemental was lurking in the cabin, I would be staying out in the fresh air.

Unfortunately, and unsurprisingly, because he'd struck me as the sort not to appreciate books, his browsing session did not last long. Dusk was beginning to fall, but his shadow appearing beside me made it seem like night had already arrived.

'We didn't introduce ourselves properly. I'm Jack Siddall. Having definitively ruled out all other options, I am convinced we must have matching books,' he said, sounding far from pleased about it. I mean, that was absolutely how I felt myself, but it was plain rude of him to make his contempt for me quite so obvious.

I grimaced, not bothering to hide my irritation.

'Molly Bramble,' I reluctantly told him my name. 'Well, Jack Siddall, I guess we'd better resolve this one way or another. Is this your book's twin?'

I removed the wrapped book which I'd been carrying tucked under my arm for half the night and placed it in his hand.

He compared its weight to his own wrapped volume, then read the clue out loud.

'Yes, that definitely matches mine.'

He passed his book across to me for inspection.

'And the book behind the wrapping is?' I prompted.

'I haven't got a clue to be honest,' he said unashamedly.

'Really?' I paused, trying to work out if this was his bad idea of a joke. 'It's *Pride and Prejudice*.'

I waited for the nod of recognition, the gasp of 'How can I have been so stupid as not to have realised that?' followed by a comment demonstrating the average person's awareness of Jane Austen's arguably most famous novel.

But instead, he frowned slightly. '*Pride and Prejudice*? Never read it. I think I've seen a screen version at some point. It was alright, I suppose.'

'It was *alright*?' I repeated with horror. What kind of a charlatan was he? His presence at an event in a bookshop for people who liked literature seemed inexplicable given his behaviour all night. He hadn't read the novel, but couldn't he have at least made some kind of positive comment along the lines of he'd always wanted to read it? To instead offer a mediocre rating of a screen adaptation was frankly offensive given his surroundings. And to cap it all, he hadn't even specified which screen version he'd found merely 'alright', which would have given me something to respond to, because like any other self-respecting Austenite, I have strong opinions about particular adaptations.

'Can I ask what made you decide to sign up for a dating event designed for book lovers when you're clearly not one yourself?' I questioned.

His nose wrinkled as he frowned in thought. 'I'm interested in your implication that not having a view on Jane Austen equates in your mind to not liking reading.'

I would have responded, but he didn't give me a chance.

'The event was one of those things that popped up in my timeline, and I guess I thought, why not?' he continued. 'I'm new to the area.'

He waved his arm around vaguely.

'Lucky old Oxford to have you gracing it with your presence,' I said, wondering if he expected me to be flattered that he'd selected my little event as his introduction to the city.

'Thanks, but I've lived in Oxford for yonks,' he corrected. 'Or rather, I used to own a flat here which I rented out while I worked in London. I've sold it now to fund my next venture. It's this area in particular that I'm new to.'

'You mean Jericho?' I pressed.

'No, the Oxford Canal itself. I should have explained before when I introduced myself. I'm your new neighbour. I've bought a narrowboat and I'm planning to open a wine bar next door.'

# Chapter Six

'A wine bar. Right next door, run by the worst possible person,' I wailed down the phone to Flick the next morning as I sat in front of my ancient laptop waiting for my accounting software to load. 'Can you imagine? What a nightmare.'

I heard her moving out of the noisy newsroom and into the relative peace of the corridor.

'It might be quite fun to have a boozer on your doorstep, so to speak,' she said, attempting to make me look on the bright side. 'Didn't you say the other day it would be nice to have someone use the mooring just along from you? Have a new neighbour?'

'I meant a quiet neighbour. Preferably someone who enjoyed reading and spent all their money on my stock. Not another business, and definitely not a business run by an uptight prick who mansplains stupid ancient Greek phrases to me. Plus, what kind of fool is irresponsible enough to open a wine bar on water?' I was warming to my theme as

Flick patiently listened. 'It'll be full of drunks who will inevitably end up in the canal and then I'll have to save them because I doubt Mr Jack Siddall will be wanting to jump in the water what with his taste in show-off deck shoes and silly linen trousers. I mean, who wears linen trousers on a canal boat? You'd only have to breathe to get muddy water on them.'

'Hero bookseller jumps in canal to save drowning drunk.' Flick sounded like a news anchor delivering the top headline on *News at Ten*. 'Now that would be a good story.'

'It would be *awful*,' I emphasised.

'Sorry, I should rephrase that. I mean it would be a strong news story. But obviously it would be a terrible thing to happen,' she said hastily. 'I'm sure it won't.'

'It'll be happening every other night,' I muttered darkly.

'You don't know that,' said Flick. 'He'll have had to come up with reams of health and safety procedures as part of the conditions of opening the place up, you know that.'

'You can bet I'll be checking up on that,' I said. 'Although from my googling, he's from some *Succession* style banking dynasty and is absolutely dripping in money and privilege, so I wouldn't be surprised if he's paid his way to ignore the inconvenient stuff while he indulges in his new hobby trying to prove himself to daddy.'

'You make him sound like he's going to be the local mafioso,' said Flick. 'The *Gazette* could do with some scandal like that to entice the readers back. Promise me you'll send any juicy corruption stories involving him my way.'

'Believe me, I will,' I said, even though I knew she was joking.

'Look, I'm sure there's nothing to worry about. And if this Jack character is as into linen and fancy deck shoes as you suggest he is, he'll probably be running a super sophisticated and classy joint. You never know, it might attract a whole new clientele to your bookshop.'

I drew in a breath. 'Are you suggesting that I don't attract sophisticated and classy customers to my bookshop already?' I said in mock offence.

'Absolutely not. The bookshop is a beacon for every right-thinking person,' said Flick. 'Can you elaborate on why he's an uptight prick, out of interest? Aside from the ancient Greek thing, which while annoying, sounds pretty standard Oxford brainiac interaction to me.'

'I don't *think* that he's an uptight prick; I *know* that he's one. He's possibly the rudest man I've ever had the misfortune to encounter.'

'Wow, don't hold back. I'm not sure I've ever heard you badmouth another human being to this extent. Who are you and what did you do with my best friend?' she teased. 'Okay, hit me with it. What else has he done that's made you so prejudiced against him?'

'Where to start? He insulted Hilda for one thing. He called her a horse.'

I had to hold the phone away from my ear as Flick's distinctive cackle rang out.

'You regularly make jokes threatening to harness her up to tow the Bookship if the engine ever fails,' she pointed out once she'd finally stopped laughing.

'I'm her hu-mum. I'm allowed to make comments like that. Other people aren't. Especially not other people who say they prefer the film to the book.'

Flick tutted. 'Why didn't you open up with that? The perpetrator of such a heinous crime should never be permitted to move next door to a bookshop. Hold on a second, let me go to my editor and tell him we need to change the front page and expose this dreadful individual for his crimes against civilisation.'

'Before you continue taking the piss, I haven't got on to the biggest issue. He was incredibly rude about the event, and he spent the whole time acting like he wished he was anywhere else. I mean, nobody held a gun to his head and made him attend.'

'That's unfortunate, but perhaps he was nervous? A dating event is a very high-emotion kind of do,' pointed out Flick.

'I promise you there were no nerves in attendance. He was an incredible snob. Which is surprising when I tell you this next thing. Guess what he's going to call the bar?'

'Now why would I do that and spoil your fun of telling me?' said Flick patiently.

'He's naming it the Jericho Wine Barge. I mean, honestly, what is the bloke thinking?' I relieved my anger by one-handedly plumping up a cushion with unnecessary force.

'What's wrong with that?' asked my much more fair-minded friend.

'Seriously? He's totally lowering the tone of the canal with his silly pun,' I said pettily.

'Says the woman whose floating business is called the

Oxford Bookship.' Flick couldn't keep the amusement out of her voice.

I flumped back against the cushions of my galley bench-cum-bed and picked angrily at a loose thread on the fabric.

'Fine. I'll concede that you make a decent point there. Why do you have to be so reasonable about it all?'

'Because I'm not the one he's moving next door to, so I have a degree of emotional separation from the problem. I get why you're feeling unsettled by the arrival of another business, but change isn't always bad. After all, you made a huge change last year by opening the Bookship, and honestly, lovely, you've been glowing ever since.'

I was glad she still believed that to be the case. I felt as far from glowing as it was possible to be right about now.

'Hmm,' I responded dubiously. 'That was change that I chose. It's not really the same thing. And I don't feel unsettled by another business coming on the scene. I would just prefer not to have a party boat move in next door.'

'I'm sure it won't be as bad as you fear. And maybe his use of puns indicates that beneath the awkward posh boy exterior he's a kindred spirit?' she pressed. 'Perhaps you'll enjoy having some fresh company on the towpath?'

'I have plenty of friends on the towpath. I don't need new ones,' I said.

'It's not possible to have too many friends. Or too much money for that matter.'

The conversation was straying into dangerous territory. Time to turn the tables.

'Speaking of new friends, where did you and Liam disappear off to? Quick work, Ms Summers, quick work.'

'Nothing of that sort happened,' said Flick sounding regretful. 'Liam merely suggested we go somewhere for a drink, so I took him to the Boaters' Ale House. Thought he might as well be introduced to the local while he's moored up on the stream.'

'How very self-sacrificing of you,' I said. 'And?'

'And what? We had a drink, and they had a two-for-one pizza deal on, so we stayed for some food as well.'

I laughed. 'Purely because it was on special offer, or was it really because you fancied the pants off him?'

'A lady never tells. And yes, I know you're about to say something along the lines of "Good thing you're not a lady",' she said, getting in there first.

'You know me too well.' My laptop chirruped, indicating my accounting software had finally opened. 'You'll tell me eventually. I know you journos can't resist gossiping. But I shall content myself with the fact that you sound happy.'

'Put it this way, it's very early days, but so far, I would say that your matchmaking skills are pretty on point. As you'll see from Liam's video whenever it drops. Yup, he's very persuasive and I even consented to a brief appearance in it.' She really was into him then. 'Right, the boss is giving me evils, so I'll love you and leave you. I don't want him to change his mind about using my feature on your do in the Saturday supplement tomorrow. Let me know when the next one is planned for, and I'll make sure the details are included at the bottom of the article so people can book on for it.'

'You're the best pal a girl could wish for,' I said,

although the fate of future Blind Date with a Book nights very much depended on what I was about to see in my accounts. 'Speak later.'

'See you.'

I stared at the figures on the screen and forced myself to focus on the positive. If I didn't take into account the wages I should have paid myself for running the event but hadn't, then I had actually made a respectable-ish profit for once. I mean, it would hardly put a dent in the figure I needed to raise to pay the mooring fees, but it was a start, and it indicated that it was worth holding the event again. Before I could change my mind, I texted Flick a date for the next one. At least I felt I was taking control of my situation, rather than sitting back and hoping for a miracle to occur.

I put the kettle on and started scrolling idly on my phone while I waited for the water to boil. To my delight there were several DMs waiting for me from people who'd attended last night and loved it, and others who'd heard about it from friends and wanted to know when the next one was being held. I quickly set up another booking page on my website, then tapped out replies, throwing in a couple of romance book recommendations to the would-be daters to tide them over until the event. The final DM was from Liam with a link to his draft video.

> As promised! Let me know if u r happy and I'll post it asap! Thanks for a fab night!! xx

I watched it through a couple of times, trying not to cringe at my awkward piece to camera. But the Bookship looked beautiful, and Flick was there, all cute blushes, acting most unlike the hardened journalist she liked to project. If I were a potential customer, I'd take one look at the video and make a beeline for the shop. But then again, I was a biased book lover.

I tapped out a reply to Liam.

> I LOVE it, thanks so much! I'm v happy for you to post. And you're welcome to come to the next BDWAB night, although you might not need to…?! 😄 x

I poured myself a cup of tea and went into the bookshop cabin to open up. After pottering around for a bit, tidying up the stock and filling the gaps in the shelves left by last night's extravaganza, I decided to take up Hilda's usual position on the well deck so I could spot any potential customers walking down the towpath towards us. A gentle breeze was rustling the leaves of the trees which lined the canal and sending the clouds scudding overhead. I took a deep breath and savoured my surroundings. The air was fresh, the delicate scent of wildflowers mixing with the clean aroma of the freshly mowed grass by the towpath. A pair of elegant swans swam past the boat, their heads turned to each other as if they were deep in conversation. Their body language was mirrored by Bill and Rozina who were marching past on their way into town, although they did briefly break off from their discussion to wave a cheery good morning to me.

'Those clouds look a bit ominous, what do you think?' said Rozina. 'By the way, I'm sending my pal in your direction. She's just had a bad break-up and I thought your dating night might be the perfect tonic.'

'That's sweet of you, but are you sure she's ready?' I asked, remembering the aching pain which had wiped me out in the immediate aftermath of my own last break-up. Eighteen months on, I had finally left it behind, despite Flick's annoying cod psychological analysis suggesting the contrary.

'They do say the best way to get over someone is to get under someone else,' Rozina said with a wicked grin.

'Rozina Murphy-Clark, you shameless hussy,' said her husband with a laugh.

'I didn't hear you complaining when we got together,' she responded, nudging him playfully in the ribs.

'Too much information, guys. I had you down as a proper Captain Wentworth and Anne duo, please don't destroy my romantic illusions,' I teased them. 'I'll reserve a ticket for your friend, but in the meantime, give me a sec.' I dived down into the cabin and pulled a book off the shelves. 'Give her this. It might help in the short term,' I said on my return. I leaned across to the shore to pass the book over.

Bill took one look at the cover and snorted. 'Should I be worried?'

'*How to Kill Men and Get Away with It*,' read Rozina out loud. 'Sounds brilliant. I think I need to read that too. How much do we owe you?'

'Don't worry about that for now. Let her read the blurb and see if she fancies it, and if she doesn't'—I knew that wouldn't be the case—'just bring it back. I know where you live after all.'

'Out of interest, have you read this book?' asked Bill, pretending to look concerned.

'Definitely. Most informative it was too,' I said. 'And spit-your-tea-out hilarious.'

'Concerning. Thanks, Molly. We'll let you know what she thinks. Remind me to keep on your good side from now on,' said Bill.

'Nana Rose has read it too,' I said. 'But don't worry, I reckon you're safe for now. It's only scumbags who are targeted by the main character.'

Bill pretended to mop his brow in relief.

I settled down on deck with a book as they continued on their way, but it seemed the reading gods had other ideas for me this morning. I wouldn't go so far as to say I had a steady stream of customers to the shop, but there were certainly more visitors than the average day, and I was more than happy to put aside my own novel to recommend one to punters. I would never tire of the thrill I got from introducing people to authors I was confident they'd love. I knew I was more hands on than the booksellers in the land-based chains, but that was the joy of running an independent bookshop. And today only two visitors took my advice and then stood in front of me ordering the book online 'because it's cheaper'. Definitely better going than usual.

The rain started coming down at about eleven o'clock, which coincided with a hopefully temporary lull in customers.

'Hilda, in you come, I'm not having you getting soaked out there,' I called, whistling between my teeth to attract her attention from the interesting clump of grass which she was nose deep in at the other side of the towpath. She reluctantly dragged herself away from whatever fascinating aromas had been absorbing her and jumped onto the boat as delicately as it was possible for a fifty-kilogram dog to do.

The boat rocked. Hilda padded after me into the cabin and settled at my feet as I started wrapping some more books to add to my Blind Date with a Book display. A few minutes later I reached for the sticky tape and frowned. Why was the boat still rocking? The effect of Hilda's jump should have long worn off. Living on a boat you get used to the gentle motion of floating, and the little noises which the vessel makes in different weathers, like the soft creak of the mooring ropes on a windy day, or the soothing percussion of rain landing on the cabin roof. But this motion was different from normal, choppier certainly, unsettlingly unusual. I started to suspect it was the churn caused by a boat travelling along the canal at a speed much higher than it should be. Sure enough, above the sound of the rain the choking noise of a badly maintained engine being gunned started to grow louder.

'Stay here, Hilda,' I said, my serious voice on so she knew that it was important. She huffed pointedly, then reluctantly curled up in her bed, burying her nose between her paws.

I hurried onto deck just in time to see another

narrowboat heading down the canal steering a trajectory which I knew would bring it perilously close to mine.

'You're going too fast,' I shouted, as the wash from the other boat hit the bank. The Oxford Bookship pitched abruptly as another wave slapped against the hull. I thought I heard Hilda howl from indoors.

'It's alright Hilda,' I called, although it very much wasn't.

I tried again. 'Turn the tiller to starboard, and ease off the throttle,' I yelled at the distant hooded figure who I could barely see hunched up in the cockpit. Unfortunately, the helmsman either couldn't hear me or didn't want to pay attention to my directions.

'Slow down, and steer in the opposite direction.' I quickly translated my instructions into hopefully more civilian-friendly terminology. The person on board was covered from head to toe in waterproofs which looked like they'd come straight off a stand at a superyacht show, and clearly had no idea what they were doing. It should be illegal for people like that to be allowed out on the water.

Some of my words must have finally filtered through to them because the other vessel began to change direction. But it was too little too late. With a terrible screech of metal on metal, the speeding narrowboat collided with the midships of the Oxford Bookship and scraped its way along the side. The force of the impact knocked my beautiful shop sign, the one which I'd spent hours designing and painting by hand, off the roof and into the muddy depths of the canal.

'You bloody idiot,' I muttered under my breath, which

was incredibly restrained of me. In truth I wanted to shriek every swear word in the dictionary at the fool. But I didn't have time to assess the damage and mourn my loss, because the sound of the other boat's engine had changed, warning me that worse was about to come.

'No, whatever you do, do not put that boat into reverse,' I yelled. 'You'll completely lose the steering. Not that you have any steering ability in the first place.'

The stern of the other boat was now tracking backwards on an erratic trajectory which I suspected would bring it crashing once again into the side of the Oxford Bookship. Without allowing myself to think about it, I clambered on the roof of my boat, ran along until I was level with the stern of the other boat and jumped the gap between the two.

I dropped neatly into the cockpit in a smooth move which would have made James Bond envious. At least, after the event, that's how I told myself it looked. I suspected in reality it was somewhat less impressive. I certainly made enough of a thump landing on the deck, the momentum from the jump making me collide with the solid form of the helmsman who automatically put his arms out to stop me felling him.

'Who? What's happening?' asked the bewildered figure in the waterproofs, keeping hold of me in his confusion.

My heart sank as I instantly recognised the voice. The uptight prick from the Blind Date with a Book night, aka Jack Siddall, my new neighbour, confirming all my worst fears about what kind of a neighbour he was going to be.

# Chapter Seven

What a way to introduce himself to the area, speeding along the canal and crashing into my beloved boat. I pushed back against Jack and removed myself from our accidental embrace.

'I'm saving you from yourself, you idiot,' I said. 'Now are you going to let me take over?' I gestured at the tiller which was swinging freely as he'd failed to grab hold of it again. The stern tone of my voice made it abundantly clear that if he didn't agree, I was going to shove him out of the way and do it anyway.

'I'm rather new to this and—' He started to say.

'Less talking, more action,' I retorted, conscious that the boat was only moments away from hitting the bank. 'Move.'

Jack nodded abruptly and tucked himself under the overhang of the cabin roof, watching me closely as I took hold of the tiller with one hand and leaned forward to adjust the throttle with my other.

The engine immediately stopped complaining and settled into a more comfortable chug. I gently pulled the tiller towards me, directing the bow of the boat out into the middle of the canal where there was a little more room.

'Slow and steady wins the race,' I said, repeating the instruction which Nana Rose had given when she'd first entrusted me with steering her precious boat. 'The speed limit on this canal is four miles per hour,' I explained. 'And that's a limit, not a target by the way.'

'I wasn't intentionally speeding,' said Jack, affronted, a man clearly uncomfortable with admitting when he was in the wrong. 'Nothing seemed to happen if I tried moving the tiller at a lower speed, and then I got concerned I was going to crash, so I accelerated to get more of a result with the steering, and then—'

'—and then you crashed anyway. Right into the side of my boat. Contrary to what you seem to think, boating is not a contact sport.' I gestured towards the Oxford Bookship, not trusting myself to turn and examine the damage properly. I dreaded to think what I would discover.

'It was more of a scrape than an actual crash,' he tried to defend himself, then his words tailed off as he saw my thunderous expression. 'But I appreciate that's semantics. I can only apologise about the incident. It was certainly not my intention to damage your boat, and I of course accept full responsibility for the cost of any repairs which are required.'

I ignored his apology, not being in the right frame of mind to deal with it for the time being. He was obviously in the fortunate position of being able to throw money at his problems, but from my initial impression, the damage was probably bad enough to require hauling the boat out of the water for repainting, and no amount of cash would be sufficient compensation for the disruption that would cause to my life, let alone the effect of the emotional upheaval.

It was easier to lock that crippling worry up at the back of my mind for now and slip into teacher mode instead so I didn't lash out at him again, or worse, burst into tears. 'We'll definitely get into that later when we're not in quite such a precarious position. But as I was trying to say, the trick with steering a canal boat is anticipation,' I schooled him. 'If you keep your wits about you, and prepare in advance for any obstacles you might be approaching, then you'll prevent dramas before they can happen.'

'When I realised I was turning in the wrong direction, I thought if I went into reverse it would act like a brake,' he said, still trying to defend his actions.

'Nope. You just quickly lose whatever control you have. Which clearly wasn't much, especially given the speed you were doing.'

'The guy I bought the boat from said it was a good technique to use.'

I frowned, which caused a rivulet of rain to go into my right eye. I let go of the tiller briefly to wipe my face, causing Jack to tense.

'There's no need to brace for impact. *I* actually know what I'm doing. And who was it who sold you the boat? They clearly don't have a clue what they're talking about. They must have seen you coming a mile off.

It's frankly irresponsible letting someone like you take possession of a vessel this size.'

'I'm not a complete novice on the water, and I did my research before buying the boat,' he said defensively. 'It had all the proper paperwork and I got it for a good price.'

'Hmm, you believe that if you want to. And pottering around on an inflatable unicorn off the back of a super yacht does not count as water experience.'

'I've never…' Jack started, no doubt intending to argue back, but the glower I sent in his direction quickly silenced him.

Once we were safely out of any imminent danger, I put the engine into neutral and turned to face him properly.

'Right. Time to talk. What exactly are your plans for this business of yours? I hope you've got more experience of bar management than you have of boat handling.'

Jack looked nervously around as if I were holding him hostage in the middle of the canal. Which to be fair, I kind of was.

'I know what I'm doing. I have a sound business background and a solid plan in place. I'm very invested in the venture, and I mean that from the financial and the emotional perspective.' He frowned. 'I don't know why I'm trying to justify myself to you. Perhaps we should postpone this talk until another occasion. Look, you're getting drenched standing there at the tiller. Don't you have a coat or something?'

'I didn't have time to grab it given I was reacting to an emergency situation. Besides, proper boat people aren't afraid of a little bit of water,' I said, although I was admittedly starting to feel rather cold. My favourite patchwork skirt and book-themed t-shirt combo was not exactly ideal gear for carrying out boating manoeuvres in the driving rain.

'I've got a spare coat in the cabin,' he said.

'Good for you.'

'I meant you can use it if you want.'

It was hardly the most generous of offers.

'I'm fine as I am,' I said. Unfortunately, my attempt at being a strong confident woman, unbothered by a bit of rain was somewhat undermined by the involuntary shiver which followed my statement.

'I'll go and fetch it,' he said.

Jack retreated into the cabin and emerged a moment later with a Henri Lloyd fleece-lined waterproof sailing jacket which had probably cost more than my shop had taken in the last month. He tentatively held it out towards me as if he expected me to snatch it from his hands and toss it into the water in disgust.

I made a great show of checking our surroundings before I let go of the tiller and reluctantly accepted the coat, feeling instantly warmer.

'Thank you,' I said grudgingly.

'You're welcome.' He dipped his head in a strangely old-fashioned gesture.

'Shall we get you moored up then?' I suggested. The sooner I could get off this boat, the better.

'You've done enough already. I wouldn't want to put you out,' he said. As a late attempt at politeness, it made zero sense.

I gestured around me. 'If you hadn't noticed, your boat is in the middle of the canal. Unless you're expecting me to swim back to mine, we're going to have to head towards the shore at some point. We might as well go to your mooring.'

Despite the logic in my statement, Jack still looked extremely reluctant.

'Or you've had enough of boating already and have decided to take the boat back to its original owner?' I asked hopefully.

He shook his head.

'Fine, I guess I am taking a dip in the Oxford Canal after all,' I said. I made as if I was going to clamber onto the stern railing in preparation for diving into the water.

'No, stop, don't jump,' he cried out. With visible effort, he adjusted his tone to one suited to calming a nervous animal. 'Why don't we go to my mooring after all? That seems like a much safer option than diving in.'

I couldn't help laughing. 'I'm an excellent swimmer, you know.'

'I'm sure you are. But who knows what's lurking beneath the surface of this water. There could be shopping trolleys and all kinds of rubbish dumped in there. And isn't there a risk of contracting … what's it called? Weil's disease? The thing from rats. It would be frankly irresponsible to get in.'

He was trying to be smart by echoing my earlier words back to me. It wound me up still further.

'It's a bit late to be worrying about stuff like that when you've already bought your boat. If you've got such a low opinion of the place, I can't understand why you wanted to move here. Do you really imagine we all sit around letting people dump rubbish in the canal? We take pride in our home. There are certainly no shopping trolleys. The water's definitely clean enough for swimming, although the Boating Association frowns upon it in case hullabaloos like you happen to be around. As for Weil's disease, there's no risk of contracting it in the water if you keep your mouth closed.'

'I'm not sure that's your forte,' he shot back.

I sucked in a breath. 'Wow, that's harsh Mr Siddall, very harsh indeed. You're being pretty bolshy for a man who's dependent on me to get safely back to dry land.'

I waited for another apology but this time there was none forthcoming.

'You were probably more concerned about your designer jacket going in the water than me,' I grumbled.

He frowned, pretty much proving my point.

'I guess this is a classic case of if you can't say anything nice, don't say anything at all,' I said, needing to fill the awkward silence. 'So you concede that our only option is for me to steer us to your mooring? Feel free to make notes on how the professionals do it. You'll find it useful when you move on to your next location.' *Hopefully*, I thought, *you'll quickly grow bored of this venture.*

'Oh I don't have a continuous cruiser licence,' he said, watching my expression to see if I was impressed that he'd got the lingo correct. I was not. 'The Jericho Wine Barge is here to stay. Permanently. Hence the name.'

'Who would have guessed it? You could call it the Wine Barge instead and then insert the location of wherever you happen to be staying at the time. It could be a quirky marketing ploy, plus you'd get to see much more of our nation's beautiful waterways.'

Jack shook his head. 'By the same token you could do that with the Bookship. What's stopping you from moving around?'

I scowled at him in lieu of a response. I didn't need to justify my decisions to anyone, particularly not him.

He shrugged. 'Like you, I am here to stay.'

'More's the shame,' I muttered.

'What was that?' he said.

'Mooring's the game,' I adjusted, not wanting to extend the conversation any longer. I'd spent too long on this boat allowing the man to wind me up. I needed to get back to work. 'Let's get this vessel tied up and out of the way before someone else needs to come through.'

## Chapter Eight

My section of the Oxford Canal wasn't the busiest, but it was a rare day when I didn't see another boat puttering past. I checked up and down the waterway and was relieved to see that it was still clear. I hoped the rainy conditions might have encouraged most people to tie up and put a brew on; it would be sod's law for another vessel to come into view as I was trying to steer the Jericho Wine Barge into its mooring. I was confident I could do it, but every boat has its own quirks, and I would normally prefer not to be handling them for the first time to carry out one of the trickiest manoeuvres you could perform on a canal.

'Should I keep watch or something?' asked Jack, once again dropping in some nautical vocabulary in another lame bid to convince me of his boating credentials.

To be honest, he'd be of more use going into the galley and putting the kettle on, but if it would get him out my hair, then I could play along.

'How far are we from the bank right now?' I asked first.

He squinted towards the shore. 'I'd say approximately two and a half metres away. Give or take a few centimetres.'

I nodded, surprised by his accuracy.

'Not too bad. Okay, let's get ready to moor up. Why don't you head to the well deck, so you can jump ashore with the line?'

Maybe he'd fall in the water while he was at it. That would wipe the smug expression from his face, which had grown bigger when I acknowledged his correct distance calling.

'Absolutely. On it,' he said, not moving anywhere.

'The well deck is at the front of the boat,' I said, doing my best to keep the irritation out my voice, which frankly was a courtesy that he didn't deserve.

'Right. I'm not completely up on my canal boat terminology yet.' He sounded unapologetic about it.

'So I see. I have a couple of books for sale on that topic which you might wish to purchase and then take pains to study. However, I will add the caveat that you'll learn the most by actually being out on the water with someone who knows what they're doing. And no, I'm not offering. Much as I love books, there is only so much theory you can absorb before it becomes necessary to engage in the practical. You wouldn't want to get a lift in a car from someone who'd only read about how to drive, would you?'

'I figured boating on a canal would be easier than driving a car. Otherwise, why would they hire these things out to holidaymakers?'

'Hmm, that theory doesn't seem to be working out very

well for you, does it?' I pointed out. 'And don't get me started on the holiday hires.'

'Something else you've got a strong opinion about?'

'Well, some of them are okay, but many of them seem to think that the best steering method is bouncing from one bank of the canal to the other, a habit which you seem to be in danger of developing. And what exactly is wrong with having an opinion?' I asked.

'Nothing at all,' he acknowledged. 'I've got plenty of my own, although I'm perhaps not quite as vocal about sharing them as you are.'

'I hadn't noticed you holding back at all. Now if you've quite finished with the idle chit-chat, will you please head to the front of the boat and get ready to moor up?'

'Aye aye, cap'n,' he responded.

I frowned at him.

'Is that not what you're meant to say on a boat?' he asked with affected innocence.

'A "Yes, Molly" will do just fine. There's no need to take the mickey.'

'I was—' he started.

'I'm not interested. Enough talking.' I gestured at the shore. 'This boat isn't going to moor itself, you know. We've been faffing about in the middle of the waterway for quite long enough. Off you go.'

He nodded, thankfully swallowing back whatever smartarse comment he had intended to make and hurried down into the cabin. After a lengthy pause, I heard his voice echo down from the other end of the boat.

'I'm in position.'

'Praise be, we're all saved,' I muttered under my breath.

I checked our surroundings and assessed my options. A burst of reverse to get us parallel to the mooring, then a slight manoeuvre starboard would do the trick I reckoned. The engine let out a pleased purr as I put the boat into a low gear and gently steered us into position.

'One and a half metres. No, actually, I think it's less than that now,' came a muffled yell from the well deck.

I ignored Jack's attempt to help and leaned as far as I could to starboard to check for myself. He might have got the distance correct earlier, but that could easily have been a fluke.

'Smoothly done,' I said to myself as I brought the Jericho Wine Barge perfectly alongside, and put the engine back into neutral. Then I hopped over the side with the stern line and tied the rear of the boat up myself, before jogging to the bow as Jack showed no sign of doing anything to help.

'It would be good if you jumped across sometime today,' I said to him as he hesitated on board, staring at the miniscule space between the boat and the shore. Surely he couldn't be scared of jumping that? There were bigger gaps between the pavement slabs in the centre of town.

'The longer you leave it, the further the distance will get,' I pointed out. 'The wind is blowing the boat off the bank. The stern might be secured, but if you wait too long, the bow will end up in the middle of the water.'

He still hesitated, apparently trying to work out how to avoid the rather large puddle on the bank.

'Now would be a good time to go for it. Or you could throw the rope across to me,' I said. For a man who exuded such an air of self-confidence most of the time, he looked remarkably unsure of himself. I was rather enjoying the spectacle. 'It's that one there,' I added helpfully before he made another rookie error like throwing the decorative coil from the roof which had probably been put there by the seller to hide some damage.

Jack considered his options, then scooped the rope up and threw it towards me like he was chucking a rugby ball at the touch line. I ducked before it whacked me in the face.

'Oops. I went a bit hard then.'

'Once again, a little bit of care and attention, please. I'd prefer not to end up as injured as my boat is. Also, before you chuck a rope, you should always double check to make sure the other end is properly secured. You could throw it like an Olympic champion, and it'd be wasted effort if the whole thing ends up on the land.'

'All I heard is that I threw it like an Olympic champion,' called back Jack with a grin, which he'd no doubt been flattered into believing was charmingly cheeky. I rolled my eyes.

'Of course you did.'

I deftly tied the boat up, wondering if he'd bother taking note of how to do a perfect bowline knot. He'd do well to, if he was serious about making a success of his hobby venture.

There was a thundering of paws as Hilda leapt off the Oxford Bookship and came running towards us, grinning with delight that I'd finally reappeared after what probably felt to her like a lengthy absence.

'Hey, don't worry, girlie, I was only gone for a short

time, I'd never abandon you,' I said. She gave me an affectionate wag of the tail before she brushed past me and jumped onto Jack's boat to greet him as well. I was glad the boat was properly secured as her enthusiastic leap set it rocking vigorously.

'Hello there, my horsey friend,' said Jack, patting her haunches. She shamelessly leaned against him inviting further attention, the treacherous beast.

I swallowed my retort, unable to help feeling somewhat jealous at my pet's transferral of affection. Instead, I whistled for her, but while her ears pricked up, she decided she'd prefer a belly rub and slumped down onto the deck to make Jack give her one. Somewhat to my surprise, he did.

While Hilda was occupied with flirting with the enemy, I returned to my own boat and precariously leaned over the side that had been struck to get a better look at the damage. The hull of my beautiful boat now sported a wide gash through the dark paintwork. It looked like it was superficial, thankfully, but even just repainting would be a big job. I peered into the canal's depths but couldn't spot the bookshop sign which had gone overboard. Despite singing the praises of the canal's cleanliness to Jack, I drew the line at snorkelling in it on a rescue mission. I would have to make do with the sign's twin on the towpath until I found the time to replace it.

Someone cleared their throat from behind me, nearly startling me into falling into the canal.

'It's probably too rainy to be hanging over the side like that,' said Jack, his hand resting casually on Hilda's head in a far too proprietorial way for my liking. 'It wouldn't take much for you to lose your grip.'

I got the impression the double meaning to his words was deliberate.

'When I want your input, I'll ask for it,' I snapped. I was cold, wet and extremely tired of dealing with this man. I'd been in a perfectly good mood before he turned up and started smashing his canal boat around. Now the joy at the modest profit I'd made last night had long vanished, with the fear that the money might have to go on repairs, rather than being put towards my mooring fees fund.

'What's the verdict?' he asked, still not taking the hint and leaving me alone.

'The paintwork will need completely redoing for starters.'

He nodded. 'No problem. I can fund that. It was my mistake after all.'

I thought how nice it must be to be able to make such promises without having to worry about the financial implications. And could I afford to take him at his word?

'While I appreciate your offer to wave a magic wand and sort it all out, it's not really about the money. Redoing the paintwork will involve leaving my mooring, sailing to the boatyard and taking the Bookship out of the water, probably for a few weeks. It's simply not practical at the moment.'

Jack frowned. I suspected he wasn't used to having people talk back to him.

'How about this for an alternative? I was going to get someone in to help with the fit out for the Wine Barge. I can send them in your direction. They could at least paint the area above the waterline so it doesn't look quite so bad. See, Hilda thinks it's a good idea.'

That tipped me over the edge.

'That's not what Hilda thinks at all. She's a dog with her own thoughts, a dog, mind, not a horse, and she doesn't need someone like you projecting their misguided ideas on to her. As for what I'd like, it's for you to leave the pair of us alone, and for things to return to the nice peace and quiet we enjoyed before you, the hullabaloo who delegates everything to other people, turned up.'

'Quaint vocabulary there. That's the second time you've called me a hullabaloo, you know,' he pointed out.

'Says the man who uses phrases like "hoi polloi",' I snapped back, daring him to patronise me still further by praising me for using it correctly.

Instead, he focused on picking apart another of my accusations. 'I don't delegate everything. I'm perfectly capable of standing on my own two feet,' he asserted.

'Sounds a bit too much like you're trying to convince yourself there.'

'I...' Then he sighed. 'Look, I'm sorry that we've got off on the wrong foot, but we're going to be neighbours. We might as well try to get along and be friends.' He attempted a different tack.

'In my experience, if you have to try, it's not an actual friendship. Now, if you don't mind, I have stuff to be getting on with. Some of us have to work for a living, you know.'

He gave Hilda one final scratch of the head. 'That's me told. You know where to find me if you change your mind.'

'There is little chance of that. "My good opinion once lost, is lost forever",' I quoted self-righteously.

'Very well, I'll leave you to it.'

I held on to Hilda's collar as Jack left, ignoring her whimper of disappointment that I wasn't letting her go with him.

'I don't know what's got into you. You're normally such a good judge of character,' I said to her.

She gave an eloquent huff at being prevented from following our new neighbour, and slumped down onto her bed, leaving me to my rage.

<h1 style="text-align:center">Chapter Nine</h1>

I'd not been back in the Bookship five minutes when there was a knock on the shop door. I quickly wiped my eyes, hoping that my visitor wouldn't spot that I'd been crying. I was annoyed at myself for doing so, but the combination of my boat being crashed into and the subsequent confrontation with Jack had thoroughly shaken me up. I was normally pretty even-tempered, but the man brought out the worst in me.

'Come in,' I called, trying so hard to be normal that I'm pretty sure I sounded anything but. I hoped it wasn't Jack returning for round two. Or maybe he'd come to reclaim his coat which I still had wrapped around my shoulders, its warm fleecy lining a comfort, despite the lingering faintly citrusy scent which made me feel like its owner was still hovering over me.

As I hastily removed the coat, Liam appeared in the doorway, and I heaved a sigh of relief.

'Hey, Molly, I wanted to stop by to ask if you're alright,'

he said. 'I saw what happened. You poor thing, you look properly done in.'

He hurried over to me and squeezed my arm sympathetically.

'It's not been the easiest day,' I replied, taking a step away, fearing that if I allowed myself to accept his kindness I might start crying again.

'I can imagine. I was live streaming on the other bank when he collided with you and ended up filming the whole thing as it happened,' he said, gesturing at his phone. 'I got some great action shots of you mid-jump. My followers were pretty impressed by your athleticism as you saved the situation, the heroine of the day. The video's engagement's already off the scale with all the comments pouring in. You can guess what they had to say about his steering ability, or should I say inability.'

I wasn't sure how I felt knowing such an upsetting incident had been broadcast live for the world to see. My uncertainty must have shown on my face because Liam added, 'I'm sorry but there was no time to ask permission to keep filming, and on the plus side the video will be good evidence for your insurance claim.'

I pursed my lips. 'I'm hoping it won't come to that. Making a claim will send my premium sky high. Jack says he'll cover the costs.'

'Let's hope that's the case,' said Liam in a doubtful voice which chimed with my own concern. 'Anyway, where are my manners? I know it's your boat, but can I make you a cup of tea? It feels like the kind of situation where a strong and sweet brew – a drink to match your personality in fact – would be a good idea.'

I laughed at the overblown compliment, as I'm sure he'd intended me to. 'Honestly, it's kind of you, but I'm fine,' I protested, but Liam was having none of it.

'It's no bother,' he said, letting himself into the galley and starting to prepare the drink, opening and closing cupboards until he found the right implements. Hilda grumbled at him as he clattered around, for which apparent sin he apologised profusely.

I settled down on one of the bean bags in the bookshop and decided I'd allow myself to be taken care of for once.

Liam soon returned with the steaming hot drink, along with one for himself, and a plate of biscuits which he must have brought with him, because I knew for a fact my cupboards were empty of any such treats. He sat down next to me and stared spooling through his socials.

'Check you out,' he said, pointing at the reel of me steering the Jericho Wine Barge to safety which he'd posted on his feed. It had already gained several hundred likes.

'And you tagged the bookshop in it too,' I said, unsure whether to be pleased or embarrassed by my new-found social media fame.

'I hope you don't mind?' he asked. 'I sometimes forget not everyone lives their life by the algorithm.'

'I probably should get better at understanding it, to boost the Bookship's following,' I said.

'Happy to help you, any time. I mean, the social media giants are constantly changing the goal posts, but I do okay.'

'You do more than okay. What is it now, eighty-five thousand followers on YouTube?' I asked, happy to think about something other than the crash for a few minutes.

'Hovering around eighty-nine actually. The hundred k mark remains elusive, alas.'

'And here's me being proud of my two thousand followers on Instagram. Some of them might even be actual people rather than bots.'

I took a sip of the tea and pulled a face.

'Sorry, did I go too hard on the sugar?' asked Liam.

'Just a little.' Nevertheless, I took another sip and started to feel the energy returning to my body.

'I figured you'd need all the help you could get after your encounter with Mr Jack Siddall.'

There was something in the tone of his voice which made me sit up straight.

'Do you know him? I mean, from somewhere other than the blind date night.'

Liam took a bite of biscuit before he answered.

'I may have encountered him in my previous existence,' he said carefully.

'You're not giving much away there. I sense there's a story to be told.'

He shrugged, trying to appear casual, but the knuckles of his left hand were white as he clenched his fingers into a fist. 'You make it sound much more interesting than it is,' he said, his tone most unlike his usual relaxed happy-go-lucky manner. 'It's not really that big a deal. Or at least, that's what I tell myself nowadays. I probably shouldn't have mentioned it.'

I took another sip of the disgusting tea, my heart accelerating as my imagination went wild over what Liam wasn't saying, then I tried a different tack. 'You can't say something like that and then go all coy about it. Look, the guy's going to be living just along the canal from me. If there's something about my new neighbour that I need to know, as my friend, it would be great if you told me.'

He pursed his lips, still considering.

'I'll be the soul of discretion,' I added. 'I've read a couple of articles about the Siddalls. Jack isn't mentioned much, but it's clear that his family are uber successful, and if you ask me, it's not possible to get that rich without there being a level of ruthlessness along the way.'

'Ruthless certainly…' Liam made a conscious effort to relax his fist, having realised I'd noticed it. 'The trouble is, I signed an NDA, and the Siddalls are a litigious bunch.'

I was getting more and more worried. 'I promise it won't go any further.'

He nodded. 'I know I can trust you. It's something I still find hard to talk about, even though it was a couple of years ago now. But you're a mate and a fellow boatie, and you're right, the guy's going to be living next door to you. You should know what you're dealing with.' He lowered his voice, and quickly looked about him before he continued speaking, almost as if he expected Jack to appear at any moment. 'Before I discovered the waterways and got into content creation, I used to work in the corporate world. I know, I know, it's hard to imagine me in a suit and tie.' He grinned, and I experienced the briefest flash of regret that I'd fixed him up with my best friend, before feeling guilty and reminding myself that I didn't have time for that kind of thing. 'Anyway, so Jack and I used to work together. He was Mr Nepo Baby Trader, and I was the guy who was working his way up from the shop floor so to speak. We were supposedly at the same level of seniority, but you know how these things go. It's all about who you know and what your name is. Some people try their best to make it on their own merits despite their connections. Others…' His voice trailed off. It was easy to fill in the gaps. 'Anyway, it went down in a disappointingly predictable way. We both went for the same promotion. I'd been working hard on a project; Jack offered to help. Then suddenly there he was presenting all my research as his, while I looked like a complete mug. He generously threw me a bone and offered to let me deliver some of his findings, which I refused to do because they were clearly acquired through questionably legal methods. Inevitably he was the one to get a massive bonus plus the corner office with the city view. I meanwhile got called in by the boss, who just so happened to be Jack's dad, and was told I was out on my ear because my work wasn't up to scratch.' He laughed bitterly. 'I don't know why I didn't see it coming. Still, I suppose it all worked out for the best. If that hadn't happened, I wouldn't have found my real passion.'

Liam was trying to see the positive, but I could tell he was still hurt by what had happened. As he had every right to be.

'What a horrible thing to do,' I said. 'That's downright dirty behaviour. If you can't get something without resorting to trickery or having to use friends in high places, then you're not meant to have it.'

Liam nodded. 'You're absolutely right. But I guess insecurity will drive people to act in ways they otherwise probably wouldn't.'

'That's a very generous interpretation of things. I'm not sure he'd afford you the same courtesy,' I said.

'It's been tough, but I've moved on with my life. The guy doesn't deserve any of my head space.'

'I don't suppose you'll be wanting to stick around for long now that he's here in Oxford,' I said, now regretting setting him up with Flick for a very different reason. I didn't want my best friend to fall head over heels for someone who wasn't planning to stay.

'Actually, I have no intention of changing my plans,' he said forcefully. 'I don't see why I should leave purely because he's turned up.'

'Good for you.' I reached out to scratch Hilda's head. 'I wonder what made him quit the family business. From trading to running a bar is quite a career change. Do you suppose his dad realised what he did to you?'

Liam frowned. 'Old man Siddall likes nothing more than a businessman who'll stop at nothing to get to the top. If anything, I'd imagine setting up his own enterprise is Jack's attempt at trying to impress his daddy still further. Mark my words, he'll have big plans, and I doubt his boutique bar will remain that way for long. He'll already be looking at ways to expand the Siddall empire and take over the canal.'

'Well, he can't expand here. I'm not going anywhere,'

I said, hoping what I said was true. But my anxiety about the mooring fees was now even more pronounced. If I couldn't afford to pay them, and there happened to be a neighbouring boat with a wealthy owner looking to grow his business, the Oxford Boating Association would be falling over themselves to move me along and offer him my mooring position so he could do precisely that. My battle to survive had just got even harder.

# Chapter Ten

Liam kept me company for a while longer, trying to cheer me up by helping to create a new video advertising my next Blind Date with a Book night, then once the rain had stopped, he returned to his own boat. I pottered around the cabin, straightening the displays and rearranging books, not with any particular purpose in mind other than to feel like I was actually doing something. My brain was buzzing with everything Liam had said, and another lull in customers did not help my spiralling anxiety about the cold-blooded operator who now lived next door to me.

'Maybe it's the weather that's putting them off,' I suggested out loud. This time I didn't even have the excuse of speaking to Hilda as she was hanging out on the stern deck, standing alert, unashamedly watching what our new neighbour was doing. I wished she could talk, because I was dying to know what he was up to, but I didn't want to be caught spying. I could hear that his engine was on, probably to charge up a generator, and I reckoned that said engine was in need of a service, judging by the clattering noise it was making. Every twenty seconds or so it would stutter, almost as if it was about to die out completely, then with a groan it would revert to its usual banging. I found I was waiting for the pause, subconsciously counting down until it happened.

I put some music on and turned the volume up louder than normal to try to distract myself from fixating on the pattern. But even with the *Bridgerton* soundtrack blasting out from my speakers I could still hear the engine, and by mid-afternoon, the thud of metal clanging against wood had entered the mix. I forced myself to stay where I was, even though my curiosity was reaching fever pitch.

'The canal is a veritable hive of activity this afternoon,' said one of my most loyal customers, Kat, as she climbed on board hand in hand with her boyfriend Leo. She'd been the first person to buy a book from me, not that I'd told her at the time because I'd already been open for a week by then, and I was grateful she continued to visit, even though, as a librarian, she had ready access to pretty much any book she could possibly want.

'Tell me about it.' I tapped my phone to turn the music down to a more reasonable volume, then flinched as yet another thud rang out from my neighbour's boat. 'What on earth is he doing in there?'

'Your new neighbour has arrived with a bang,' said Leo. For a moment I thought he was referring to the noise from the boat, then I realised what he actually meant as he gestured at his phone and continued with, 'Thank goodness you were on hand to save the day.'

'How much traction is Liam's video getting?' I worried out loud. 'I really don't want Nana Rose to come across it before I tell her about what happened. She'd be so worried about the boat, and me, and she doesn't need that kind of stress in her life.'

'I'd tell her pretty soon in that case,' said Kat. 'We popped into work on our way here—'

'She can't keep away from the place, even on her days off,' interrupted Leo, his voice full of affection.

'It was your idea, you gorgeous geek,' she pointed out with a grin. 'Anyway, the video was all the folk from the Seniors' Social Media group could talk about. It was causing quite a stir. It's definitely trending in the Oxford area, and probably further afield I'd say. It looked like a pretty dramatic chain of events. You did well to take control and sort out the situation.'

I groaned. 'Thanks, but it was only what anyone would have done. And becoming the talking point for the Seniors' Social Media group is the last thing I need. I was hoping to generate some positive publicity for the Oxford Bookship, but I'd prefer to go viral for something literature-related. If Nana's seen the video, she'll be out of her mind with concern.'

'Why don't you give her a call now?' suggested Kat. 'We're happy to have a browse by ourselves. We've got some serious book shopping to do. Leo treated me to a new bookcase to celebrate us buying the house together.'

'I thought you could use it for the thousands of books

you already have,' he said, his grin growing wider as he anticipated her response to his provocative statement.

'Very funny. You knew exactly what you were getting into when you asked me to move in. A new bookcase means buying new books to fill it with, any fool could work that one out.' She nudged her hip playfully against his, and they carried on with their happy bickering as they went to inspect my recent arrivals shelves, Leo standing with his arms out ready to hold the pile of purchases which Kat would undoubtedly make. I experienced a moment of envy at their carefree happiness, although I reminded myself it had not always been that way for them.

I slipped into my living space, leaving them to it, and quickly called Nana Rose.

'I was wondering when I'd be hearing from you, my adventurous darling,' she said as soon as she picked up. I felt instantly guilty for not thinking to ring her earlier. It was strangely quiet in the background. Normally when we chatted, I could hear the hubbub of activity from the care home's lounge where she spent most of her time. I wondered if she was resting in her room and worried about the reason why.

'I guess you've seen the video then,' I said, although my fear she'd be upset by what she'd seen had been somewhat allayed by the cheery tone she'd answered in.

'Haven't I just? I've been showing it to all the girls and boys here, and let me tell you, they're terribly impressed by your skills. That was quite the leap, my darling. You didn't hesitate. You saw somebody in trouble, and you jumped instantly to his aid. I'm so proud of you.'

'It wasn't quite like that,' I said. It was typical of Nana Rose to think the best of me, but my motivation at the time had been entirely selfish, aiming to save the Oxford Bookship from further harm, rather than being concerned for the person who was so obviously out of their depth on the other boat.

'And that footage of you bringing the boat to shore. My chest was practically swelling when I saw that. Not an easy task on a strange boat, no indeed. Mind you, you've always been a talented helmswoman. You could steer a boat almost as soon as you were able to stand up.'

'If I'd known there was going to be such a big audience for my efforts, I'd have done it with more finesse,' I said.

'Pshaw, now you're fishing for compliments,' said Nana Rose with a laugh. 'And in case you're wondering whether to mention it, I've also seen that the Oxford Bookship got a little scrape from the other boat.'

*Not so little*, I thought silently, then added out loud, 'I'm really sorry about that, Nana.'

'There's nothing to apologise for. These things happen. And worse things happen at sea, or so they say. Let me tell you, it's not the first scratch the boat's had in her lifetime, and I'm sure it won't be the last. She'll survive; she's a sturdy bird.'

'Like her previous owner.'

Nana Rose laughed again, although this time it evolved into something which sounded worryingly like a wince of pain.

'Perhaps not quite as sturdy as I used to be,' she said, an

unusual admission for her to make which got me feeling anxious all over again.

'Nana…' I started to say, but she interrupted me.

'Anyway, I've kept you far too long. You get back to your customers, Molly love. You've got more important things to do than spend your time talking to me. And don't forget to give Hilda a hug for me. Such a shame she only made a fleeting appearance in the video.'

'Nothing's more important than talking to you, oh Nana mine. And maybe if Hilda had appeared, there would be fewer comments about me.'

'I love talking to you too. Embrace the fame, my darling. It's about time the rest of the world recognised your shine.' She coughed. 'I think that's my cue to go and fetch a drink. The sun is over the yardarm somewhere in the world, am I right? Enjoy the rest of your day, it was lovely to hear from you.'

'Take care. I'll be round to see you later.'

'That would have been lovely and I hate to be a party pooper, but can we take a rain check? I've already got plans this evening,' said Nana Rose.

'That's nice, what are you up to?' I asked.

She hesitated for a little longer than felt natural, and I wondered if this might be a manufactured excuse because she was too tired to see me.

'We're having a bingo night, and I said I'd do the calling,' she said.

There was a note in her voice which made me even more convinced that this explanation didn't ring true. But I knew better than to push her.

'Two little ducks…'

'Twenty-two,' she said, managing to put on an appropriate calling voice. Thankfully this time she didn't break down into a cough again.

'Have fun. Don't do anything I wouldn't.'

'Oh, my darling, I'll do much worse,' she replied with a cackle. I really hoped that was true.

# Chapter Eleven

'How are you getting on? Very well, I see,' I said to Kat and Leo when I returned to the bookshop cabin. The latter was laden down with an armful of books, and there was another pile of volumes next to the card machine. The pair of them might be about to become responsible for the Bookship turning a profit this month.

'I'm concerned we may have to start looking for a bigger home already,' said Leo. 'By my calculations, the new bookcase is full and then some. Did I mention I've developed this recurring nightmare about being trapped under an avalanche of books?' He didn't seem too bothered about it, his expression soft as he looked at Kat.

She rolled her eyes. 'He's one to talk. His stack is the one by the till.'

'I confess, you've got me bang to rights.'

'You know what they say: there's no such thing as too many books, just not enough bookcases,' I said with a smile.

Kat nodded. 'Exactly that.'

'I'll throw this in, as a house-warming present,' I said, picking a copy of *What You Are Looking For Is In The Library* from the central display. It was one of my go-to comfort reads and I knew these two would adore it.

'Thank you. The author's obviously very wise as it turned out to be true for me,' said Leo, nodding towards Kat.

She smiled back at him, then reached across the counter and gave my hand a squeeze. 'That's so kind of you, Molly. I've heard a lot of good things about it but haven't got round to reading it myself yet. You always make the best recommendations.'

As I rang up their purchases, I decided to turn the conversation back round to my new neighbour to see if they'd spotted anything on their way past. Leo ran a private investigation business after all, so he was bound to pay careful attention to his surroundings at all times.

'Is it me or has it gone quiet at last?' I asked, nodding my head in the direction of the soon-to-be Jericho Wine Barge. There was another thunderous sound of banging before they could respond. 'Nope, sadly not.'

'We did think that he's got his work cut out for him as we walked past,' said Kat. 'It looked like he's single-handedly stripping the interior completely back. It's going to be quite the job carrying everything along the towpath to get rid of it.'

I nodded. That would explain the banging then. It was concerning that Jack hadn't bothered waiting for help with the work. Maybe his claim that he was going to get someone in who could also work on the damage to the

Oxford Bookship had been just that, a claim, without any basis in truth. Given his track record of poor behaviour, it wouldn't surprise me.

'He's not hanging around,' I said. 'He's only just arrived. I was hoping he'd take a few days to recover from the experience before he started work. I guess he wants to catch the summer trade with his new enterprise.'

'From experience of starting up a business, it's best to get stuck in as soon as possible,' said Leo. 'The early days can be challenging.'

'I know that,' I responded with feeling. Did a year in still qualify as being early days? I knew Leo had started his business around the same time as I had, but judging by the number of books he was buying, I suspected he was doing a lot better than I was out of it, although at least today's sales figures would reap the benefit of his success.

'What's he planning to do with the boat? Is he going to be living on it full time like you?' asked Kat.

I quickly told her about the Jericho Wine Barge. To my disappointment, she looked delighted.

'What fun, and in time for the good weather too. We'll have to go and check it out, won't we, Leo? And maybe you could arrange a joint bookshop and bar night. We were saying last night we hoped you'd do an event that wasn't only for singletons, now we're practically smug marrieds.'

'*Bridget Jones's Diary*,' said Leo, looking pleased with himself for getting her reference. These two were too cute. If I'd even dreamt of mentioning the M word around my last boyfriend, he'd have fled in a panic, but Leo seemed completely relaxed. 'I've been working my way through all

Kat's favourites,' he added, making me like him even more.

I smiled. 'Good for you. And I bet you're not the type of guy to say he preferred the film to the book.'

Kat drew her breath in with a hiss. 'He wouldn't dare. Although the *Bridget Jones* movies are also excellent.'

'They are; it's true. And you make a good point about events for a wider audience. I want to share the Oxford Bookship with as many people as possible. I've been mulling over a few ideas. How does a bookish afternoon tea sound? I was thinking of theming the treats with specific books, like carrot cake for *Anne of Green Gables* as a nod to her touchiness about her beautiful hair colour. Do you think there'd be much of a market for that?'

'I love it,' said Kat. 'You can't go far wrong with a books and cake combo.'

'It would of course rely on the weather being good,' I thought aloud. 'There's not enough room to set up more than a couple of small tables for afternoon tea in here. Most people would have to sit on the decks or by the towpath. And I'd have to find someone to make the cakes for me. The galley isn't exactly designed for fine patisserie work, that's supposing I was even capable of such a thing, which I'm not.'

'You've thought about author events, right?' said Kat. 'I'm happy to pass your details on to the authors we've had into the library if you want.'

'That would be great, thank you. Signings, readings, whatever they want, I'd love to host them. It's one of the reasons I wanted to open a bookshop in the first place.

I've reached out to loads of authors and am desperately hoping my emails didn't go into their spam folders.' I didn't articulate my real fear that no one had replied because my bookshop was considered too small fry to be worthy of consideration.

'Persistence is key. In my experience, authors are very busy people. Most of them have to juggle day jobs with the writing after all, but I'm sure you'll find some takers before long.' Kat checked her watch. 'Heck, we're running late. We're going to have to love you and leave you.' She gave me a quick hug. 'Make sure we're top of the invitation list for your bookish afternoon tea and your first author event. See you soon.'

It was only after they'd left that I realised I should have asked them to drop Jack's coat off for me on their way past, but at least this way I had an excuse for doing some snooping. I joined Hilda on the stern deck and pretended I was checking the towpath for customers, while glancing surreptitiously across to the Jericho Wine Barge. Was that a pile of wooden cabinets on the well deck? He'd better not be dumping those on the side of the canal and cluttering up the area I liked to think of as my private garden, even though technically it was shared between the moorings.

'You're staring so hard, you might as well come across and take a closer look.' Jack poked his head out of the cabin door, which by nature of our respective moorings meant he was only a couple of metres away from me.

I jumped at his sudden appearance. 'I thought you might want this back,' I said, holding up the coat.

'You can leave it by the mooring once you've had it dry-cleaned,' he said, his expression solemn.

I gaped at him. 'I only wore it for half an hour, tops. Getting it dry-cleaned seems a little excessive.'

He continued looking steadily at me, then his right eyebrow quirked slightly upwards. 'I was making a joke,' he said, as if it was obvious.

'Hilarious. Maybe you should consider a career in stand-up comedy?' I suggested. 'Although you might have to reconsider the deadpan delivery. It could make you sound like you're grumpy instead.'

Jack seemed unbothered by my assessment. 'I'm quite happy with the career path I've chosen, thanks.'

'I'll chuck this across for you,' I said, preparing to throw.

'I'd prefer it didn't end up in the drink,' he said, which was rich coming from a guy who'd shown himself to be incapable of throwing a mooring rope ashore properly. He was probably worried about his ability to catch it safely, I thought.

'Fine, I'll bring it across. Stay here, Hilda,' I instructed. She settled down on the deck, but when she realised I was about to get off the boat, she jumped up and leapt onto the towpath, leading the way to the Jericho Wine Barge, tail wagging furiously.

'At least someone's pleased to see me,' said Jack.

'I think she spotted a bird,' I lied, jumping ashore myself and quickly checking my mooring ropes were still secure out of habit.

I took my time covering the short distance to the Jericho Wine Barge so I could get a proper look at the boat. Unlike the tasteful dark blue exterior of the Oxford Bookship with her painted swirls of faded, burnished gold around the portholes, the Jericho Wine Barge had a colour palette of red, moss green and yellow. The colours were all normally used on traditional boats, but to my critical gaze, they seemed garish, like a cartoon interpretation of what a canal boat should look like.

'What do you think? I asked the boatyard to freshen up the paint before I took full ownership,' said Jack, Hilda making herself at home beside him.

'It's a shame you didn't get them to sort your engine out while they were at it,' I said.

Jack frowned. 'Yes, it has been making a strange noise. I hope they haven't been putting sawdust in there.' He must have seen my blank expression, because he elaborated. 'Like Mr Wormwood does in *Matilda* to make the engines in the dodgy cars he sells sound like they're running more smoothly. At least, they do for a short while, before they break completely.'

He'd know about dodgy business practices, I thought, but restricted myself to saying, 'Another film you've watched in preference to the book?'

'No, I've read the actual book. I admire a character with the courage of her convictions.'

'Right,' I said, rather taken aback.

'And as we're on the subject of children's literature that still resonates, like you, I'm a big fan of the *Swallows and Amazons* books by Arthur Ransome,' he added, his eyes sparkling in an irritatingly pleased-with-himself way.

'How did you...?' I started to ask, before stopping

myself. The whole charming book chatter was clearly a ploy to soften me up.

'Only someone who likes *Swallows and Amazons* would use the term "hullabaloo" to describe a person who's failing to control their boat properly.'

'It was justified,' I said, unashamed of my use of the word, but surprised at his knowledge of my reference point. It would have been an easy shot to make a snide comment about his apparent love of books intended for children, but I would never stoop so low as to criticise a person's reading habits. Reading was reading, whether it was the back of a cereal box or *The Iliad* in the original. Although remembering Jack's ancient Greek pedantry, I wouldn't be surprised if he'd actually done the latter. It was probably only a matter of time before he'd make some comment designed to show that off.

'Perhaps in that moment. But I promise I'm much more than a hullabaloo,' he said, looking at me steadily. 'Maybe you would agree, if you allowed yourself to see past the first impression, that is. After all, isn't that what the message said on our blind date book?'

I fought the urge to drop my gaze, feeling uncomfortably exposed, fixed in his hazel eyes. I clamped down on the stirring of curiosity. He was playing with me. I didn't need to know anything more about him. I was a good judge of character, and I knew quite enough already.

'Hmm,' I said dubiously. 'Delightful as it's been to talk, I've got work to do. Here's your coat back.'

I held it out to him, but instead of taking it, he gestured for me to follow him.

'Dump it on the side somewhere. Come and take a look inside, if you like.'

I folded the coat carefully and placed it on the cleanest-looking bit of deck. No matter what my thoughts were about its owner, it was too expensive an item of clothing to be dumped on the side. 'I really am very busy at the moment,' I said half-heartedly.

But there was no point in trying to deceive Jack.

'Sure you are,' he said, pointedly looking over at the empty towpath. 'You've had, what, a grand total of half a dozen customers so far today?'

'There were more than that. And at least two of them were very good customers who bought a significant number of books,' I pointed out, omitting to mention I'd undermined my bottom line by giving them a book too.

Jack looked unimpressed.

I sighed. 'Fine, I suppose I can take a look, but if any customers arrive at my shop, I'll have to leave.'

'Naturally. I would expect nothing less. Follow me,' he said. 'Or rather, Hilda will lead the way. She seems to have taken quite a liking to me.'

'There's no accounting for taste,' I retorted.

He drew a sharp breath in. 'Ouch. Molly Bramble by name, Molly brambly by nature, I see.'

I unleashed an icy glare on him which would have been enough to wither most people, but Jack returned my gaze with a distractingly concentrated focus.

'Lead on, MacHilda,' I said, tapping her gently on the haunches as I sought to break the intensity of the moment.

'I hope that doesn't make me Macbeth,' muttered Jack.

I tried a different approach and smiled with sweet sarcasm at him, which he took at face value, surprising me with a smile of his own, a sudden change which threw me even more off guard and made me feel unaccountably flustered.

Hilda nosed her way into the cabin, and I gestured to Jack to go ahead of me too, somewhat taken aback by my reaction.

'Shall I explain My Vision as we go?' he asked.

'I'm definitely hearing the capital letters in there, Mr Wine Barge,' I said, back on the defensive. 'Go on then, fill me in on your Big Plans.' I injected a note of weariness into my voice to disguise my eagerness to discover exactly what horrors I was going to have to endure from my new neighbour's enterprise.

'So up there on the well deck where we were standing,' he glanced at me to check his vocabulary, and I nodded, 'I'm going to have some bench seats fitted with large cushions for people to lounge around on while they're enjoying their drinks. I'll string fairy lights up from the roof, and there'll be a proper gangplank with guard rails so people can get on board and off again easily.'

'Drunk people and water are never a good combination. What time will you be staying open until? And what will your policy be on serving people who've obviously already had too much? How strong will the outside lighting be? What noise controls will you have in place?' I fired a load of questions at him. Flick would be proud of me. Jack nodded as if he'd been expecting them.

'I envisage the lighting being soft and cosy, atmospheric

shall we say, but obviously bright enough so people can see where they're going. My hospitality licence is until 11 p.m. And before you ask, I've done plenty of risk assessments. It was a requirement of getting the licence in the first place. I don't have a policy per se about people getting too drunk, but I don't think I'll be attracting that kind of clientele. I highly doubt they'll be rowdy or even that noisy.'

I frowned. 'That seems foolishly optimistic. This is a city full of students and tourists. People out for a good time who like to let their hair down rather than sticking to being sensible. And I can't imagine they'll be quiet about it.'

'There's nothing foolish about optimism,' he said simply.

It was a sentiment I'd normally agree with, but whatever optimism I used to have was being slowly crushed out of me thanks to the challenging financial circumstances I faced.

'Easy to say when you can afford it. Where is the bar going to be?' I asked.

I could see him considering whether to respond to my statement, but he decided it wasn't worth it and answered my question instead.

'In this main cabin over there, approximately where Hilda is standing at the moment. In fact, she's a similar length to the actual bar. Maybe I could get her to lie down so I can draw around her on the floor and mark out where the rest of the furniture will go.' His features softened with an infectious flash of humour.

'Good luck persuading her to stay still for that,' I said, smiling despite my best intentions. Given Hilda's inexplicable interest in the man, she'd probably do exactly as he wanted.

I followed him further into the body of the boat and walked slowly in a circle, taking in the stripped back interior. I could see marks on the walls where a set of bunks must have been, and the floorboards were bare and in desperate need of a good sweeping. The portholes were grimy on the inside, and a pile of wine boxes was stacked up next to the interior door, which was hanging off its hinges. It was echoing in its emptiness.

'It's a good space, isn't it?' said Jack, the starry expression on his face telling me that he was impervious to any flaws. In truth, it was an expression I recognised from seeing it in my own mirror in the early days of the Oxford Bookship before the reality of the day-to-day battle for business took over. He'd soon realise the errors of his naivety, I tried to reassure myself. On the other hand, it was obvious he had a much bigger financial buffer to protect him from the stresses I had to face. Perhaps I was the one being naive.

'The floor is in good condition, so that will stay as it is. Yes, I will give it a good clean first,' he added, as he caught my dubious countenance. 'I've got a reclaimed bar from a pub that closed down. I'm planning to disassemble it and then rebuild it in here. It's made of beautiful old oak, smoothed to a shine by the touch of generation upon generation of punters. I love that it'll bring some history to the place. A few barstools and then some small tables, and that will be all the furniture I can fit inside. Again, I've reclaimed them from the same pub. It was sad to see such an institution shutting down, but I'm glad that I can give them a second life. I'm going to fit a ledge running along one side of the cabin so people can rest their drinks on it. I don't want to cram too much furniture in. That way there will be more room for people to mingle. And the overflow will be on the deck and the towpath garden.'

'The towpath garden too?' I repeated. There was no clear boundary between my bit of the garden and Jack's so it was inevitable that people would spill over into my space, tramping on the herbs and flowers I'd planted with such optimism, and shattering their wine glasses in Hilda's favourite snoozing spots. I was going to feel under siege in my own home. I was used to lying in bed and hearing people walking past on the towpath, but it would be another thing entirely to lie there and hear them rowdily socialising probably only inches away from my head for hours at a time. I might as well go out to join the party in my pyjamas.

'Exactly how many people do you think you'll get in here?' I asked, picturing hordes of noisy drinkers partying into the night. 'And does the Oxford Boating Association know about the overflow into the garden thing?'

'Yes, the Association approves entirely. If you think about it, it's not really that different from your Blind Date with a Book night, where I seem to recall several people were hanging out on the towpath. In fact, hadn't you set up a table for drinks there? Did you clear that with the Association, out of interest?' I remained silent. If he was trying to threaten me, I wasn't going to give him the satisfaction of appearing worried by it. He shrugged and continued. 'As to numbers, there will be maybe a dozen who could fit in the cabin, if people don't mind getting a little cosy.' He lowered his tone. 'I want to keep things … intimate.'

I scowled at him, annoyed at the involuntary frisson I'd experienced at his choice of vocabulary. I knew he'd only done it to try to get a rise out of me. 'And what about the other facilities?' I asked primly, refusing to rise to his bait.

'I got the bathroom re-fitted before I took possession of the boat. Two heads – correct nautical term for the loo, right? – and a pocket handkerchief-sized shower for me to use. Tiny house living might be all the rage, or tiny boat living in my case, but it's a challenge to find fittings when you're six feet tall. But you'd know all about that.' He gestured at me.

'You're six feet? Really? Are you sure?' I asked provocatively. 'I would have put you at more like five nine, maybe five ten on a good day.' He was definitely six feet, judging by the fact that we were pretty much eye to eye when we stood next to each other, but I wasn't going to pander to his ego by agreeing with him about it. I knew from experience that most men were notoriously sensitive about their height. I went through a period of only wearing flats and hunching my back when I was dating the awful ex, desperately trying to appease his feeling of being threatened by my superior height. My superior everything, I reminded myself. I was definitely better off without him.

Jack, however, seemed unbothered by my dig, not even trying to refute my words.

'The only thing left for me to do on the bathroom front is

re-hang the door properly, which I'm hoping will take me all of five minutes. I am on a schedule, after all.'

'So, you'll be living on board?'

'To start with.'

I waited for him to elaborate but it soon became clear that that was as much as I was getting.

'And when do you intend to open?' I pressed.

'Two weeks tomorrow,' said Leo. 'That should give me plenty of time to get the rest of the place shipshape. Despite current appearances, I'm confident that between me and the work crew, it'll be ready in plenty of time. I'm going to launch with a wine tasting evening, admission to ticket holders only.'

'But you can't launch then. That's the night I'm going to have my next Blind Date with a Book event,' I said, before I could stop myself.

'I don't think the two are mutually exclusive,' he said.

'The noise from your bar opening will spoil the event for my visitors,' I retorted. 'They'll be coming to enjoy an evening of culture, to discuss books and maybe meet someone special. They won't want to mingle with beer-swilling louts clogging up the towpath and being dickish on your deck.'

Jack's laugh was infuriatingly dismissive. 'Let me set the record straight. The Jericho Wine Barge is a wine bar; the clue is in the name. Yes, I'll sell a couple of beers for those who want them, but be reassured, there won't be any louts. I'll put up a "No Louts Allowed" sign if you like.'

'Stop taking the mickey, I'm being serious. Look, you're obviously set on your plans for this place, good for you, but could you not launch on any night other than that one?' I hated even asking him for this favour, but I had to try.

'I'm struggling to see why you've got such a problem with it,' he said, his exaggeratedly reasonable tone irritating me still further.

'The Blind Date with a Book night really matters to me. I need it to work. It's about the only profitable aspect of my business right now.' I regretted the words as soon as they were out of my mouth. It was beyond foolish to expose that particular weakness to a guy who had a proven track record of putting his own interests first and playing dirty. But it was too late now.

'I need my wine tasting launch event night to be a success too,' said Jack in a clipped tone. 'As far as I can see, we're in the same boat.'

'We might be physically standing in the same vessel right now, Jack, but you and I might as well be sailing in different canals. And frankly, I really wish you'd do that.' I threw my hands up in frustration. There was no reasoning with some people.

I clicked for Hilda to follow me and stomped off the Jericho Wine Barge, my fears for the future of the Oxford Bookship stronger than ever.

# Chapter Twelve

F lick was suitably indignant about Jack's bad steering and poor attitude when I joined her to drown my sorrows in the King's Arms on Sunday night. It was one of Hilda's favourite pubs, mostly because the staff never failed to give her treats, plus she got lots of attention from students who were missing their pooches back at home. She was currently sprawled out at our feet, using her long tongue to her advantage to search for any crumbs which might be lurking on the floor.

'Eurgh, Jack may be pretty but that doesn't give him permission to behave terribly,' said Flick, taking a large slurp of her G&T without the G, her favourite tipple. Flick had never been a boozer, but despite the teetotal nature of her drinks, she always managed to end up acting tipsy by the end of a night out, high on social energy.

'Do we think he's pretty?' I asked doubtfully.

'Okay, so pretty's maybe the wrong word. Dishy.

Handsome. Swoony. Take your pick,' said Flick, trying the words out for size.

I frowned as I pictured him. 'Not sure any of those fit exactly. How about surly? Entitled? Posh boy?'

Flick leaned forward and brushed something off me.

'What was that?' I asked.

'Just removing the chip off your shoulder,' she said with a teasing glint in her eyes.

'Ha ha, very funny.'

'He can't help what family he was born in,' she said. 'What's wrong with being posh?'

'Nothing whatsoever, unless it makes someone believe they can swank around doing whatever they like, which is unfortunately the case with Jack Siddall.'

She pursed her lips. 'Let's rewind a little. His previously discussed sins still stand, and yes, like you, I'm horrified that he crashed into the Oxford Bookship. Someone with no sense of direction like that absolutely shouldn't be allowed in charge of a boat on the canal. But you've said yourself he apologised and offered to pay for the damage, which a spoilt posh boy wouldn't have thought of. And he lent you a fancy coat when you were getting soaked in the rain. So, he's not all bad.'

'The only reason I was getting soaked in the first place was because I was having to rescue him. If he knew even the very basics of steering a canal boat, I would have been able to stay nice and dry indoors. Every time I think about what happened, I seethe. There's something about him which makes me...' My voice trailed off as I struggled to articulate exactly how he made me feel. Irritated, pissed off, whatever other synonyms for annoyed you could come up with. And something else as well. Jumpy perhaps? On edge? Definitely hyper conscious of his every move. From a self-protection perspective, I elaborated in my internal narrative.

Flick raised an eyebrow. 'Interesting,' she said in a pointed manner.

'Bloody hell, no, nothing like that. He really … *riles* me.'

'Right,' she said, still maintaining that irritating I-know-better-than-you voice. 'Look, at the end of the day, you can't change the facts. The guy's there now. There's no point in letting him spoil your happy place for you. And they do say there's a thin line between hatred and love,' she added with a devilish grin.

'I know you're winding me up. Jack Siddall is the last man in the world I would ever love. Whoever "they" are need their head examining,' I said. It was about time I turned the tables on her. 'Speaking of all things romantic, when's your next date with Liam? I'm assuming there'll be one.'

'We're texting a lot, and he's promised to give me a guided tour of his boat, which I think is a genuine offer rather than being a pretext to lure me back to his, although I wouldn't be devastated if it was. She's called *Lydia* apparently.'

'Lucky you. He did a whole series of videos about doing her up. She was a complete wreck when he bought her and he's completely transformed her, so cool.' Flick assumed her ultra patient expression. 'Sorry, that's not the point, I know. I'm thrilled you guys have hit it off.

He seems really lovely, such a positive outlook on life despite it all.'

'Despite what?' asked Flick.

I hesitated. 'He swore me to secrecy, otherwise I'd tell you myself, but you might want to ask him about his experience of Jack Siddall,' I said.

'Sounds intriguing. You do realise telling your best friend doesn't count,' pointed out Flick.

I fought an internal battle. 'I'd absolutely love to, but I made a promise, plus I don't want to put you in a difficult position. You're a journalist after all and although I totally trust your discretion, it would be plain mean to hand you a story when you can't do anything with it. Ask Liam. Honestly. I'm sure he'll fill you in. And then you'll understand why Mr Siddall is not to be trusted.'

'Order twelve, portion of chips?' asked the waiter, providing a welcome distraction from potential awkwardness by arriving at our table to deliver our food. 'Any sauces with that?'

'Tomato ketchup,' started Flick.

'And lots of vinegar, please,' I completed our request.

'The mark of true friendship,' she responded. 'Can you imagine if one of us preferred mayonnaise and salt with our fries?' She shuddered at the very idea of it, and I felt relieved that she hadn't taken offence at my reluctance to share Liam's story with her.

'I'm afraid I'd have to end our friendship,' I said with mock seriousness.

'Or we could order two portions for once,' said Flick with a smile.

'Yes, of course, splash out, why not,' I said hastily. A bit too hastily.

'Is everything alright, Molly?' she asked. 'There's nothing you're not telling me, is there? I mean, apart from the thing you've explicitly said you're not telling me.'

I forced myself to take a moment before replying. If I came in too quick again, she'd definitely know I was holding something back. Flick and I had grown up together and been by each other's sides through all the significant firsts – boyfriends, jobs, homes. But time and time again I'd seen her take on other people's problems as her own, and I truly didn't want to burden her with my worries. Her job was high pressure. She should be focusing what energy she had left over on herself, not me.

'All's good. Apart from Mr Annoying McAnnoyington next door, of course.'

'Catchy nickname,' she said, smuggling a chip to Hilda under the table.

'I suppose you think I should ignore his presence and carry on as normal,' I replied.

'Ignore him? Now that would be a shame. At least allow yourself to enjoy the novelty of having some eye candy on your doorstep. Is doorstep the right word?'

'Not exactly. His bow is in close proximity to my stern.' I regretted the words as soon as they were out of my mouth.

'Ding dong, oo-er Matron,' said Flick in her best *Carry On* voice. 'That sounds like an extremely interesting position to be in.'

'Alright, alright, there's no need to keep making the same point. Jack could be described as objectively hot.

When he's not scowling, that is, which is hardly ever. But he's in possession of a terrible personality and there's nothing that will make up for that.'

'Is he really though? Or are you prejudiced against him, Miss Elizabeth Bennet, because he hasn't read your favourite book, and you're more of a cider girl than a wine drinker? Remember how it works out for our lovely Lizzy.'

I snorted. 'Well, I've been on board his barge, and trust me when I tell you it's no Pemberley. And despite his terrible steering, he's yet to have a wet shirt moment in the canal.' I held up my hand to stop the interruption I anticipated. 'Before you call me a hypocrite because that only happened in the TV series and not in the book, I don't care. Mr Darcy's wet shirt moment is iconic, and I won't hear otherwise.'

'Don't worry, that's a point I certainly won't argue with you about. But I maintain he has some claim to Darcy looks. You're sure he can't be tempted to join your next Blind Date with a Book night? You might get a few extra ladies signing up if he appears in the posters.'

I nearly choked on my drink. 'He is the last person I'll be putting on the posters. I want the right sort to come along. You know, men who are well-read and—'

'—good in bed,' added Flick with a snigger. 'You can have that marketing tagline for free.'

I pretended to consider it. 'Hmm, maybe, although trade descriptions would probably get me into all kinds of trouble with those sorts of claims unless I verified them for myself, and frankly I don't have the energy.' Flick was snorting with laughter, but I ploughed on regardless. 'As to the next do, there's another very good reason why Mr Siddall won't be attending. He's holding his Wine Bar launch event the very same night. He absolutely refuses to change the date. And no, I will not even consider doing a joint event, before you suggest it.'

'Sounds like this new revelation calls for further discussion which can only mean dessert. Shall we spoil ourselves?' said Flick.

'Why n—' The words died in my mouth. 'Actually, why don't we head elsewhere for dessert?' I suggested casually, trying very hard not to make the reason for my sudden change of heart obvious. Unfortunately, Hilda had no such qualms. As soon as she clocked the man who'd just walked into the pub she was on her feet, thumping her tail in anticipation, and looking at me expectantly for permission to go and see the person she now considered a friend, even if I didn't. Although I had her lead hooked onto the bottom of my chair, I grabbed hold of her collar, just in case. The furniture in the King's Arms was no match for Hilda when she put her mind to it.

'Stay, Hilda.' I delivered the command softly, but she knew I was serious. She let out a little whimper and quivered in frustration. I could practically read the thoughts running through her mind – confusion as to why she wasn't allowed to say hi to him, and betrayal that her number one human was holding her back from something she really wanted to do. I willed the new arrival to decide it was too busy and leave, but no, he stood casually surveying his surroundings like he owned the place. I wouldn't be surprised if he was considering adding it to his empire.

I shrank back in my seat, trying to make myself invisible, but it was practically impossible to remain incognito given my own height and the fact that I was accompanied by a large dog who was very keen to be noticed. She let out a plaintive 'Harrrwuull' of frustration as I continued to keep hold of her collar, and the game was up.

# Chapter Thirteen

Jack's gaze fell on our table. He seemed to falter then strode across, greeting us with a curt nod. 'Good evening, ladies.'

Hilda whined in response, while Flick chuckled. 'I reckon she's the most ladylike of us lot,' she said, pointing at my pooch. I'm Flick by the way. It's short for Felicity in case you were questioning the sanity of my parents.'

'It's nice to meet you. I'm Jack.'

'Oh, I know exactly who you are,' said Flick. 'Do you want to—'

I shoved my elbow against her ribs, stopping the invitation which I knew my treacherous so-called best friend was about to issue. I didn't bother trying for subtlety, and judging by the expression on Jack's face, he'd seen the move and knew exactly why I'd made it, which was probably why he took such perverse delight in his answer.

'Actually, yes, I will join you,' he said. 'It's rammed in

here tonight. I think I'd be hard pressed to find a table elsewhere.'

'We are truly honoured,' I muttered sarcastically.

'Meeting someone special?' asked Flick. I fought the urge to jab her in the ribs again. She had the subtlety of a brick sometimes.

Jack shook his head.

I tutted. 'You're missing an opportunity for flattery here, Mr Siddall. Surely everyone knows that the only correct response is, "I am now"?'

'Is that so?' he replied, refusing to rise to my bait.

'Ignore Molly, she's got a bee in her bonnet tonight,' said Flick. 'Her favourite Jane Austen style bonnet that is,' she added with a wink.

'Apologies if I am failing to conform to expectations,' said Jack, taking our banter at face value. 'I wasn't anticipating having to be sociable.'

'Even though you've chosen to come to the pub? Surprising. What did you expect was going to happen? You'll have to get used to the whole being sociable concept once your bar is up and running,' I said, unable to resist making the dig. 'Most people tend to prefer a genial mine host, rather than a grumpy so-and-so who hates having to chat.'

'I didn't say I dislike talking,' pointed out Jack. 'I was merely trying to explain that I talk when there's something worth saying.' Unlike some, was the unspoken implication. 'I had intended this visit as business research,' he continued, impervious to my fizzing irritation. 'I wasn't expecting to see someone I'd recognise.'

'Business research? Way to put a dampener on a night out,' I muttered.

'Checking out the … opposition?' said Flick, quickly changing tack from her intended comment after I pointedly cleared my throat at her.

'Sort of. I know my endeavour is on a different scale to this place. But it's solid practice to see what other Oxford venues are offering and try to work out what makes them popular with the punters.'

'I'd say the chips they serve here are a good place to start,' I said. 'But you're not serving food, right? Just letting people drink without providing anything to line their stomach. I read the press release you sent to the *Gazette*.'

I got a perverse kick out of seeing the frown lines furrowing his brow again.

'I won't be running an all you can drink happy hour, if that's what you're worried about,' he said. 'I may offer some snacks – olives, maybe some artisan pretzels and the like – but that will be the extent of it.'

'Sounds deliciously pretentious,' I said.

'I'm not much of a cook,' continued Jack, ignoring my comment. 'I mean, I'm perfectly capable of creating a balanced meal for myself, but I have neither the ability nor the ambition to extend my catering to a wider circle than my family and friends.'

He glanced across to the bar, reading the drinks listed on the chalkboard with a critical eye. Flick gave me a significant look which I pretended to be oblivious to.

'Where are my manners? What can I get you to drink?'

she asked after her telegraphed instructions to me went ignored.

Jack started. 'No, absolutely not. I'm the one intruding on your table. I should get drinks for you two. Three, if Hilda would like a top up of her water bowl.'

'Nope, I insist,' said Flick, standing up and starting to make for the bar already. 'Same again, Molls? And you're a wine man, aren't you, Jack? Shall I surprise you? Perhaps something rich and full of character?'

She didn't say 'Just like you', but it was obvious from her tone that that was exactly what she was implying.

'Thanks, that sounds good,' said Jack, oblivious to Flick's teasing or at least pretending to be.

'De nada,' replied Flick, winking at me as she disappeared into the crowd. Judging by the amount of people vying for the barman's attention, she'd be there some time, even supposing she made any effort to catch his eye. I knew perfectly well she'd disappeared off to leave Jack and me alone together in a touchingly optimistic attempt to encourage us to mend our differences. When she spoke to Liam, she'd realise why they were irreparable.

We sat in awkward silence for a few minutes. At least, I felt awkward. It was very hard to tell what was going through Jack's mind with that impenetrable expression of his. Even when he wasn't speaking, he had a way of making me feel unsettled. I shifted in my seat, wondering if I could get away with going to hide in the toilets for a bit. But that would mean leaving Hilda in his care, and I was reluctant to give him an opportunity to further ingratiate himself with my pet. As if reading my mind, Hilda pointedly put her paw on my foot to encourage me to let go of her collar. I acquiesced, as always unable to resist the power of her pleading expression. She went straight to Jack, wiggling in pleasure as he scratched her behind the ears. Then with a contented sigh, she settled down at his feet, curling herself up like a giant hairy croissant.

'It's like having my own personal hot water bottle,' he commented eventually. Then he winced. 'She has remarkably bony elbows for a dog her size.'

*Well played, Hilda*, I thought.

'I suppose I should be grateful you've at least stopped referring to her as a horse,' I responded.

'You seemed to find it offensive. Although Hilda informs me she was never bothered by that. She has her mind on a much higher plane.'

'Yes, mostly food related, or so she tells me. If she shares other thoughts with you, I hope you'll keep her confidence.'

'I am the soul of doggy discretion.'

We lapsed into a prolonged silence again.

'Goodness, Jack, you really must stop with all your chitter chatter, I can barely get a word in edgeways,' I said eventually, tired of the discomforting sensation of him sitting there beside me.

'I don't feel the need to fill the air with any old comments for the sake of it,' he responded.

'That's me told.'

'That's not what I... Oh never mind,' he said. 'What do you think I should be saying?'

'I didn't know you held my opinion in such high esteem. Perhaps you should use your initiative? Surprise me.'

He frowned, then took a deep breath, as if steeling himself for something difficult.

'How long have you lived in Oxford?' he asked eventually.

'Wow, insightful question, I can't believe it took you so long to come up with it,' I said, then regretted my bitchiness. Normally I went out of my way to keep a conversation flowing, to the point where guys sometimes believed I was really into them when in fact I was only trying to calm their nerves out of a misguided sense of empathy. Not that Jack needed or even deserved that kind of treatment.

'I've lived in Oxford my whole life,' I said.

'Right,' he said, sounding surprised.

'What's that supposed to mean?' I asked, my hackles rising.

'Nothing at all. I was merely acknowledging what you said.'

'Sure you were. It's funny how one word can be so loaded with stuff that isn't said.' I was back being defensive and snappy again.

He spread his palms. 'I really don't know what you're talking about.'

'You were being judgemental and dismissive because I've only ever lived in one city.'

'I think you're projecting your own insecurities on to me,' he said in an infuriatingly calm tone, but I was warming to my theme. Why I felt the need to justify myself to him, I didn't know but somehow it felt important to explain.

'I have travelled elsewhere, don't get me wrong. But I've never spent longer than three weeks away from this city. And no, that doesn't mean I studied here. I went straight into work at eighteen. Some of us have to, you know,' I added, a little wistfully. Plus, I didn't have the grades to get in. My teachers had always told me I was bright, generally before they then went on to shake their heads disapprovingly and mutter something about me needing to concentrate more and apply myself. The trouble was, my brain and formal exams did not get on with each other. Given how my shop was doing, those teachers would probably say the same thing was true about my brain and business management. I pinched my finger and thumb together, trying to settle my anxious thoughts, and decided to turn the tables on him. 'How about you? Was the university what brought you to this city?'

'Me?' he asked.

'Yes, that's generally how conversations work. You ask a question, I answer, then it's your turn. Or I could guess if you prefer?'

'I prefer to answer for myself,' he said.

There was a long pause, during which I started constructing a tower out of beer mats.

'Note to self, get better quality beer mats than this place,' Jack said as the tower collapsed onto the table. He reached across and began his own, much more successful, attempt. 'Scratch that. It's all in the architect.'

I shrugged. It was a fair cop.

'Go on then. I'm guessing you read something like Classics here, Mr Hoi Polloi,' I said.

'Yes, I studied at Oxford, and I initially started reading Classics. But in the end, we decided it would be better to go for something more practical, so I switched to E and M. Economics and Management,' he explained, catching my blank expression.

'*We* decided?' I pressed.

'I decided,' he corrected, although it didn't ring true.

'Sounds … fascinating,' I said.

'It gave me the knowledge I needed to succeed in the world of high finance, particularly my area of speciality in the family business. And now I'm looking forward to applying those skills to running my own business.'

He sounded like he was reciting an answer in a job interview. But I could see the light of ambition in his eyes. He was definitely out to prove something.

'What was your area of speciality, out of interest?' I asked, trying to keep my question casual.

'Mergers and takeovers,' he replied.

Why was I not surprised? My sense of impending doom increased.

'Your turn,' he added.

'What?' I snapped, half believing he'd declared his intention to take over the Oxford Bookship then and there.

'Your turn to answer a question,' he said. 'You did say that was how it's meant to work,' he pointed out, looking a little too pleased with himself.

'Oh that. I guess so. Hit me with it.'

'Have you always lived on the Oxford Bookship?'

I examined his expression suspiciously, wondering whether this was the innocent question he was presenting it as, or part of a fact-finding mission by a takeover expert.

'No, I grew up in a normal terrace house off Cowley Road with my parents, but I spent practically every minute I could on the water in Jericho with my grandma. She taught me what it means to be part of a community, to look out for each other and to contribute to the bigger picture. That's what I was determined to do when I opened the Oxford Bookship. I want it to mean something more to the community than just the physical place. I want it to be a home for them, somewhere people can find friends, and perhaps even get to know themselves better through the books I have on the shelves. I care about the connection I make with my customers.' I fixed him with a serious look. 'Can you honestly tell me that you're going to achieve the same with your Wine Barge?'

Jack thought for a moment before replying.

'A business is a business at the end of the day. But I also see the true value in creating that sense of community. Start off small and develop it into something which can make a real impact.'

'By opening a place where people go to get drunk?' I said dubiously, my anxiety over his allusion to expansion plans making me sound all puritanical.

'Yes, it's a wine bar. But I hope it'll be a place where people can come and chat and feel welcome to visit by themselves or with others. I want the Jericho Wine Barge to have the kind of relaxed vibe you get when you're in Italy or Greece, to be a place where the atmosphere is friendly and warm, where people are comfortable to be themselves and savour their drinks rather than downing them like it's going out of fashion.'

I was surprised by his speech and nearly found myself being taken in by his obvious enthusiasm for his vision.

'That's not normally the way things are done in a student city. I imagine most people will hear the name Jericho Wine Barge and assume they're in for a booze cruise.' I was making myself sound more and more uptight, but I'd seen the city centre bars at closing time and carnage didn't begin to describe it.

'I know you're wrong, and I'll prove it to you. It's the way I'll do things,' he said firmly.

'Oh of course, if it's the way you'll do things, I'm sure the rest of the world will click its heels and obediently fall into line.'

'Perhaps not clicking its heels, but I know that I will make it work.'

'You're very confident in yourself,' I said.

'You say that like it's a bad thing,' he responded.

I shrugged. 'I suppose you do have the male advantage of self-confidence being a trait which is applauded, as opposed to it being reframed as arrogance or "being difficult" if you happen to be of the female persuasion.'

'Tough, and unfair,' he acknowledged.

'Too damn right.'

'But that's not my fault,' he added. I opened my mouth, ready to respond that a 'not my issue' attitude was part of the problem, but he continued with an earnestness that even I couldn't deny. 'And that's certainly not how I think.

I have great respect for women with strong opinions who aren't afraid to voice them.'

He looked at me steadily, and I glanced down, feigning a renewed interest in the beer mats. Had he just paid me a compliment? It seemed like he might have, but I didn't know how I felt about it or how to respond. Thankfully Flick saved me by finally returning with our drinks.

'Have you been giving him one of our feminist lectures, Molls?' she asked, handing Jack and me a glass of rosé apiece.

'Some things still need to be said,' I said self-righteously.

'Absolutely,' agreed Flick. 'And as I'm sure Jack is a fully signed-up ally, why don't you enjoy the drink I went to great pains to acquire? I had a dilemma, but in the end, I thought it would be good for you to push yourself out of your comfort zone and have wine for a change. I went for something subtle and light for you both,' she continued, diverting me before I could climb too far onto the moral high ground. 'I hope you approve, Jack. I felt the pressure buying wine for the expert.'

'The proof is in the tasting,' said Jack.

I expected him to take a sip and swill it around his mouth in the slightly pretentious manner of all self-professed connoisseurs, but instead he looked expectantly at me.

'I'm of the opinion that people should be able to enjoy what they enjoy, without feeling the need to appear a certain way. You go first, tell me what you think,' he invited. 'And before you say anything, I'm not trying to test you.

I'm genuinely interested in your opinion. You do after all seem to like expressing it.'

I frowned at him, unsure whether he was criticising or merely stating a fact. I generously decided to give him the benefit of the doubt and took a small sip, then a larger glug. 'Good choice, Flick, fresh and fruity. What is it you say? Very quaffable.'

Jack raised an eyebrow. 'That sounds like a ringing endorsement to me. I shall have to stock it in the Jericho Wine Barge.'

'Don't bother on my account,' I said quickly, not wanting him to get the wrong idea. I didn't have time to be popping out to wine bars, even if they were right next door to me. Especially when they were right next door to me and owned by someone I frustratingly couldn't fathom. Tonight's socialising at the pub was an aberration. 'Your turn, Mr Siddall. What's your informed opinion?'

Jack lifted the glass, and gently wafted it under his nose, a dreamy expression softening his features.

'I wouldn't sniff too deeply, I think Hilda's just let one slip,' I said facetiously, hoping my dog forgave me for my little white lie.

But instead of frowning in disapproval at my coarse comment, his face crinkled into a warm grin.

'That's dogs for you. Don't worry, my smell receptors are pretty much immune to *eau de* dog, thanks to growing up with a particularly flatulent Labrador. What he delivered in gas attacks, he more than compensated for in love and affection. I always thought of Henry as my four-legged brother.'

Was it me or were Jack's eyes turning a little watery as he remembered his childhood pet? Despite my misgivings about my new neighbour, I couldn't help feeling the empathy any dog parent would. I fought the urge to pat him sympathetically on the shoulder, and instead nudged Hilda gently with my toe, encouraging her to sit up and rest her head on his lap.

Jack immediately started stroking her, thankfully unbothered by the string of drool which she deposited on his previously immaculate jeans.

'All dogs are special. We don't deserve them, really,' I said quietly.

'You're right there,' said Jack.

This time there was a different quality to our silence.

'What's the verdict on my drink choice then, Jack?' asked Flick eventually.

'Absolutely. Sorry, let me try it properly now.'

I found myself almost hypnotised by the way he pressed his lips to the glass and took a sip. His throat moved as he swallowed, and then he glanced up and caught me staring at him.

'Delightful,' he said.

I knew he was only talking about the drink, but something about the way he said that word while looking at me made my insides lurch. I tried to dismiss the disconcerting sensation as vinegar-and-chips related. The rosé must have gone straight to my head for me to be feeling... No, I pushed the false thought away. I was in an emotionally vulnerable state, with all the stress I was under at the moment. Whatever bizarre imaginings were going on, I needed to get myself out of here, and smartish. I put my glass down and made a great show of checking my phone, before standing up abruptly.

'Goodness, is that the time? I should be off home. Some of us still have to work in the morning.'

'May I—'

But I didn't let Jack finish whatever it was he wanted to ask. 'Thanks for a lovely evening, Flick. Come on, Hilda, let's get going.'

Hilda blinked up at me, surprised by my sudden change in tone, and clearly telegraphing her intention to stay right where she was.

'Come on you, Hilly-billy. It's way past your bedtime.'

She slumped down and shuffled herself into an even tighter ball, burying her face under her haunches, apparently thinking if she couldn't see me, I wouldn't be able to see her.

'She can stay here, and I'll bring her back with me later,' offered Jack, as she signalled her intention to remain glued to his side. I was rational enough to realise Hilda would be perfectly happy with that scenario, but instead of being gratified my loving pet parenting had resulted in a dog who no longer had separation issues, I felt sad she seemed to be picking him over me. It was the final straw.

'You can move into my neighbourhood and destroy my peace and quiet, but there's no way I'm letting you steal my dog too,' I said.

And with that, I grabbed hold of Hilda's lead and bribed her with all the treat-related buzz words I could come up with to follow me reluctantly out of the pub.

# Chapter Fourteen

H ilda and I emerged on deck to set off for her early walk at the normal time the next morning. I usually loved the canal when the sun was still low on the horizon and the only other occupants of the towpath were sleepy ducks with their beaks still buried in their feathers, or the occasional vole scampering into the undergrowth. Today, however, I hopped ashore to discover my peaceful haven had been invaded by a platoon of high visibility-bedecked blokes wielding a variety of paintbrushes and power tools.

'Good morning,' said one of them, doffing his hard hat. I did a double take as I recognised my new neighbour in an outfit most unlike his usual garb. He should have looked like he was messing about in fancy dress with his paint splattered ripped jeans and toolbelt hanging low over his narrow hips, but his characteristic air of confidence meant he appeared completely comfortable. I became acutely conscious of his physicality in a way I hadn't been before, suddenly aware of the strength in muscles which had previously been concealed by immaculately tailored clothing.

'What on earth is going on?' I asked, flustered and trying to cover it by going on the offensive.

'The guys will be working here with me all day,' said Jack. 'They're going to help fit out the bar.'

'Are you sure they're all going to squeeze on board? How many venture capitalists does it take to change a lightbulb?'

'I'm not a venture…' With a visible effort, Jack changed tack. 'Very witty,' he said. 'I'll make sure they stay out of your hair.' His eyes lingered on my mane with an amused glint, and I shuffled awkwardly, fighting the urge to smooth it.

I cleared my throat. 'I hope they won't put people off visiting my shop. If there are loads of workmen around, customers might think I'm not open for business.'

'I'll ask the team to make sure every passer-by knows that's not the case,' said Jack. 'In fact, I can get them to actively encourage the crowds to enter your lair if you like. Anything my neighbour desires, I'm happy to help.'

His tone was teasing, but I decided not to rise to the bait.

'That won't be necessary. I would, however, appreciate if they could take pains not to block the path and to keep their stuff out of my part of the garden.'

'Not a problem. I can send them across to spruce up the Bookship later, if you like,' he added.

This time he really had overstepped the mark.

'I beg your pardon, but what exactly do you mean by that? The Bookship certainly doesn't need "sprucing up".'

Hilda slumped down on the path, sensing we might be here for a while.

'Let me rephrase. They'll take a look at the damage I caused the other day and see if they can fix it,' said Jack. 'I have high standards and they come recommended.'

'By whom exactly? Because as I've already told you, that scrape on the hull is above and below the waterline, which means the boat will have to go into a dry dock for the paintwork to be done. I know all the specialist boat maintenance workers around here and none of them are standing on the towpath right now. If those guys have claimed they can fix my boat in situ, then they're lying to you. Your standards clearly aren't high enough. You should have a word with the person who recommended them and let them know they don't have a clue what they're talking about.'

The crease in Jack's brow reappeared and he folded his arms defensively. 'I was merely trying to find a quick solution.'

'Quick solutions do not necessarily equate to being the best solutions,' I pointed out.

He tried to stare me down, but I returned his glower and eventually he sighed. 'Fine, if you don't even want them to take a look, that's your prerogative. I'll get my insurance expert to come across and arrange repairs on another date.'

'Yes to the repairs on another date, and no to getting your "expert" to sort them out. I'd prefer to appoint my own actual expert, thank you very much.' He opened his mouth, preparing to argue back, but I didn't give him a chance. I had no intention of letting him think I needed saving by him. 'Trust has to be earned, and I'm not going to let some random who's never stepped foot on a boat before try and earn it on my Bookship. Now if you'll excuse me, I have chores to do.' I clicked my tongue. 'Come on, Hilda, we're behind schedule as it is.'

I set off at a pace which Hilda found unusually fast judging by the little glances she kept sending in my direction, but I could feel Jack's critical gaze burning between my shoulder blades as we hurried away. Once we were around the corner, I slowed down and tried to focus on enjoying the walk, but I kept replaying the conversation with Jack and overanalysing every word, hating that I was allowing him to live rent-free in my head, but unable to stop it happening.

My mood plummeted still further as I approached the post office ready to carry out the weekly check of my PO box. The only correspondence which landed there was money-related, and sure enough when I unlocked it, there was a brown envelope emblazoned with the logo of my bank waiting for me. I toyed with shutting it back in the box, but I knew it wouldn't help me in the long term, so I ripped it open and quickly scanned the contents which immediately sent my anxiety levels rocketing. The letter informed me that the interest rate on the loan I'd used to buy the Oxford Bookship was increasing by 2 per cent. There was the usual spiel about getting in touch for support if I was struggling, but the threats in red capitals about missed payments and repossessions didn't exactly make me trust that the bank would show mercy if I fell any further behind. A 2 per cent increase sounded like such a measly amount, but the effect on my monthly repayments would be significant as the letter handily spelled out for me. I translated the sum into the number of books I would have to sell and felt even more sick.

I left the post office in a daze, not even finding the energy to do more than nod in acknowledgement as one of the ladies behind the counter waved a copy of *The Secret History* which I'd recommended to her a couple of weeks ago and gave me a big thumbs up. I walked down the street, letting Hilda lead the way as I read the letter again. How on earth would I be able to afford these repayments as well as finding the cash to cover the mooring fees? Was this the way the situation would continue, me fooling myself I might be able to get a handle on things, before yet another financial blow wiped out that tentative optimism?

'Not bad news, I hope?' asked a familiar voice as Hilda suddenly stopped in her tracks and started wagging her tail vigorously.

I quickly stuffed the letter back in the envelope and screwed a smile on, not quite ready to articulate my fears out loud, even to my best friend.

'Flick, hi, are you on your way to work? And no, only the usual boring business correspondence, dull as dishwater, as always,' I said in as sunny a voice as I could manage.

The fact she took my words at face value was an instant warning. In normal circumstances there would have been no way she'd have been taken in by my forced grin, and knowing her, she'd have eyeballed the letter's contents too, her journalist's eye automatically seeking out the salient information because she couldn't help being curious about the world around her. But today that curiosity was strangely absent.

'Good, good,' Flick said distractedly, glancing down at her phone and chewing her bottom lip, her usual tell for when something was bothering her.

I forced my financial concerns to the back of my mind and focused on my friend, looping my arm through hers to escort her to a nearby bench.

'Try again, Summers. You can't fool me. What's the matter?'

She sighed. 'I think I've messed up with Liam.'

She passed her phone across so I could read the exchange of messages on the screen.

I'm sorry hun but I won't go on the record, not even for u. Liam xx

But you could help stop him doing that kind of thing again! Plus, why shouldn't you set the record straight? YOU did nothing wrong! You can trust me to tell it properly I promise F x

'I stopped by his place after the pub last night and he told me about the whole Jack screwing over his career situation,' she explained. 'I should have just listened, but I wanted to help, to do something practical. I offered to write about it in the paper because people shouldn't be allowed to get away with treating others like crap, and Liam's story deserves to be heard. I mean, no matter how well he's doing with his social media stuff, his original career has still been stolen from him. But he got all worried and couldn't get rid of me fast enough. And then like a complete muppet, I kept pursuing the thing over text as I was walking home and he's stopped replying. I think he's going to break up with me. Well, I mean, he can't break up with me because we're not officially an item yet or anything, but you saw what he said.'

My fury at Jack increased exponentially.

'Jack Siddall has a lot to answer for. I'm so sorry, lovely. I feel responsible. I was the one who suggested Liam might have a story for you. I probably shouldn't have said anything in the first place.'

She squeezed my hand. 'Don't be silly. Of course you told me. We've never kept secrets from each other.'

Now I felt even worse. It wasn't the time to add to her distress by confessing my financial woes, but I made a silent resolve to speak to Liam as soon as possible to try to clear things up. He didn't strike me as the type to ghost someone, but I could understand his extra sensitivity when it came to Jack.

Flick's phone buzzed and she checked the screen hopefully.

'Liam?' I asked.

'Sadly not. The boss nagging me for this week's prospects list. I thought I was going to have something really good to present him with, but it'll have to be the usual dull council fodder. And now that makes me sound even more awful, like I was only interested in Liam for the exclusive.'

'I know that's not the case, and I'm sure he does too.

He's probably busy with his socials and it won't have occurred to him you might be worried he's not replied.'

She pulled a face. 'I'm afraid it's another classic Flick scenario. You know me, it's always all or nothing. It's just … I really like him, and so I went too hard trying to fix the situation for him.'

'Classic Flick,' I said with a smile. 'That's why I love you, and if he's got any sense, he'll love you for it too.'

Hilda showed her agreement by resting her head on Flick's lap. Flick scratched her behind the ears and smiled as she was rewarded with a rumble of pleasure.

'There's no beating doggy therapy. And best friend therapy too, of course,' she added quickly.

I laughed. 'It's okay, I know where I fit in the hierarchy. Hilda's deservedly at the top. You're very welcome to borrow her for the day, if it would help cheer you up.'

'If only I could. The newsroom would be much improved by the presence of a news hound, but the boss doesn't like animals. Massive red flag, obviously.'

'Huge red flag. You should complain to HR.'

Flick checked her watch. 'Speaking of which, I should dash. There's a full team meeting later this morning and I need to get some writing done before then.'

'Don't worry about Liam. I'm sure it's all a misunderstanding,' I tried to reassure her.

I went the long way round back to the Oxford Bookship, hoping to accidentally on purpose bump into Liam so I could clear up the Flick situation, but there was no sign of life on the *Lydia*. Unfortunately, the peace of Castle Mill Stream was not replicated on my section of the canal where half the members of the high-vis gang were busy using a collection of extremely noisy tools to batter and chop pieces of wood, while the other half faffed around trying to untangle various lengths of power cable.

I pointedly ignored them as I swept past and opened up the Bookship for business. Mondays weren't always the busiest of days, but thankfully today proved to be the exception with a steady succession of student visitors looking for some much-needed escapism from exam revision. I sold my entire stock of adult colouring books to a pair of undergraduate welfare officers who promised to send their friends along to the Bookship, then I encouraged a sallow-faced individual in a college hoody to curl up on one of my squishy beanbags with Hilda and a copy of *The Things You Can Only See When You Slow Down*. I gently steered a shaky-looking med student towards *Wintering*, then prescribed a stack of second-hand *Beano* annuals for the Blues rower whose spirit was clearly crushed by her arm being in a sling. As I was putting them in a bag, the college hoody guy leapt up from his bean bag, the colour rushing back into his features as he offered to carry them back to town for her.

'I see your matching skills aren't confined to your Blind Date with a Book nights,' said Liam, climbing on board soon after the pair had left chatting happily.

'Call it my bookseller's alchemy,' I said. 'Speaking of which, how do you fancy this one?'

I pointed at a copy of *The Man Who Didn't Call*. Hilda backed me up by raising her hackles and delivering a disgruntled bark.

Liam frowned. 'Hmm, I think I know where this is going, and before you give me a hard time, I dropped my phone in a sink full of washing up last night as I was about to reply to Flick. I can see how tight you two are, so I'm sure she must have told you about the chat we had and the fact that I've been MIA since. I promise it was unintentional.' He pulled a sealed bag full of rice out of his messenger bag and waved it at me. 'Exhibit A, phone in recovery, another sorry victim of Jack Siddall.'

'I agree with Flick. He shouldn't be allowed to get away with how he's treated you. But she would never write about you without your permission, you know,' I said. 'She's a good journalist, but more importantly, she's a good human being too. Believe it or not, the two are not incompatible.'

Liam chuckled. 'Flick and I may have only had a couple of dates so far, but you're preaching to the converted. I was really touched by her offer to write about what happened to me, but putting aside the thorny issue of the NDA, I've always promised myself to find a better way of dealing with Jack Siddall's behaviour than going to the press. And if you'd be kind enough to lend me your phone, I'll give her a call and explain all that myself. I'm not letting Jack mess this up for me too.'

I winked at Hilda as Liam went off into my cabin to speak to Flick. At least one problem seemed to have resolved itself. If only my financial situation could be sorted as easily.

## Chapter Fifteen

There was a gentle sigh beside me, then a tongue softly traced its way from my ear lobe and along my jaw. I let out a sleepy groan and turned my head over on the pillow, hoping to be left alone after my late night. Instead, I was treated to a cold wet nose which started its campaign with a pointed sniff, then escalated to a persistent shoving at the back of my neck.

'Later, Hilda,' I muttered. 'Go back to bed. It's still sleepy time. I know it's light, but the alarm hasn't gone off yet.'

I really could do with another couple of hours of sleep. After making things up with Flick, Liam had invited me to appear live on his socials doing a tour of the Oxford Bookship. I'd thought it would feel unnatural interacting with a virtual audience, but I'd soon forgotten they weren't there in front of me and had darted around the cabin taking books off shelves and eagerly matching members of what had turned out to be an international audience with their new favourite reads. Sadly most of them hadn't followed through by placing orders to acquire the books from me, but I'd comforted myself with the thought that maybe the exposure would turn out to be more valuable in the long run.

Hilda gave me another shove then breathed heavily on my face for good measure. Her early-morning doggy breath was nearly as effective as smelling salts in rousing me from my semi-conscious state.

'Why is canine toothpaste liver-scented rather than minty?' I grumbled, sitting up and running a hand through my hair. I frowned as my fingers caught in the tangles and quickly decided to give up on trying to make myself presentable. I reached out and picked up my phone to check the time instead, but the screen was blank.

'Great, that's all I need,' I said. I'd got so tired last night I'd obviously forgotten to turn the switch on when I plugged my phone in to charge overnight. I swung my legs out of bed and leaned down to reach the socket. But as I ran my fingers over the switch, I realised it was already in the on position.

'Shit.'

Suddenly I felt wide awake. I hurried across the cabin and scrabbled through my drawers until I found my watch. It was nearly nine o'clock. No wonder Hilda had been pestering me for her breakfast. She normally had it at half seven on the dot. Even a 7:31 a.m. mealtime usually resulted in baleful looks and telegraphed threats to report me to the RSPCA for doggy cruelty.

'One minute, one minute I promise Hildy-girl,' I said,

moving to the doors and trying to click on the main cabin lights, more out of hope than expectation. As I'd feared, nothing happened. Even though I knew there was no point, I repeated the exercise in the bookshop, but everything was dead in there too. The power was most definitely off. And no power meant more than no lights. I could survive without lighting at this time of year. But it also meant a useless fridge, a freezer, albeit tiny, stuffed with food which I couldn't afford to replace once it thawed out, and most importantly of all, it meant no Wi-Fi. I could live without checking my emails and scrolling through my social media, but I couldn't open my shop without being able to process payments and search for orders online. And I couldn't even use my phone to do any of those things because that was dead too. How could I run my business without that basic facility? The answer was I couldn't.

I quickly pulled some clothes on and got Hilda her breakfast, then while she was munching contentedly on her kibble, I set about trying to work out why on earth my boat was experiencing a complete loss of power. I inspected the fuse box, but everything was as it should be. But that was where the similarities between a land-based power cut and a water-based one ended. There were a couple of systems which kept the lights on for the Oxford Bookship. Being at a permanent mooring meant I was in the privileged position of having access to shore power, so running out of juice wasn't usually a problem I encountered. I needed to check the connection. It worked by means of a heavy-duty cable, one end of which plugged into a socket on my boat, and the other into the junction point on shore. I tried not to have it plugged in all the time for economy reasons, mostly using it to charge up the boat's storage batteries overnight and relying on those for as much of the day as they lasted. For none of the power outlets on the Oxford Bookship to be functioning right now, the problem must have started not long after I turned the lights off and went to bed, my phone charger and other electrical outlets draining what little had been left of the boat's batteries after a full day of use. If I could afford solar panels, I wouldn't be facing this problem, but it was pointless dwelling on that thought.

I went out on deck and inspected the connection point where the cable should have been plugged in, but there was no sign of it. I frowned in confusion. Heavy-duty cables didn't just disappear into thin air. I looked across to the shore in case the cable had somehow detached at my end but was still connected to the power bollard on land which I shared with the neighbouring mooring, but the Bookship's socket was neatly closed off by the plastic cover and there was no sign of the thick cable which had been plugged in last night. The Jericho Wine Barge's cable on the other hand was still firmly in position.

I was starting to get a very bad feeling about this. I examined the connection point on my boat more closely, frowning at the scratch marks around it. I could have sworn they weren't there before. It would be highly unusual for one end of the cable to come loose accidentally, but for the whole thing to vanish… That couldn't be by chance. I jumped ashore and checked all round for other signs of anything wrong, but aside from the missing cable, everything looked as I would expect.

I shook my head. I was no Sherlock Holmes. What had I been expecting to find? A trail of muddy footprints along the towpath leading me to the guilty party who'd pinched the cable? Who would bother to do such a thing? It was a bit of kit designed for use on boats only. The average person walking past on the canal wouldn't have a use for it and surely there were far more obvious items to nick for someone who was carrying out a prank or a dare, which was always a possibility in a university city.

No, I was getting carried away. The more obvious explanation was that I was mistaken. Plugging into shore power was such a routine thing that I'd conjured up the memory of doing it on another night and convinced myself it was yesterday evening. I was under a lot of stress at the moment. I'd open up the storage locker under the stern deck and find the cable there in its usual place. I'd be able to plug it in, get everything working again and continue with my day as normal, albeit a little behind schedule.

Accompanied by a now-sated Hilda, I fetched the key from my cabin and opened up the locker. Usually I found it strangely calming looking in there because of the way I had everything neatly stowed in place. Nana Rose had always impressed upon me the need for order on a boat, 'You never know when you might need to find something in an emergency.' And yes, as I knew it would be, everything was in its proper place. Everything, that was, except the missing power cable.

'No, this cannot be happening,' I muttered, lifting each item out of the locker and checking underneath it: the heavy metal windlass which worked like a key to open and close canal locks; a box of spare light bulbs both for internal lights and the headlight which I was legally obliged to have glowing when navigating the canal after dark; a couple of thick ropes neatly coiled; a retractable boathook which was the backup for the one stowed on the roof. All very useful and important items, but not the extremely vital bit of kit I was searching for. Apart from startling a couple of stowaway spiders, I achieved precisely nothing with the exercise.

I sat back on my heels and stared at my surroundings in an attempt to quieten my racing thoughts, but for once the serene environment of the Oxford Canal did not work its magic on me. I tried to quell the rising sense of panic by telling myself that maybe I'd absent-mindedly put it elsewhere for the first time ever in my boat-owning existence. I opened up the other lockers on deck and then continued my search in the cabins, rummaging through my clothes, books and even food cupboards with an increasing sense of desperation. My beloved, formerly beautifully neat living space looked like it had been ransacked, which felt nearly as violating as the theft of the power cable. Because that must be what had happened. My first horrified instinct had been the correct one. However much I wanted the cable to be hidden away somewhere on board, it quite clearly wasn't. The scratch marks around the connection point told the tale – someone had disconnected the cable on land and then yanked very hard to detach it from my boat too.

'Shiiiiit,' I said again, the elongated vowel coming out as something close to a wail of frustration, bordering on panic. If the rush from the students yesterday had been anything to go by, I might be in for another decent day of much needed trade. I couldn't afford to turn these new customers away because I had no power. But panicking wasn't going to help me sort this situation. I needed to pull myself together and solve the problem, fast.

'Time for a backup plan,' I told Hilda, not that she seemed in the least bit concerned by the crisis. She'd taken advantage of the commotion to haul herself up on my bed and was stretched out under my duvet as if she belonged there. I smiled as she smacked her lips contentedly, welcoming the brief distraction from my anxiety. If she got the slightest indication I was amused by her behaviour, she'd do it all the time. Although theoretically the bed was designed for two humans, the expectation was that the two humans would have to snuggle closely to sleep. I knew for a fact that Hilda liked to stretch out in bed, and I'd probably end up on the floor if we attempted to share. Plus, the aforementioned doggy morning breath made it a distinctly unappealing option.

'Get down, Hilda,' I said firmly. 'Your bed is there.' But she yawned pointedly and ignored me. 'Might have known you'd take advantage of any sign of weakness, my girl,' I said. 'But yes, you're right, I should chill out. At least there are other options, albeit not ideal.'

The backup plan was running the engine. It was something I tried to avoid doing when I was moored up because fuel cost more than shore power, and it was noisy, which didn't help the peaceful ambiance I tried to cultivate in the shop. But I didn't have a choice about it now.

I scooped up my other set of keys and opened the little

cupboard by the stern doors where the engine control panel was hidden away. I checked the gauges first, grimacing as I realised I had very little fuel left. I thought back, trying to remember when I'd last filled up. Not recently enough. Another impending expense to add to the ever-increasing tally.

I turned the ignition key, and the engine spluttered in response.

'Come on old thing, you can do it,' I said reassuringly.

'That's an interesting technique,' came a voice from the towpath garden. I looked up from my task to see Jack watching me. He'd ditched the builder get-up and was back in his usual 'Man in finance' garb, although I couldn't un-remember the unexpected muscles which had shown themselves underneath his t-shirt. I was suddenly very conscious of my raggedy appearance. I crossed my arms protectively, wishing I'd taken the time to put proper underwear on rather than merely pulling clothes on over the top of my pyjamas. I glanced down and realised that my pyjama bottoms were in fact sticking out below my skirt.

'What is?' I asked, stupidly allowing myself to engage.

'Talking to the engine to get it to function,' he said, nodding his head at the control panel. 'Does the technique normally work?'

'Look, Jack, I'm having a bit of a day of it, and I'm really not in the mood for your brand of humour today,' I said, praying he'd get the message and leave me alone.

He did not.

'As a novice boater observing a much more experienced one in action, I was merely making enquiries for my own potential future use,' he said, still keeping a completely straight face, although his overly elaborate explanation told me he was continuing to make a joke at my expense. 'Can I help with it at all?' he added, stepping closer to the boat.

I couldn't stop myself from letting out a surprised laugh. 'Seriously? The man whose engine sounds like it's held together by rubber bands is asking me that question? Do you honestly think you could be in any way helpful right now?'

'I thought you could do with a laugh. It felt like the polite thing to say. I mean realistically you and I both know I'd be as much use as a frozen teapot.'

At least he was self-aware enough to admit it.

'Well, thanks for being neighbourly and trying to cheer me up,' I said begrudgingly.

'Go on, I know you're itching to say it,' he added. Now he was letting the spark of mischief show in his eyes.

'Fine, you know the phrase is chocolate teapot, right?'

He nodded, contemplating me like I was the most interesting person he'd seen in a while. 'Sure I do, but I thought I'd put my own twist on it, give you something to take your mind off your woes for a second.'

I pulled a face, torn between amusement and irritation at his game.

'Cheers for the thought. It was a kind gesture, I guess,' I said. 'Now you've made me smile and we've established there's nothing practical you can contribute, feel free to carry on your normal business. I've got everything under control.'

Jack put his hand on his heart, pretending to be

overcome by my statement. 'I made you smile. And now you've made me smile.' He gestured between us both. 'See how this could work, new neighbour? We don't have to be at odds with each other.'

'Don't push your luck,' I said, although there wasn't any real rancour behind my words.

Painfully conscious of his steady gaze on me, I tried to focus my attention back on the control panel and turned the key again, muttering a plea for it to start working.

'Come on, good little engine, you can do it,' said Jack. I actually think he was being serious.

Thankfully, it proved second time lucky, and the engine woke from its slumber and started purring smoothly. I glanced over the gauges and checked all the dials were at the correct levels. To my relief, everything was running as it should.

'Now that is how a well-maintained engine should sound,' I couldn't resist pointing out to Jack with satisfaction, my stress levels temporarily reduced.

'After a few attempts, of course,' he said. Did he wink at me?

I nearly winked back in a reflex response which I caught just in time and covered by glancing at my watch.

'Late opening, is it?' asked Jack.

'My alarm didn't go off,' I said, my tension headache ratcheting up once again.

Half an hour late opening. At least it was only half an hour. It could have been significantly worse. I could carry on with my day nearly as normal. Although the next pressing problem to deal with would be either replacing the power cable or filling up the fuel tank. The former option would be both a cheaper and more long-term solution, but the chandlery run by the Oxford Boating Association only operated for ad hoc hours, and I'd be lucky to catch the volunteers opening up the shop before the official start of the summer holidays. Most of us full-timers kept a stock of extra kit for emergencies, and I was kicking myself for not including a spare power cable among my just-in-case supplies.

Perhaps someone could lend me one. Once my phone was charged up and functioning again, I'd drop Bill and Rozina a text to see if they had one, I decided. If they didn't have a spare, Eric would probably know someone who did. I glanced across at the Jericho Wine Barge. There was another option which I hadn't explored, and I'd seen only yesterday that my neighbour had a plethora of spare electrical cables. I pushed the thought back. There was no way I was going to ask Jack for assistance. I hated appearing anything less than capable, even to my friends, let alone to my irritating new neighbour. He'd never let me live it down. But what was the cost of a bit of personal dignity compared to the price of a tank of fuel, the practical side of my brain reminded me. My priority had to be getting my business up and running for the day.

'Jack, can I...' I started to say, then I spotted another figure walking down the towpath towards us. I waved at Liam, who greeted me with a beam in return, although it unsurprisingly dimmed when he spotted my neighbour.

'Morning, Molly,' he called out. 'How are you this beautiful day?'

'What were you going to ask?' asked Jack, emphatically ignoring Liam's presence.

'Not to worry, it's all in hand now,' I said, greatly relieved Liam had shown up when he had.

Jack hesitated, his shoulders tense.

'Honestly, everything's fine,' I insisted.

'I wouldn't be so sure,' said Jack, turning on his heel and stomping back to his own boat.

'Was it something I said?' said Liam with an expression of exaggerated offence on his face.

'I think he had something to check on,' I said, somewhat surprised to find myself making an excuse for my neighbour.

'I don't mind. I'm used to being on the receiving end of Jack Siddall's attitude problem.' Liam's laughter was clearly forced. 'Anyway, that's enough about him. How's your day going?' He held up his vlogging camera.

'It's not the best. Is that thing recording?'

'Sorry, what was that?' Liam cupped his other hand around his ear. 'I can't hear very well because of the engine noise.'

He still looked blank and gestured towards the engine, miming for me to switch it off.

'No can do. I'm afraid I have to leave the engine on for the time being. I'm having a cable issue,' I repeated.

'A table issue?' Liam looked confused.

I gestured for him to come aboard. He hopped on with alacrity, the little red light on his camera still glowing away.

'That's better,' he said. 'What's wrong with your table?'

'It's actually a cable issue. Or rather, a lack of cable issue.

The cable in question seems to have gone walkabouts. And would you mind turning the camera off? I'm sorry to be a pain, but I'm not really in the mood for being filmed today.'

'Someone's pinched your cable?' asked Liam, his shock making him not notice my request. 'That's terrible, I'm so sorry.'

'It certainly is.'

'Who would do something like that?'

'The camera?'

'Oh heck, sorry.' He fiddled with the camera, and the red light went off. 'It's become second nature for me to vlog as I go along. It saves me the regret of missing something important. Don't worry, I won't use any of it if you don't want me to.'

'Thanks,' I said.

Liam put his head on one side thoughtfully. 'Although having said that, there's a good chance one of my sponsors might offer you a free shore power cable to replace the one that's disappeared. My viewers really connected with you during last night's live, and I know they'd be shocked if they found out what's happened to you. They should understand the reality of life living on the water. It's not all perfect Instagram moments after all.'

A beep from the engine panel distracted me before I could respond. I checked the gauge and realised the fuel level had dropped a lot more quickly than I'd anticipated. It certainly hadn't been on anywhere near long enough to charge up the boat's batteries to full capacity. I'd have to turn it off now, otherwise I wouldn't have enough fuel to make it to the boatyard to top up. There was a fuel boat which occasionally travelled the Oxford Canal filling up boats along the way but Katie, the woman who ran it, normally needed a day or two's notice so she could get a list of customers and make sure the journey was worthwhile. I silenced the engine, hoping it had been on long enough to do what I needed it to.

'Excuse me a second,' I said to Liam. I hurried into the cabin and checked my phone. That at least had quick charged to 50 per cent, so I could use it for vital shop transactions until I came up with another solution. I texted Katie, asking if she could head this way before the end of the week.

When I returned to the cockpit, Liam was in the middle of recording a piece to camera.

'So yeah, that's the reality of boating life, folks. Ultimately us boaties are quite vulnerable living on the water. It only takes someone stealing the shore power cable to leave a person high and dry. My lovely friend Molly is resourceful, and I'm going to help her find a solution, don't you guys worry, but things like this shouldn't happen. And look, here she is.' He put his arm around my shoulders and gave me a squeeze. 'And before she says anything, because she's the kind of person who doesn't want to put anyone out, I'm more than happy to help. That's what friends are for. It's what anyone would do.' He paused, and I saw he was panning the camera over towards Jack's boat. 'Let me correct myself. It's what most decent people would do. It's what I love best about the boating community. Most of us are all there for each other, and we take care of our own, don't we?'

I nodded automatically, then caught myself, feeling a tad guilty I hadn't contradicted his heavily implied criticism of Jack. For once, my neighbour didn't actually deserve it, given that I was the one who'd failed to be clear about what help I needed when he offered it. I broke free of Liam's embrace and tried to keep my voice casual.

'Look, I really appreciate your kindness, and I understand it's how you make your living, but can we call it a day on the filming. I've had a pretty trying morning so far, and I'm not in the right frame of mind.'

In fact, my head was aching in a way which I feared could turn into a full-on migraine if I didn't take action soon. I pinched the bridge of my nose, suddenly longing to go back to bed and pull the duvet over my head.

'Sure, don't worry, I'm all done now.' Liam put the camera away and gave me his full attention. 'How can I help?'

'I don't suppose you've got a cable going spare, have you?'

Liam frowned. 'Hmm, let me go and check. The *Lydia*'s got all kinds of odds and ends knocking around in her lockers. And if I don't, I have a collection of power banks which I use to charge up my camera kit. They would tide you over. Give me ten minutes.'

It had been surprisingly easy to ask for help, and his eagerness to give it made me feel bad about having a go at him over the filming thing. He was only doing his job, after all.

He hurried off towards the *Lydia*. Tempted as I was to give in to my desire to retreat to my bed, I quickly re-dressed in a more professional manner instead, gave myself a brief mental pep talk and set the Oxford Bookship sign out on the towpath to indicate that the shop was open for business.

Liam was significantly longer than the promised ten minutes, but I didn't mind because I was kept busy by a customer who was clearly desperate to sign up for the Blind Date with a Book night but was nervous about doing so. After some gentle reassurance and encouragement from me, he bought a ticket and then scurried away, as if he feared he'd change his mind if he hung around a moment longer. I was particularly amused that a woman who'd been loitering by the second-hand section while he deliberated, came across to the counter and bought a ticket for herself the second he left the boat. I smiled to myself as I processed her transaction. Perhaps I'd seen the start of another budding romance.

My phone battery had got down to only 18 per cent charge when Liam reappeared.

'Ta-da,' he said, waving a reel of cable around triumphantly. 'Look what I managed to find.'

I experienced a surge of relief.

'You're a lifesaver. And it looks like it's the perfect length as well, thank goodness.'

He shrugged self-effacingly. 'It's no bother. Keep it as long as you need it for. I can't get shore power where I am, so I've no use for it at the moment.'

My problem was solved for the time being at least. But the niggling concern remained. Who had stolen the cable, and why had they targeted my boat?

# Chapter Sixteen

Thankfully after the stress of the stolen cable, the next few days passed peacefully. Well, as peacefully as they could with a full-on renovation happening next door. Although I pretended to myself I wasn't interested in the Jericho Wine Barge and its owner's behaviour, I couldn't help keeping track of the efforts of the crew as they worked to their tight deadline for the transformation.

Although I'd seen no sign of them today, the noise from next door had reached quite possibly its worst level yet. The constant racket was driving me to the edge. It was like somebody was following me around bashing a saucepan by my ears. It was the hottest day of the year so far, but there was no way I could sit up on the deck and enjoy the sunshine. Instead, I was stuck in the bookshop cabin, the windows shut tight despite the rising temperature. The combination of the stuffy atmosphere and raucous soundtrack meant nobody was browsing for long and every task I attempted was interrupted by the incessant din from my thoughtless neighbour. The accounts were soon put to one side, as I kept messing up my spreadsheet, at one point making the figures go so scrambled that it looked like I was making a million pounds a day. If only.

I tried instead to relax with the advance copy of a book due out next month. I was hoping to tempt the author to do a signing, or perhaps even a talk, but as I kept having to read the same page over and over again, she'd probably be releasing her next book by the time I actually finished it. I settled reluctantly on doing a stock take, figuring even I could manage to scan bar codes without getting distracted by the thumping from the Jericho Wine Barge. I was wrong. I ended up scanning one book five times before I admitted defeat and stomped next door to confront the creator of the din.

I tried knocking on the cabin door, then rapped on the side of the boat as well, but Jack was causing such a palaver indoors he didn't register I was there. I hovered for a second, then decided the necessity to stop the noise outweighed the need for politeness, so I opened the cabin door and went in, bracing myself for the confrontation. But I should have braced myself for something else altogether. My normally buttoned-up neighbour was back in his working garb, but this time he'd ditched the high-vis. In fact, he'd dispensed with wearing a top all together. His feet were bare, which struck me as being hazardous while he was messing around with hammers and nails. I had a sudden vision of him walking barefoot across a beach, white sand glistening between those tanned toes. I didn't have a thing for feet, and my only excuse for fixating on them was that I couldn't quite bring myself to look upwards again. I tried to convince myself I'd imagined it, that the whole Poldark scything topless thing Jack had going on was a mirage created by my over-stressed brain. I mean, men who looked like that did not exist outside of the world of fiction. For one to exist in the form of my infuriating next-door neighbour was astonishingly unfair. The universe was having a laugh.

Jack cleared his throat and I was suddenly conscious I'd been standing there for an indeterminate amount of time, but definitely too long to justify remaining this quiet for. I finally dragged my gaze back from his feet to his face. He raised an eyebrow at me, and I blinked back at him in embarrassment.

'Mr Siddall,' I started, feeling the need to address him in a formal manner to make up for his very informal mode of undress. I hoped my voice didn't sound as strangled as I feared it did.

'My dad is Mr Siddall. I'd really prefer you stuck to Jack,' he replied. 'And calling me Mr Siddall doesn't make up for the fact you let yourself in. I could have been doing DIY in the buff.'

Why had he felt the need to evoke that image in my head? 'You might as well be,' I retorted, wishing I didn't blush so easily. He grinned with the easy air of someone completely comfortable in their own, admittedly spectacular, body. 'And I did knock,' I added lamely.

'I guess I mustn't have heard. I tend to get quite focused on tasks.'

'I noticed.' My voice was stronger now. 'You've been

focused on this particular task since 7 a.m. Without stopping.'

He took his phone out of his back pocket and checked the screen. 'Time flies when you're having fun. You must have been paying close attention to have noted exactly when I started work.'

'I couldn't have failed to notice. I didn't need an alarm call this morning due to your banging and crashing. I'm of half a mind to complain to the Oxford Boating Association about you causing a noise nuisance,' I said. I had no real intention of doing so, but perhaps the threat of it would make him be more considerate.

'I didn't realise the Oxford Boating Association had a remit over such things,' he said.

'They like to keep a close eye on all residents to make sure nobody's doing anything which could damage the environment around here. Welcome to canal life,' I said.

'I'm not too worried about it. The noise is for a limited amount of time and is well within guidelines. I've found the Association extremely helpful so far, and I'm sure they'd agree what I'm doing is reasonable. *They've* made me feel very welcome,' he said.

Of course they had. They didn't have to live next to his building work.

'Look, I appreciate you have to do the work, but can you please try not to make such a din while you're about it. You're giving me a headache. And more to the point, you're putting off my customers. Nobody wants to browse in a bookshop where it sounds like a juggernaut is doing battle with a pile driver next door.'

'I think that might be somewhat of an exaggeration,' said Jack, in an emphatically polite tone.

I sighed. 'You're missing the point. I shouldn't have to put up with it.'

Jack looked contrite, although I wasn't buying it. 'I do apologise. If it's any comfort, it's only for a short amount of time longer. As you can see, I'm nearly finished with the conversion.' He gestured around him, and I finally took in my surroundings. The floor was neatly sanded apart from a final patch surrounding the vintage bar which was now fixed into position. Behind the bar was a large fridge with a clear door, presumably for white wine and other drinks that needed chilling, while shelves stood ready for glasses and more bottles. The lower part of the cabin's walls had been transformed by the addition of warm oak-coloured panelling, which explained the reason for all the noise. The furniture was stacked in one corner, ready to be set out in time for the grand opening. It was starting to look like a really classy venue. Not that I was going to tell him that.

My expression must have given away I was impressed because he added, 'My living area isn't looking quite so polished, but that's not really a priority at the moment. I'm still working on the plans for my private residence. It's good to keep one's options open. Who knows what other opportunities might come up in this area of the canal?'

His seemingly offhand comment was perturbing, especially given his earlier mention of cosying up to the Oxford Boating Association. Everything I'd heard suggested Jack Siddall worked five steps ahead of the rest of the world. If his plans involved expanding into the neighbouring mooring, i.e. mine, then I needed to disabuse him of that idea. I decided to try my luck and see if I could get any more information out of him.

'I've got a few minutes now, and having done up the Oxford Bookship only last year I can probably give you some good tips for your living space,' I suggested. 'Why don't we take a look?'

I didn't give him the chance to disagree with me. I picked my way past the construction detritus and opened the door leading into the rest of the boat. Behind it was a neat bathroom space which consisted of two tiny toilet cubicles on one side with whitewashed wooden doors, and then a couple of sinks with classy matt black fittings on the other. A glossy green plant hung between the two sinks, plump round leaves cascading towards the black and white tiled floor. I surreptitiously reached out and stroked a leaf, surprised to find the plant was real rather than the plastic replica I'd expected.

'Nothing fake around here,' said Jack.

I frowned doubtfully at him. 'I'm guessing the sink area doubles as a wet room?' I asked, indicating the showerhead on the ceiling.

He nodded. 'That's correct. And before you say anything, the guys have fitted a master switch so bar patrons can't accidentally turn the shower on while they're in here and get themselves drenched.'

'Probably wise. Although it would be one way of quickly sobering up any difficult customers.'

Jack opened his mouth like he was going to argue back but decided against it.

'Onwards to your private cabin,' I said.

'It's really not fit for viewing,' repeated Jack, but I stared at him, or rather slightly past him in the manner of someone protecting their gaze from the sun during an eclipse, until he reluctantly unlocked the linking door and indicated for me to go in first.

'Goodness, I see what you mean,' I said, taking in the spartan interior. Actually, even to describe it as spartan felt generous. There was a camping stove set up in one corner and a rolled-up yoga mat and sleeping bag in another. And that was about it, apart from a single packing case which I suspected doubled as a table, and a couple of suitcases I assumed held the rest of his possessions.

'Really living the high life, I see. Is this an exercise in self-discipline, or do you like existing like this?'

'It's only like going camping,' said Jack.

I turned slowly on the spot, trying to see if there was something I'd missed. But there wasn't. There was nothing comfortable about the space at all.

'But you don't look like you're camping. You're always so meticulously dressed,' I said, then immediately regretted saying the words out loud.

Jack cleared his throat and indicated his current state of disarray. As if I was likely to have forgotten about it.

'Apart from now, obviously,' I added.

'I'm flattered you think I look good,' he said.

'I didn't say that exactly,' I retorted. He responded with one of his disconcertingly devastating grins. The way it transformed his face with warmth never failed to surprise me, giving a glimpse of a normally hidden side to his personality. I started to smile in return but caught myself in time.

'It's all smoke and mirrors. My shirts may look like linen, but they're actually a cleverly designed non-crease variety. Life's too short to be constantly pressing stuff, and I'm certainly not going to waste space by having an ironing board on the boat.'

'It must be tough slumming it without staff,' I said, still trying to get back on the offensive.

'I'm more than happy standing on my own two feet,' he said quietly.

'How very commendable of you. But you're not telling me you're using that thing as a mattress?' I gestured at the yoga mat.

'Admittedly it isn't ideal, but I'm still trying to get a feel for the place, and I've been too busy to get a proper bed sorted.'

'Or in fact any kind of furniture at all. Be careful, it's making you look like a commitment-phobe.'

'I wouldn't say that. I'm merely a man who considers choices carefully so any commitment I make is a meaningful one. As you can tell by the amount of work I've put into creating the bar, I'm extremely committed to making it a success.'

'And what exactly does success look like for you?' I decided I might as well come out and ask it.

Jack chuckled. 'That sounds painfully like the type of question I was expected to answer in my previous corporate life.' He plucked at his shorts. 'I'm a little underdressed to play the interview candidate right now.'

I frowned. 'I was only asking. You keep stressing how important it is for the bar to do well, but what does that actually mean? From what I've heard, you've climbed to the top of the corporate ladder in the past and not minded the price others had to pay for that along the way. Are you intending to do the equivalent here? Are you looking to create a Siddall monopoly on the Oxford Canal?'

Okay, I'd got a bit carried away, but the questions were out there now, and I really wanted to hear his answers.

Jack folded his arms defensively, and despite his dishevelled appearance, his stance was now one hundred per cent confident, steely-eyed businessman.

'It sounds like you've been paying too much attention to gossip, and I bet I can guess exactly who has been feeding it to you.'

'Let's leave Liam out of this,' I responded.

'Why?' he asked simply. 'You clearly set great store by his opinions.'

'I'm perfectly capable of forming my own opinions, believe me. And bringing Liam up sounds like a classic tactic for trying to avoid answering my questions.'

He shrugged. 'You were the one who mentioned his name. But there's little point in me having the Liam discussion with you at the moment, as you've obviously made your mind up that what he says is gospel. Fine. If you insist, yes, I have a long-term plan for the Jericho Wine Barge. What sensible businessperson doesn't? And as part of that plan, I've considered options for further development. The Oxford Canal and the beautiful permanent moorings in this area in particular offer a plethora of possibilities. I'd be a fool not to consider the opportunities which might present themselves were another space to become free.'

'You'll get my mooring over my dead body,' I declared.

'Why wou—' started Jack, but I left before he could even ask the rest of his question.

# Chapter Seventeen

**W**hy wouldn't he be able to take my mooring? I was pretty sure that was what Jack had been going to say before I practically ran away from him. I'd felt that awful pricking at the back of my eyes warning me I was close to bursting into angry tears. It frustrated me that my emotions manifested themselves in waterworks like this, making me seem weak when it was so important to show strength, especially to someone who could be as coolly calculating as Jack. I was so befuddled by him. There were times when I thought I saw glimpses of a funny and interesting human there, someone I might actually have liked were the circumstances different, but then the uptight and ruthless businessman would reappear, reminding me of all the reasons I had to be on my guard against him.

I texted Liam to vent, knowing he of all people would understand.

Between you and me (pls don't worry Flick about this) I'm worried the Siddall is up to his old tricks… He's got his eye on taking over my mooring space and he's cosying up to the OBA to make it happen. Feeling pretty powerless at the mo tbh

His reply came within seconds.

OMG that sucks, so sorry hun. Can he get your space?

I hesitated. The honest answer was yes. But it was hard enough thinking about it, let alone putting that fear in writing. It would make it so much more real.

This is Jack Siddall we're talking about…

enough said…I've got ur back x

Thanks. You're a mate x

I tried to busy myself with work, but every time I looked at the shelves of the Oxford Bookship, I felt the pang of potential loss. The fact the shop was quiet for most of the afternoon didn't help either. By closing time, my anxiety had grown so acute I could barely sit still. I shut up shop in record time and took Hilda for a run, the pair of us pounding the streets of Oxford until the endorphins from my exertion slowly started to work their magic on my psyche. As my tracking app bleeped to tell me we'd hit 5k,

I paused for a breather and realised we were only a couple of streets away from the Jericho Grange Care Home.

'Fancy stopping to say hi to Nana Rose, Hildy-girl?' I asked.

She wiggled joyfully and set off again at a trot.

Nana Rose was on good form, temporarily alleviating one area of concern. She was sitting on a bench in the care home garden, enjoying the late evening sunshine when I arrived, and greeted me with a cheery wave.

'I've got some good news for you, my darling,' she said as soon as I sat down next to her.

'Have they managed to get your pain medication sorted?' I asked.

She lightly tapped the back of my hand. 'Stop fussing. You're as bad as your father. No, this is much more exciting than boring old medication.'

I considered pushing harder, but she seemed so happy I thought it would be a shame to spoil the moment.

'I've found an author who'd like to launch her debut book on your boat,' she said, the words spilling out in delight. 'She's written a murder mystery set on a cruise ship, and she thought spending publication day on a boat would be perfect.'

'Of course I'd be very happy to help her. But wouldn't she prefer to be on an actual cruise ship?'

Nana Rose waved away my objection. 'Pshaw, why would she want to spend time on one of those floating tower blocks? She'd be better off staying on dry land than going on one of those things. No, she agrees a canal boat would allow her to be close to the water, and it would be a quirky line to sell for the media coverage.'

I raised an eyebrow. 'Does she agree, or have you strongarmed her into agreeing? I know what you're like, oh Nana mine. Your powers of persuasion are unparalleled.'

'Between you and me, she did try to get on a cruise ship, but they weren't interested. Her grandmother was telling me all about her disappointment over dinner the other night. Anyway, we came up with the perfect solution, and now everyone can be happy.'

I chuckled. 'I might have known it would be a grandparent conspiracy.'

She pouted. 'We've got to look after our grandchildren's best interests,' she said. 'I'll text you her number and you can get it all sorted. I'm not exactly sure when her book is due to be published, but you'll be able to iron out all the details.'

'As long as she brings plenty of fans along to buy copies, I'll be happy. Now, Nana, are you sure I can't tempt you to come to the next Blind Date with a Book night? It would be lovely to have you visit the Bookship and see her in all her glory. It's been a while since you last came. You'd definitely be the catch of the evening.'

Nana Rose pulled a face. 'That's very sweet of you, dear, but I'm otherwise engaged next Saturday evening.'

'Bingo calling again?' I asked.

'What? Oh, that. No, I decided one time was quite enough. In actual fact, I have a date of my own to look forward to. Eric invited me round for dinner and I said yes.'

'Eric? As in Eric Sanderson?' I swear she actually blushed. 'Nana Rose, you dark horse.'

'We're old friends. We thought we'd get together to reminisce.'

'Is that what the young people are calling it nowadays?' I teased, delighted by the happy expression on her face.

Nana Rose gave a throaty chuckle. 'It does me good to hear you refer to me as one of the "young people", although I know you're only humouring your old gran.'

'You're definitely young at heart,' I said. 'Old is as old does.'

'You're absolutely right. And before you start worrying, I'm not trying to seduce him into giving you a discount on the mooring fees.'

'What? How?' I stuttered, then realised I'd fallen into a trap.

'A-ha,' she said triumphantly. 'I was right. I knew you were worrying about them.'

'Nana, are you seriously telling me you've come up with a story about dating Eric to try to get me to confess I'm worried about the mooring fees? I'm not, by the way. Yes, it's a chunk of money, but it's a basic part of my business costs, and it's all in hand.'

I felt deeply uncomfortably spinning this less than true line to Nana, but it felt more important to protect her from my concerns. My problems were mine to deal with. She shouldn't have to worry about them.

'You were never a convincing liar, my darling.'

'I'm not going to argue with you about this, Nana,' I said firmly, knowing I'd need to try harder to deflect her. 'If I was worried, which I'm not, it would only be on the same level as being concerned about other hypothetical things like the Oxford Bookship flooding, or setting on fire, or Hilda breaking her leg.'

I winced, wishing I hadn't said those fears out loud. Logically I knew voicing them wouldn't make them come true, but the thing with worry was that it was rarely diminished by logic.

'Hmm,' she said doubtfully.

'The fees are well within my budget, and they will be paid when they're due, and not a moment later.' If I said it enough, maybe I would be able to convince myself too. 'And that is all you're getting from me on that subject. You worrying about me worrying only makes me actually start to worry.'

Thankfully she laughed, although I knew she was still watching me carefully. I'd have to work harder at putting on a brave front.

Hilda and I didn't stay as long as we'd have liked because Nana Rose started looking tired, although she claimed otherwise. I made an excuse about needing to get an order in for more stock and we headed home.

As I stepped on board, I found an envelope pushed halfway under the door of the bookshop and instantly recognised the luxurious stationery of the Oxford Boating Association.

With a feeling of trepidation, I reached down and picked it up, weighing it between my fingers as if I could psychically glean the contents. I'd had the invoice for the mooring fees, what else could they have to communicate with me? I opened the envelope, my heart thumping rapidly as I read the scribbled note warning me that the Oxford Boating Association was going to carry out an inspection of my narrowboat and check my canal licence to make sure that I wasn't in contravention of its terms.

I spluttered with indignation and picked up my phone without allowing myself to think about it. Eric answered on the first ring.

'I was expecting to hear from you,' he said, not bothering with pleasantries. His voice was resigned.

'I bet you were. What's all this about a licence inspection?'

'Hold on a minute.' I could hear the sound of him moving around and a door opening and shutting. When he spoke again, his tone was hushed, but more informal.

'It's exactly what it says in the note, Molly love. The Oxford Boating Association is obliged to carry out regular inspections of the boats mooring in our waters. We need to make sure everyone has the appropriate licence to be here. It's purely routine, nothing to worry about.'

'With all due respect, that's utter boll—balderdash.' I hastily corrected myself before I accidentally let slip an expletive. I'd only make things worse for myself by alienating him. 'I've been living here over a year, Eric. How come nobody's needed to inspect my boat in all that time? And as far as I know, Nana Rose never experienced a snap check like this, in all her decades on the water. What's brought it on now?'

'Why do you say that?' he asked, carefully avoiding answering my question.

'I'm saying something must have inspired this. Nothing's changed in my circumstances since I signed the contract for the mooring. I showed my canal licence then, you know it's for a permanent mooring because otherwise I wouldn't have been allowed to settle here in the first place.'

'I know that, but we still have to do our due diligence.' There was something in his tone which I couldn't quite figure out.

'Did somebody put you up to this?'

Eric cleared his throat. 'Molly dear, be careful with what you're asking. It sounds awfully like you're accusing me of doing something wrong.'

I took a deep breath. 'Sorry, that wasn't my intention.' I thought carefully about what he'd said and decided he'd been hinting at something. 'Okay, putting my situation to one side for a moment, theoretically, what sort of thing could trigger a snap inspection of this kind?'

There was a short pause. 'That's an interesting question. Of course you could consult the Association's handbook, but I'm happy to talk you through it now, if you would prefer.'

'That would be helpful. As a responsible canal boat owner moored on the Oxford Canal, it's important to me to have a full understanding of the rules and regulations of the water.' I was beginning to get the hang of how he wanted me to play this game.

'Absolutely. You're a sensible woman, Molly. The guidelines are very clear. When a boater signs a contract for their mooring, their credentials are scrutinised at that stage. Further inspections of documentation and boat can be carried out if there are reasonable grounds for believing the terms and conditions of the mooring are not being adhered to.'

'And what kind of thing would constitute reasonable grounds? Speaking hypothetically, of course,' I said.

'Speaking hypothetically? The scenario which comes to my mind is if the Association were to receive a report claiming a boater was not fulfilling the terms of their occupation. For example, a suggestion that they'd switched to a continuous cruiser licence without informing the relevant authorities, namely the Oxford Boating Association. Obviously if we were to have someone permanently moored who didn't have permission to do so, we would have to act immediately. We would issue a week's notice to move on, unless there were extenuating circumstances such as illness of course.'

'But I don't need extenuating circumstances because I have the proper licence.'

'And once you've proved that in the inspection, plus a few other minor little details have been cleared up, then I'm sure everything will be fine,' said Eric. I didn't find his statement reassuring.

'What other little details are you talking about?' I asked.

'Health and safety. The usual red tape.'

'What particular aspect of health and safety?'

'Electrical safety. Pipe cleanliness. Appropriateness of bathroom facilities for events. That kind of thing.'

I started to feel sick. The Oxford Bookship was immaculate; she had to be. I was meticulous when it came to keeping the boat's services in good condition, and the only issue I'd had was the disappearance of the power cable, which had been beyond my control. I filled up my water tanks using a series of pipes which I connected to the mains supply managed by the Oxford Boating Association, and I kept those pipes pristine. I tested the quality of the water every other week, not because I had to, but because I cared about keeping on top of these things. There was always a chance Nana Rose would come for a visit, and I wanted to be in a position where she could look at the Oxford Bookship and know she'd done the right thing by allowing me to buy it from her. I was outraged someone would even suggest I didn't care enough to keep on top of these things.

'When will this inspection take place?'

'The thing with a spot inspection is that there isn't any notice about it,' replied Eric.

'If that's the case, how come I received a warning letter?'

He cleared his throat again. 'A warning letter? Are you sure you received it? I know when I was living aboard full time, it was amazing how many leaflets I'd find stuck under my door when I returned to the boat. Most of them were junk.'

He was being far from subtle, and I felt a deep appreciation for the risk he'd taken in giving me an advance warning. He'd aspired to be chairman of the Association for many years before he finally was awarded the role. If his colleagues were to find out he'd tipped me off, he could lose his position. I was touched he'd gone to such lengths to help me. I wasn't under any illusion I'd earned it on my own merit, but I was grateful his loyalty to my grandmother had proved beneficial to me.

'You know, you're right. I wish all these takeaway places would stop spamming me with all their leaflets. The best place for them is the recycling. As long as they stay in there without Hilda ripping them to shreds, of course.'

'It would be a shame if that happened,' said Eric solemnly. His voice suddenly changed. 'Thanks for your call, but I'm afraid I'm not interested in changing our broadband provider at the moment.' Somebody else had obviously come into hearing distance.

'Not to worry, it's been good to talk to you. Do give us a call if you fancy a great deal,' I said quickly playing my part.

As soon as I hung up, I ripped up the note and then looked around for a place to hide it. Just how thorough was this inspection going to be? I didn't want to leave it somewhere where it could be discovered, even if it was shredded. I stuffed the tiny pieces into my pocket and turned my attention to the biggest problem of all. What had triggered this inspection? I shook my head. Or should I be asking myself who had triggered it? Jack had told me himself that he was pally with the Association. What if this was part of his scheme to take over my mooring?

# Chapter Eighteen

I took out my phone, then decided it was too much to explain by text, so instead I tucked Hilda up in her bed, then stomped up the towpath and over the bridge to speak to Liam in person. It had felt unexpectedly reassuring to share my concerns with him earlier and to receive his message saying he had my back, and I wanted his take on this latest development.

Dusk was falling as I made my way to Castle Mill Stream. The backwater was home to temporary moorings, and in the height of the summer holidays it was normally busy, but at the moment the *Lydia* was the only boat tied up on this stretch. The motor cruiser stood out even more than usual because her deck area was lit up by a collection of ring lights. Liam was standing chatting away to a camera fixed in the centre of one of them, animatedly holding up a water bottle which contained a sludgy green concoction.

I hovered on the bank, not wanting to interrupt his flow.

'Travelling around like I do, I have to make sure I'm

looking after number one. That's why I drink Prasinos Viridis Protein smoothies, who I'm proud to say are the sponsors of today's video.' He paused and held the bottle closer to the camera, then took a big glug. 'Mmm, so tasty,' he added, although the slight gagging noise he made after somewhat contradicted his words. 'Nutritious and totally delicious, these smoothies are my absolute favourite. Honestly, if I wasn't sponsored by these guys, I'd still be recommending them to you. Did I mention they're super tasty and full to the brim with goodness? Check out the description below to get 25 per cent off if you sign up for a subscription using the code Boaty Liam. Yes, folks, you heard me right, a whopping 25 per cent off. And now back to the video.'

He reached forward and covered the lens with his hand, then turned the camera off and spat over the side of the boat into the river, pouring the rest of the bottle's contents in as well. I took a step back, deciding it would be better to pretend I hadn't been standing there the whole time, but I ended up treading on a stick which broke in half with a loud crack.

Liam looked up from the railings and grinned ruefully at me.

'Caught in the act. I can never keep the disgusting stuff down for long, plus it gives me a dicky tummy.'

'If that's the case, why do you advertise it online?' I asked, disconcerted by the contrast in his behind-the-scenes behaviour.

'Straight to the point, Molls. It pays well and needs must. The company's giving me a percentage of the sales from my discount code as well as the usual sponsorship fee, so I had to make it convincing. Don't worry, I believe most of the claims they make on the packaging are true, even if it does taste absolutely rank to me.' He gave an exaggerated shudder then laughed in his usual charming manner, but I couldn't smile along with him. I understood the pressures of trying to get by, but to be actively deceiving your audience like that? It didn't sit right, and I was unsettled by this different side of him. I wondered whether I'd made a mistake coming here this evening. But Liam was carrying on in his usual chatty manner like there was nothing wrong in what he was doing, and before I knew it, he'd ushered me on board the *Lydia*.

'Welcome to my crib,' he said.

I'd watched his online tour, but seeing the place in person made me realise how much money he must have spent on fitting it out.

'I had to get inventive to make sure I could get all the mod cons installed, but as my social media following started growing, I saw an opportunity to monetise and I've not looked back,' he explained as he took a couple of ciders out of his fridge and gestured for me to sit down on deck. 'Cheers.' He clinked his bottle against mine. I hesitated, then took a sip of the chilled liquid and surveyed my surroundings, trying to relax into the moment. The river was gently bubbling past the boat, carrying a collection of blossom petals on the surface, while insects danced around in the golden light from the setting sun. There couldn't be many more beautiful places in the world. I was desperate to be able to continue living here. Undoubtedly Liam was equally as keen to continue his live-aboard lifestyle. Was I being too quick to judge his disingenuous behaviour?

'Shoot, what's on your mind?' he asked.

I dragged my thoughts away from my current dilemma back to my original reason for coming to visit him.

'Am I that transparent?' I said, playing for time as I questioned whether it was a good idea to confide in him further.

'I know we've only known each other a short amount of time, but I can see something's bothering you. That sunny Molly disposition has a few clouds on the horizon.' He waved his hand around, as if trying to brush them away. 'What's he done now?'

'I don't know for definite that Jack has done anything,' I prevaricated.

'You don't know, but you have a strong feeling, I can tell. You should trust your instincts,' said Liam. 'Let me guess. Is it something to do with the lengthy chat I saw him having with the head honcho of the Boating Association a little earlier? The pair of them looked as thick as thieves. I got a bad vibe about their conversation.'

'Eric is a decent guy. He follows the rules. I know he wouldn't be involved in anything dodgy,' I defended him, even as my pulse accelerated in panic as I realised my hunch must be correct.

'Is that his name?' Liam reached across and squeezed my hand. 'Your friend Eric might be one of the good guys, but the man he was talking to certainly isn't, and that's how trouble starts. Tell me. What's happened?'

I reluctantly explained about the looming boat inspection. 'I'm sure I've got nothing to worry about, but I can't help being concerned regardless. Everything on the Bookship is in order, I know it is. But I hate being put under such scrutiny, plus the inspector could turn up at any moment. What if they make an appearance in the middle of my next event and start being difficult? It wouldn't be a good look and it's exactly the kind of thing which could start rumours flying around and damage the shop's reputation.'

Liam took a drink of his cider. 'I can understand why you're worried. Let's examine the evidence and see if we can prove who's behind it.'

'That's the thing. There isn't any evidence. Eric couldn't or wouldn't tell me who'd given the Oxford Boating Association the tip-off which triggered the need for the inspection.'

'I wonder,' said Liam thoughtfully. 'It's the second questionable thing that's happened to you of late, isn't it? First the cable theft, then this. Don't you think it's strange these things started occurring not long after Jack Siddall appeared on the scene? It can't be a coincidence. This kind of behaviour is straight out of his playbook, trust me.'

I chewed my bottom lip. Liam seemed so convinced, but I was getting more confused by the second. 'Perhaps. But actual sabotage? Wouldn't that be rather an extreme way of doing business?'

'Exactly the way Jack prefers it. I was like you back in my corporate job. The warning signs were there but I kept ignoring them because I thought he was my friend, then it was too late and I was out on my ear. I don't want the same thing to happen to you, Molls.'

'I won't let it happen,' I said. 'I still don't understand why Jack chose his mooring in the first place. Yes, there aren't many going spare in Oxford, but if he's so keen to create a business that will scale, why didn't he choose somewhere on land for it?'

'As you know a floating shop has a very unique selling point. Jack appreciates a challenge. Opening a wine bar like everyone else's wouldn't be as interesting to him. He looks down at the rest of the world, yet still has this desperate need to show he's the alpha businessman.'

I thought back to Jack's disparaging comments during the first Blind Date with a Book night. He'd certainly demonstrated his superior attitude then. 'And never mind who might get hurt along the way?'

'Exactly. You saw that for yourself when he smashed into the Bookship.' He frowned thoughtfully and took another sip of his cider.

'What is it?' I asked.

'Molls, you trust me, right?'

If he'd asked me half an hour ago before the whole protein shake incident I would have immediately answered with a wholehearted yes, but I still felt a niggling sense of unease about his somewhat unscrupulous sales technique.

'I enjoy spending time with you,' I answered instead, but thankfully Liam didn't seem to notice my hesitation.

'As your friend, can I give you some advice? Given the escalation of events, it's time for you to take back control. Up until now, Jack's plan has been going perfectly. He's got you seriously worried with his underhand tactics, but it's only a matter of time before he makes his move and does something even more dramatic to force you out of your mooring so he can take it over. The only way you can stop him doing that is by being proactive.'

'And how do you suggest I do that?'

'You should call him out. On camera. Trust me when I say there are tens of thousands of reasons why he would have to behave himself if you confronted him live on my channel. My viewers would be so shocked to see the true colours of the Siddall heir.'

'But couldn't he sue me if I made accusations like that without proof?'

Liam shrugged casually. 'He wouldn't dare. The court of public opinion would back you.'

I wasn't convinced. And I didn't think Liam believed that either, otherwise why hadn't he done his own Jack exposé video? I looked around the deck, suddenly conscious of the cameras he'd got fixed at strategic positions.

'You're not filming our conversation now, are you?'

Liam looked hurt. 'Of course I'm not.' He sounded genuinely upset I'd even think that of him.

'I'm sorry. I guess I'm feeling a little paranoid what with everything that's been going on.' I shook my head. 'Thanks for the offer, but it's not something I want to do at the moment. I need to carry on gathering evidence, and then when I've got incontrovertible proof he's been trying to sabotage me, I will talk to him about it. Most likely off camera.' Although whether that would make any difference, I had no idea.

'You've got to do what you feel is best,' said Liam doubtfully. 'I can only speak from my own experience, but you need to look out for your own interests where Jack Siddall is concerned.'

I had every intention of doing just that. But I wanted to do it on my own terms. I certainly didn't trust Jack, but now I wasn't so sure I could fully trust Liam either.

<h1 style="text-align:center">Chapter Nineteen</h1>

I made my excuses and retreated to the Oxford Bookship where my fears grew even stronger. I'd tried to share my problems, but I'd chosen to share them with the wrong person, and it had made me feel worse. I checked my watch. Was it too late to call Flick? I could imagine her offended response to me even asking that question. It was only my stupid pride that had stopped me from confiding in her before. She was my best friend. Perhaps it was time to tell her everything that had been on my mind. Before I could chicken out, I hit her number, but when she picked up, I put my own issues to one side because I knew instantly something was up.

'Hey lovely, what's the matter?'

'I'm all good,' she insisted in an overly bright tone. 'How's life with you?'

'Absolutely fine,' I responded, quickly deciding that this was not the moment after all to burden her with my worries.

There was a pause as we both considered how to persuade the other to share her woes.

'Is everything alright with you and Liam?' I asked.

'Liam? Yes, I think so,' she said distractedly.

'Work then?'

I heard her swallow.

'Tell me,' I urged.

'It's no big deal, honestly. I'm probably overreacting.'

'Flick, you are the most together person I know. If you're upset about something, it's because it's justified.'

She made a noise which sounded suspiciously like she was trying to hold back a sob.

'The paper's making changes. Well, that's how they're describing it, but everyone knows it's code for cutbacks.'

I wished I was with Flick instead of at the other end of the phone from her.

'I'm sorry. I'm sending you a virtual hug. And if you want, I'll set off right now with Hilda to come over and give you a hug in person. We can be with you in less than an hour.'

'It's practically the middle of the night. Much as I'd love a Hilda hug, please don't worry. I'll be fine.'

'The offer stands. You can change your mind at any moment, and I promise I'll be there. Have they given any indication who might be affected? They do realise if they got rid of you, they wouldn't be able to fill the paper? You have to be the most prolific, hard-working reporter they've got.'

Flick gave a wobbly laugh. 'That's sweet of you to say. They haven't got as far as telling us who's at risk, but all the indications are that they're going to try to combine our team with the sister paper in London, so we work over both titles. And of course, that means anyone who does the same job as someone from the London paper is at risk.'

'But shouldn't that mean you're okay? You're the expert on council matters in Oxford. Nobody in London is going to be doing that role.'

'Ah, but the London paper doesn't have a local democracy reporter at the moment, so that's my big news. They're going to send me there for a trial run for the next fortnight to see what "added value" I could bring to that team. Basically I'm spending this weekend packing a bag and trying to brace myself for life in the big city.'

Hilda rested her head on my lap, and I gently stroked her ears as I thought about how to respond to Flick. I couldn't bear the thought of my best friend moving away permanently. If it was what she chose, then I would be happy for her, but I could tell from the tone of her voice it wasn't what she wanted at all.

'A trial run? I'm assuming that means it's a trial for all parties involved. They can't make you move there if you don't want to, right?'

'That's the one thing I'm trying to cling to. A permanent move is definitely not on the cards, according to Neil anyway. He says it's because they're too stingy to pay me London rates for a start. No, if they decide I "add value" to the London paper's coverage with my expertise, I'll get that added to my remit. So, I'll have to look after Oxford and London council news, potentially commuting down there every few days, which means I'll be even less likely to get the opportunity to do the stories I actually want to do.'

'That sucks.'

'It does indeed.'

'Try not to worry about the bigger picture. Just concentrate on getting through the next fortnight and seeing how that goes, and then once that's out of the way, you might have a better sense of what will happen next. You can only control how you react to each situation as it arises. Worrying about hypotheticals won't help.' Even as I said it, I knew I was being hypocritical. I was giving her advice which I struggled to follow myself.

I could hear the smile in Flick's voice as she responded. 'How's that technique going for you?'

I hesitated and she laughed.

'Yeah, I thought so. Spill, Bramble. What's been playing on your mind for the past few weeks? I know there's something, even though you've tried your best to keep it from me.'

'I thought I'd done a pretty good job.'

'You were *almost* convincing. I would have had it out of you sooner if I hadn't been distracted by Liam.'

I had to tell her. 'Speaking of Liam, there's something you should know about him,' I said, quickly relaying the whole protein shake incident.

I could picture her frowning at the other end of the line. 'Okay, that's not ideal behaviour. But if they're selling that shake in this country, then it will have been tested and passed by the relevant food authorities, so it's not like he's flogging something that's going to make people ill. It's not Liam's fault he doesn't like the taste.'

I was relieved by her reassurance. 'You're right. I was surprised, that's all. I felt I should tell you.'

She laughed. 'We've been on a few dates and I like the guy, but it's not like we're getting married. But I appreciate the heads-up. I shall be on my guard against questionable green concoctions. And you're not going to get away with distracting me any longer. What's been worrying you, lovely?'

After a moment's hesitation, I summoned up my courage and told her. My crippling anxiety over the mooring fees; the added pressure from my increased loan payments; my paralysing fear that Jack Siddall was going to swoop in and take over my home. As I spoke nothing materially changed. The problems were still there, and still apparently insurmountable. But as least I felt less lonely in dealing with them. The seemingly permanent tension in my shoulders eased a little.

'My love, why didn't you tell me before?' The compassion in Flick's voice was nearly my undoing.

'I didn't want to worry you. And I didn't want to disappoint you,' I added quietly.

There was a splutter of indignation at the other end of the line.

'I'm your best friend. I worry more if you don't tell me things. And you could never disappoint me. I'll return the "don't worry" lecture you've just delivered me. You're doing your best to raise the capital for your mooring fees. As to the other issue, even if Jack wants to create a bigger venture one day, the point is that his current one is based on a single berth on a single boat. And he hasn't even opened that for business yet. Any changes are way down the line, and as you've kindly reminded me, there's no point in worrying about what might happen in the future. You've got to focus on the here and now. Everything else will fall into place and you'll deal with whatever situations arise as and when they do so. Right?'

'You're correct, my wise friend.'

'Don't get too carried away, you'll make me big headed,' said Flick with a laugh. I was glad that she was sounding more like her usual self.

We chatted for a bit longer, until it became obvious that Flick was so tired she was nearly falling asleep on the phone, and after extracting a promise from each other not to dwell on our worries, we said goodnight.

Unfortunately, I only managed to keep my promise for a short while after I hung up the phone, because in the silence of the early hours, my annoying brain started picking over the impending inspection again. Logically, I knew everything was in order and that the inspector wouldn't be able to find any issues. However, it didn't stop my mind summoning worst-case scenarios. Losing my mooring because I couldn't pay the fees was one thing, but having it taken away because an inspector had found me lacking would be beyond mortifying. How on earth would I explain that to Nana Rose?

What I should have done was ignore the spiralling thoughts and gone to bed with a sleep meditation playing on my phone to quieten my mind. Instead, I went into hyper mode and decided the best way to distract myself was by staying up late rearranging the displays in the bookshop.

There was something about the physical act of moving books around the shop that made me feel like I was achieving something practical, although if I was being completely honest with myself, all I was really achieving was creating a great big mess. I needed to assert my authority on the space while I still could, a particularly intrusive thought which I struggled to ignore. If the bookshop failed, what would I do next? My CV, such as it was, was a patchwork of random jobs taken for practical reasons rather than because I had a passion for the profession I was trying my hand at. Nothing had ever felt right until the Oxford Bookship. And barely fourteen months of running my own business would only tell a prospective employer I was no good at sticking to something and making it work.

'Hilda, please tell me it'll all be okay,' I said to my pup who was snoring gently in the corner of the bookshop. It was way past her normal bedtime, and I knew she'd much prefer to be curled up in her actual bed rather than lying on the wooden floor of the shop, but she was keeping close to me, a loyal pooch as always. She gave a little grunt in her sleep which I decided to interpret as her version of a pep talk. 'Thanks, lovely girl, I don't know what I'd do without you. Time to focus on undoing the mess I've created in here.'

I stood back and surveyed the bookshop cabin. There were now gaping holes in the shelves and piles of books littered the floor. It was in no fit state to be open to the public for business as usual, let alone to be a venue for the upcoming Blind Date with a Book night.

'Little steps, little steps,' I told myself. 'I can do this.'

I moved the Blind Date with a Book trolley to the opposite corner of the cabin and then stared thoughtfully at the shelves. Despite the unconventional location of the shop, I'd always stuck closely to tradition when it came to setting out the stock with the classic divides of different genres and whether the books were new or second-hand. But as I thought about my usual sales technique, that wasn't really how I worked. My approach was holistic, connecting readers with the book that they needed, a volume which would cast light on a problem, give them confidence to choose a new path, or provide that much needed escape from the pressure of their day-to-day existence. It was the way I chose my own reading material after all. I'd always been a very intuitive reader, selecting books because I felt inexplicably drawn to them at a particular time in my life, rather than reading books I felt I had to. Sometimes I would wander up and down beside a bookcase, hand outstretched, softly running my fingers along the spines. Every so often I would pause and contemplate the title, perhaps pulling the volume out to gaze at the cover and read the blurb. Some I would set aside as a maybe, others would go straight back on the shelf for another occasion. But then when I found the one, the book that I needed at that particular point, I would know it with my whole body. The tension would disappear, to be replaced by a feeling of utter rightness. I had found my literary companion, the book that would hold my hand

and walk me through whatever challenge I was facing in my life – or enable me to escape it for a precious while. Perhaps I needed to recreate that browsing experience in my shop.

I picked up a few books and started shuffling them into different piles, not allowing myself to think too hard about why I was grouping certain volumes together. But as I worked, I realised I was starting to feel calmer and more in control of my situation. A couple of hours later, I sat back on my heels and took stock. In all honesty, the bookshop looked like it had been broken into. But despite the appearance of chaos, I could see the order there. Instead of neatly delineated divisions between the usual genres, the books were with companions which complemented them, gathered together by feelings rather than the conventions dictated by the categories set out by a marketing team. What my customers would make of this eclectic system, I didn't know, but the most important thing was that it felt right to me.

I spent another hour dusting the shelves and putting the books back in their new sections. Then I took out my label maker and started creating signs to help readers navigate the system.

'Books that give you the warm fuzzies' for one sign. 'Books with answers' for another. 'Heavily marketed but they actually deserve the hype' for those readers who, like me, tended to avoid the books they saw plastered on billboards everywhere, fearing that they wouldn't live up to their promise. 'Hidden gems which should have been heavily marketed' was the largest section. I had to do my bit for the authors who deserved more attention than what publishers' meagre marketing budgets whipped up.

As dawn approached, I stood back and surveyed my surroundings. To the casual observer, it looked like I'd hardly done anything at all. But a Bookship regular would spot the difference immediately. I hoped it would improve their browsing experience, rather than putting them off. I couldn't afford to alienate those who'd been loyal to the shop from the start. At least the exercise of sorting out the shelves had given me plenty of time to get my thoughts in order too. The inspection was going to happen regardless of my feelings about it. But I wasn't going to let the fear of it bog me down. The Oxford Bookship was my passion, and I would fight for it until my very last breath.

## Chapter Twenty

My new shelving system seemed to be having a positive impact on sales, but the real test would be the second Blind Date with a Book event, which was quickly approaching. It was of course also the launch night for the Jericho Wine Barge. I'd been studiously avoiding Jack since our last encounter, but I couldn't fail to notice his preparations for the big night. I'd spotted he'd taken over an old storage shed which the Oxford Boating Association had been trying to sell for months, and I had observed his frequent trips wheeling boxes of supplies along the towpath between it and the Jericho Wine Barge as he stocked up. The fairy lights had gone up, and he'd set out tables and chairs in the towpath garden. That had felt like a particular invasion as I was so used to having the whole space to myself. I'd been waiting for the moment the furniture encroached over the halfway point, but he'd been scrupulously pedantic at sticking to it, raising an eyebrow when he'd caught me watching, as if challenging me to have a go at him about it.

However, my avoidance tactic failed when he saw me setting up a rope to create a boundary line between our respective outdoor spaces.

'I'm not sure that's a good idea. It strikes me as being a health and safety hazard,' he said in a deceptively chatty tone as he came over to take a closer look at it.

'I thought it was best to be on the safe side. As we've got events running simultaneously, I don't want your customers coming to take advantage of the free drinks I'm offering to my customers while they browse.'

Jack smiled. 'While your lemonade is reasonably nice, I'm afraid it offers no competition to the crisp bubbles of the free Prosecco which my guests will be greeted with on arrival.'

'Even so, I think it's best to keep the two events clearly separated,' I said, unwilling to back down.

'The Oxford Boating Association might have something to say about the rope too,' he added.

If I were Hilda, my hackles would have risen at his words.

'I beg your pardon?' I said, fighting to keep my voice steady.

'You mentioned they're keen on things like noise regulation. I imagine a brown-coloured rope hanging at shin level might be something they'd also be interested in. I mean, it's almost designed to trip people up.'

If I'd had any doubts about who was behind the

inspection I was facing, they vanished now. I clenched my hands into fists to try to steady their sudden tremble.

'Fine, if you're going to be like that, I'll get rid of the rope. But if any of your customers come and spoil my event, I shall hold you entirely responsible.'

Jack held his hands up with an expression of faux innocence on his face. 'You and I both know we can't be held completely responsible for the behaviour of our patrons. However, I give you my word I'll do my best to keep them in line. Does that satisfy you?'

'Not really, no,' I retorted.

Jack frowned. 'I assure you, my word can be trusted.'

'That's not what I've heard. Besides, I prefer to judge people like you on their actions rather than their words,' I said.

'A surprising stance from a person whose business is based on the power of words,' he pointed out.

'Perhaps. But when certain people are involved, I am left with little choice.'

He folded his arms and studied me closely. 'I don't know why I keep trying to justify myself to you. It's very clear you've made up your mind about me. Or is it the case that somebody's helped you make it up?' he added darkly.

'What exactly do you mean by that? I'm perfectly capable of forming my own opinions, thank you very much.' I realised I was mirroring his stance and decided to start removing the rope instead, which unfortunately brought me closer to Jack.

'Yes, very strong ones, as we've already discussed,' he replied. He reached down to help just as I moved to grab the same bit of the rope, his hand brushing against mine. I snatched it away, and tucked my hair behind my ear, still feeling the tingling sensation of his fingers on mine.

'And what precisely is your problem with a woman having strong opinions?' My words came out forcefully as I reacted to Jack's growing smile.

'Nothing, when they have a reasonable basis. I'd like to point out that your gender has absolutely nothing to do with my concern about the stance you're taking, before you start accusing me of being a misogynist.'

'I was doing no such thing. Look, you obviously have something you'd like to say to me, so why don't you come out and say it in plain English? All these obtuse mutterings implying something isn't right are making no sense whatsoever.'

For a moment, I thought Jack was going to answer me, but then his expression grew steely again and he merely stared beyond me.

I glanced round and saw Liam approaching.

'Go on, tell me what you were going to say.' I waited, then shrugged. 'And answer came there none. Guess there's nothing for me to worry about then.'

'I wouldn't go so far as to say that,' said Jack.

'Be careful, Jack. That sounds very much like you're threatening her,' said Liam, stepping forward and standing protectively at my side.

'I'm not—Oh what's the point?' said Jack. He ignored Liam and looked directly at me. 'If I were you, I'd be careful about who you trust on this canal. Not everyone is as they seem.'

He directed his gaze towards Liam to make his meaning perfectly clear, then he turned on his heel and stomped back on board the Jericho Wine Barge, closing the cabin door with a bang. I wanted to laugh off his theatrical exit, but there had been something so earnest about his words that I almost found myself believing his warning. I frowned, telling myself to get it together.

I turned round and caught Liam fiddling with his phone and experienced a pang of irritation.

'You weren't live streaming again, were you? I already told you I didn't want to have my conversations with Jack being broadcast to all and sundry on the internet. I prefer to keep a low profile.'

'Don't worry, nothing was going out live. As I came up, I could see there was some kind of confrontation going on. It felt like a good idea to start recording as a form of insurance. I'll delete it if you prefer.'

'I do prefer.' I frowned. 'That was a weird conversation. It sounded like he was trying to warn me to stay away from you. He was playing mind games with me, right? There's nothing I should be worried about?'

Liam looked hurt.

'Sorry, that's a crappy thing for me to say. I'm sure there's no actual basis in his implied warnings,' I added hastily, although in truth, I was feeling conflicted, torn between the apparent sincerity that I'd seen in Jack's entreaty, and what I knew of his history with Liam.

'It's not your fault,' said Liam in a resigned tone. 'The Siddall powers of persuasion are lethal and even the best people find themselves being taken in by them.'

'What's he hoping to achieve by making out you can't be trusted?'

'He's trying to make himself feel important. I can't believe the guy still feels threatened by me, even though we don't work together anymore. I'm sorry you were caught in the middle.'

Liam sounded convincing, but I wasn't sure I agreed with his interpretation. The only time I'd seen Jack look anything less than one hundred per cent confident in himself was shortly after he'd crashed into the Oxford Bookship. He didn't strike me as being the type of person who would need to make himself feel important. He knew he was important.

'Maybe,' I said, my doubt obvious.

Liam exhaled. 'I see. Okay, let's try this. How are you feeling right now? Confused? Unsettled? Worried?'

'All of the above,' I admitted.

'Exactly.' His tone was triumphant. 'This is what Jack Siddall does. He likes putting people in their place. He won't have appreciated you showing him up by saving him when he first arrived on the canal. So he's getting some payback by delivering cryptic statements and making you question your own judgement.'

'That seems a little … far-fetched.' Sure, Jack had the knack for rubbing me up the wrong way, but I needed to keep a proper perspective and not let my prejudice against him influence me into getting swept along with Liam's conspiracy theory. But if I didn't believe Liam, wasn't I then doing exactly what Jack wanted? I didn't know what to think anymore. I pinched the bridge of my nose, my head starting to ache with confusion.

'You're a decent person. You want to believe the best in people. I hope you're right. But remember, I'm here, if you need me.' Liam lightly touched my elbow.

'I appreciate your support. But I reckon I'm getting myself wound up over nothing.'

'That's what I thought. Then I found myself out of a job,' said Liam ominously.

# Chapter Twenty-One

The day of my second Blind Date with a Book event dawned full of promise. I woke with the birdsong and lay in bed running through my plan of action over and over again until I was completely confident. Nana Rose was a great one for having faith in the powers of manifestation, and while I was slightly more sceptical, believing that the universe had better things to do than worry about making things perfect for me rather than anyone else, I figured it wouldn't do any harm to indulge in a bit of positive thinking myself. I closed my eyes and pictured a happy crowd of guests mingling in the shop, faces beaming as they made new connections, shoulders weighed down by the bags of books resting on them. Customers gathered around me, eager to share their delight at discovering their new favourite author in their new favourite bookshop. Then the crowd parted, and Jack walked towards me, his linen shirt casually untucked with the buttons undone, his hand resting on the smooth skin above his heart in an attitude of humble apology. His eyes raked my features, and I felt like he was seeing through to my very soul. He reached forward and rang a bell, wanting to draw everyone's attention to the important words I knew he had to say to me.

The bell rang again and I realised it was actually my phone ringing. I blinked my eyes open, glad nobody had been privy to the strange turn of events in my imagination. The very last thing I wanted to manifest was a sexily rumpled Jack, even if this imaginary version of him had been about to apologise for all the trouble he'd sent my way. I scrabbled around to find my mobile which had somehow ended up on the floor.

'Good morning. To what do I owe the honour of this early call from London's hottest new journalist?' I said, treating Flick to a very unflattering facial angle as I answered her video call.

'London's coldest new journalist more like,' she replied, moving her phone so I could see the blanket she was bundled up in. 'It might be practically July, but the grotty digs I'm being put up in did not get the memo. Did I mention the walls are mouldy too?'

She gave me a close-up of the dark bloom extending from the windowsill by her bed.

'Grim. That looks uncannily like the protein shakes that Liam's been sponsored to promote,' I said, trying to make her smile. Unfortunately, it had the opposite effect. 'Hey, what's up?' I asked, as her brow furrowed.

'Is Liam well at the moment? He's not sick or anything?'

'Not as far as I know. He looked fine yesterday when he walked past the barge. He was on the phone, so we didn't get a chance to speak. In fact, I assumed he was chatting to you.'

'Ah. No. Not me, I'm afraid. In fact, I've had all of one text from him since I arrived here. Hence, me wondering if he was sick. Just sick of me it would seem.'

'Aw, Flick, I'm sure it's not like that. It's scientifically impossible for anyone to be sick of you. Maybe he's busy with a big video coming out or something.' I wasn't making excuses for Liam, just trying to make my friend feel better.

'No, it's definitely not like before, when he'd drowned his phone. I've tried calling but each time it went to voicemail after only a couple of rings, and you know what that means. It's not like he owes me. We hadn't gone official or anything, but…'

But Flick had a track record of falling hard and fast, and the fact I'd essentially set them up with each other could have made her even more susceptible to the idea of developing a serious relationship with him. I was furious Liam was messing her around like this. He was responsible for his own behaviour, but it didn't make me feel any less guilty about him ghosting my best friend.

'Do you want me to have a word with him?' I said. 'I can't understand why he's ignoring you.'

She laughed bitterly. 'Out of sight, out of mind. I guess I'm not worth remembering about when I'm not on the scene. Please don't say anything about it to him. I feel humiliated enough as it is.'

'Flick lovely, you're kind and caring, a super successful powerhouse of a woman, and drop-dead gorgeous to boot, if we're going to be superficial about it. If Liam can't recognise he's hit the jackpot by meeting you, then frankly he doesn't deserve the honour of even having your number.' I jabbed my finger towards the screen to emphasise my point.

'Mmm,' she said doubtfully. 'You're biased because you've been my best friend forever and have developed a Stockholm syndrome-like attachment to me.'

I snorted in disbelief. 'Am I going to have to come up to London and make you see sense? Stockholm syndrome isn't even a proper thing. I read an article in a scientific journal which argued it's a constructed concept. I've got a copy in the shop, and I'll send it to you if you like. You're wonderful and I refuse to hear otherwise.'

Flick rolled her eyes. 'Only you would read a scientific journal for fun.'

'It was part of some house clearance stock I got at the beginning of the year. I was drawn towards it, and now I know why. Will you admit that I know what I'm talking about?'

'Fine, Molly Bramble is very wise. Please don't make me start repeating mantras about being a strong and confident woman.'

I examined her features closely. 'Maybe not right now. But I can think of a few choice phrases about Liam I'm happy for you to chant back to me.'

That at least provoked a small smile.

'That's more like it,' I said. 'Time to send in the big guns.' I moved my phone across to Hilda's bed and treated Flick to a close-up. 'Say hello to your Aunty Flick.'

Hilda leapt to her feet, setting the boat gently rocking.

'I'm here, sweet girl,' called Flick from the screen. Hilda sniffed it in confusion, making my friend laugh. 'You two are the best tonic,' she said.

'We miss you.'

'I miss you as well. But today I shall distract myself by attending a residents' meeting on mansard roof extensions. It's all kicking off in this borough of London, let me tell you. I'm actually feeling nostalgic for Oxford's low traffic neighbourhood dramas.'

'You'll write the best article ever and bring an exciting new perspective to the debate,' I said, keen to continue rebuilding her confidence.

'I'll try my best. As for you two, best of luck for the Blind Date night tonight. May you sell all of the books. And if Liam dares show up to find the next love of his life…'

'…I'll shove him in the canal, don't you worry,' I promised.

We blew air kisses to each other and said goodbye.

'Poor Aunty Flick,' I said to Hilda. 'No, actually, I'm not going to feel sorry for her as she's clearly better off without him.'

I briefly considered texting Liam to ask him what he was playing at, despite Flick's wishes, then decided to choose a more productive path. Time to do something I should have done a while ago. I did an internet search for Prasinos Viridis Protein and started scrolling through the reviews. The ones on the first few pages were full of praise, but as I read more, I started to get a feeling of déjà vu. They weren't identical, but the phrasing was similar enough to make me suspicious. Then about seven pages in, I stumbled on a

Reddit thread called Boaty Liam protein scam and what I read shocked me. Dozens of people had posted saying they'd written comments on his sponsored videos about being made sick by the smoothies, but their warnings had been deleted, and they'd been blocked from following him. What was he playing at? I berated myself for not acting on my gut instinct after seeing his behaviour while recording the ad. Liam was not the man I thought he was. He'd hurt my friend, and he was clearly hurting a lot of other people too by promoting a dodgy supplement. What else might he have been lying about?

## Chapter Twenty-Two

I stewed on the matter for the rest of the day and had to take a couple of hours out to read *Bad Men* to try to cheer myself up, which didn't exactly help me with my preparations for the Blind Date with a Book night. It took several attempts for me to wrap the books, and then when I'd finished, I couldn't remember whether I'd put the necessary two copies of each in the pile so had to unwrap them all and start again.

As the allotted hour arrived, I set up the lemonade table, added a sign stating that it was for the use of bookshop guests only and then I stood behind it, nervously staring straight ahead, waiting for the influx. The reason I was staring straight ahead was that I was painfully conscious of Jack standing behind a similar table outside the Jericho Wine Barge, only that one was set up with ice buckets and bottles with condensation gathering on the glass. I tried to tell myself that the book lovers wouldn't allow themselves to get distracted by the sight of chilled wine, but I couldn't help worrying my set-up looked painfully amateur in comparison with the sophisticated offering from my neighbour.

I'd hoped I'd enjoy the evening more this time round as it was the second time I was running the event and I knew what I was doing, but I felt even more on edge than previously. It wasn't helped by the fact that an hour into the Blind Date with a Book night, the shop was empty and nearly half the brown paper parcels were still lying unclaimed. And I had a very good idea why. I glared at the Jericho Wine Barge, which was sitting low in the water as a vast number of guests laughed and enjoyed themselves on board. The atmosphere was buzzing, beautiful people casually sipping on their drinks, everything as flawless as if a commercial for the perfect summer night out in Oxford was being filmed. Even the blind daters who'd stayed loyal to my event were glancing enviously across, clearly debating joining in themselves. I was blowed if I was going to let Jack steal any more of my customers. I needed them to spend their money on my books, not his expensive wines.

I quickly checked around my guests, encouraging them to have a proper browse in the bookshop, then headed across to the Jericho Wine Barge, weaving my way among the crowd, trying to look for likely book lovers who'd got diverted by my competitive neighbour.

'Decided to join us after all?' said Jack, materialising at my side and putting a glass of Prosecco in my hand before I could say anything. 'You're very welcome here.' The genuine tone of his voice rather took the wind out of my sails. He proffered a plate of plump olives, their centres stuffed with what looked like feta cheese.

'Erm, no, thanks. I'm not here to socialise, and I'm not hungry,' I said, as my stomach made a vocal growl. I hoped the hubbub from his guests had prevented him from hearing it, but apparently not.

'Can I tempt you with these instead perhaps?' he suggested, his eyes sparkling with amusement as he put the olives down and offered me a bowl filled with crisps which were undoubtedly of the fancy artisan variety. 'It's important to keep your energy up when you're running an event. They're salt and vinegar flavour. Or sea salt and cider vinegar if we're being strictly accurate,' he added. He helped himself to a handful. 'Yum. They still taste delicious, despite the pretentious branding.'

He wafted them towards me, the sharp vinegary scent making me feel even hungrier.

I begrudgingly accepted a couple. I couldn't actually remember when I'd last eaten.

'Go on then. Thanks,' I muttered.

'My pleasure. You're doing me a favour, in truth. I fear I've rather over-catered. But I suppose it's better to have too much rather than too little.'

'Is that why you've been stealing my guests?' I asked, determined to stop him distracting me any further.

Jack laughed. 'I haven't stolen any guests.'

'How come my boat is practically empty then?' I hit back.

He gave me what I guess was meant to be a sympathetic look, which riled me still further. I didn't need to be patronised by him feeling sorry for me. 'I'm sorry if that's the case,' he said. 'But if they happened to end up here instead of in your bookshop, then that was their choice. They're grown adults with free will after all.'

He made it sound so reasonable that I felt even more frustrated.

'I know that, but you promised me your event was an invitation only affair. Why did you let them in if they didn't have a ticket?'

He shrugged. 'I was feeling generous. They seemed very keen to join the fun, and at the end of the day, I'm a businessman. I've got to be pragmatic about these things, as I'm sure you understand. I would expect you to do the same in my position.'

'You could at least have pointed them in my direction.'

'How do you know I didn't?' he asked. Again, with that oh so reasonable tone. I wasn't going to let him get away with gaslighting me into thinking that nothing was going on here. I'd had it with men messing with me. First Liam ghosting my best friend and having a problematic relationship with consumer standards, and now Jack being unbearably infuriating. Again.

'The same reason I know you set the Boating Association inspector on me,' I said indignantly. When I'd stepped foot on the Jericho Wine Barge, I'd had no intention of confronting Jack with my suspicions, but he'd been so nonchalant about the idea of stealing my guests that I couldn't help myself.

Jack frowned in what looked like confusion. 'I'm sorry, I

don't have the faintest clue what you're talking about,' he said.

'I think you do,' I hit back.

He shook his head. 'I promise you I don't.'

'Think harder,' I suggested.

He helped himself to another couple of crisps and crunched them thoughtfully.

'Nope, I've wracked my brains, but none of this makes any sense. Are you accusing me of conducting some kind of dirty tricks campaign? Why on earth would I do something like that?' I nearly applauded his performance of the blameless innocent.

'Ever since you arrived, I've been beset with problems, and it can't be a coincidence. I know you've got designs on my mooring. Fine, everyone has a right to be ambitious. But to be so underhand in the way you go about it?' I shook my head in disgust. 'I suppose I should be flattered you're so threatened by my business that you think this is the only way you can go about defeating me. I've lived and worked on this canal for over a year and never experienced any issues. Then you come along and suddenly it's all kicking off: my cable's disappeared and the Boating Association's told I have the incorrect licence. What else am I supposed to think?'

I'd managed to keep my voice steady throughout my speech, painfully aware that we were in public and there were potential Bookship customers among this crowd. But it had been an effort, and I could feel the betraying stress tears forming in my eyes. The last thing I wanted was to give him the satisfaction of making me cry. I took a sip of

Prosecco to try to conceal my emotion, then choked as the bubbles went the wrong way down my throat. At least it gave me an excuse for crying, I thought dimly, as I struggled to regain control of myself.

Jack patted me firmly between my shoulders and magicked a glass of water out of somewhere. He watched me as I drank it, his palm still resting steadily on my back.

'Feeling better?'

I wasn't sure if he was asking me about the choking or getting the accusation out of my system. In truth saying the words out loud hadn't made me feel better at all. Although this conclusion seemed to be the only logical explanation for the challenges I was facing, was I completely certain that Jack was responsible for it all? I'd watched his expression throughout my speech, seeing it change from disbelief to the outright indignation of the falsely accused. I tried to remind myself that he used to work in the city in a highly competitive environment where he'd have been accustomed to playing mind games in order to get ahead. Pretending not to know what I was talking about would come easily to him. He was acting this way in order to keep me off my guard, and to manipulate me into feeling exactly as I did right now – guilty that I'd made such a ridiculous accusation against him.

'I'll feel better when you stop messing around and putting my livelihood at risk,' I tried one last time, belatedly taking a step back.

Jack's hand fell back to his side and he flexed it slightly before he spoke. 'You've obviously been having a tough time of it lately. I think I know where this is all coming from.'

'You know because you did it,' I snapped back.

'I didn't. But I can see that someone else is pulling the strings here, so there's not much point in me defending myself.'

'If it's Liam you're referring to as "pulling the strings", then I'd really rather you left him out of this. I've had enough of the pair of you. And I'm perfectly capable of coming to my own conclusions about people, and it would be respectful if you would acknowledge that.'

'I apologise. I fully appreciate you're a woman who knows her own mind. Even if it is mistaken in this instance. I'm sorry you've been experiencing such trials. I can't imagine how frustrating and worrying it must have been to have those things happen. But I would like to tell you once and for all that I am not behind your troubles. Frankly I wouldn't need to descend to such petty depths. If I wanted to expand into your mooring space, which for the record I don't, I would do it in a much more professional manner than you're giving me credit for having.'

I sucked in an angry breath. 'You wouldn't know the meaning of the word if I opened up a dictionary and showed you the definition. You might be professional on land, but when it comes to canal life, you don't have a clue. You may think you rule the waterway with your fancy boat – which you clearly paid far too much for, by the way – but you're the epitome of the phrase "all the gear and no idea". You don't have a clue what it takes to look after a narrowboat, and you've only set up business here because you think it'll give you a cutesy USP which will make you stand out from the million and one other bars which are already in Oxford. Well, I've got news for you. The novelty will soon wear off, and the customers will move on to the next trendy venue, and then what will you do? Hopefully you'll go back to the city where you belong and leave the Oxford Canal to those of us who really love it and who actually deserve to be here.'

I slammed my water glass down on the bar top and stormed out, shaking all over, angry as much at myself as at Jack for the way I'd lost control.

# Chapter Twenty-Three

I couldn't tell you how the rest of the Blind Date with a Book night went. The whole evening passed in a blur as I wallowed in my embarrassment, following my confrontation with Jack. Somehow by the end of the evening the brown paper wrapped books had all gone, and there were gaps on the shelves in the bookshop suggesting that on one level the event had gone reasonably well. On the other hand, I could have given a blow-by-blow account of how Jack's night went because after the argument I was hyper conscious of his every move. Everyone who'd stopped by for a drink had seemed charmed by the venue and even more so by its host. He had laughed and chatted, looking more relaxed than I'd ever seen him as he poured drinks and went round making sure all his guests were enjoying themselves. It had been steadily busy all evening at the Jericho Wine Barge right up until closing time, at which point Jack had had to ring an old ship's bell to indicate it was time for people to leave, a sound which had given me an uncomfortable flashback to my morning imaginings.

The last remaining Blind Date with a Book guests had taken it as their cue to go as well, two new couples departing together, clutching matching copies of *Mansfield Park* and *Great Expectations* respectively, to continue getting to know each other elsewhere. It hadn't taken me long to tidy everything away, but somehow I'd found myself lingering on the deck, aware of Jack's steady movements on shore as he collected glasses and started turning off the fairy lights. It felt like we had unfinished business, but I was unclear what kind it was.

My sleep was disturbed that night, full of stressy dreams about failing to hit my financial target and losing everything. At dawn I woke with a start, convinced I'd heard the splash of the Bookship starting to sink, but a quiet snore from the dog bed calmed my racing fears, and I managed to doze off again. But I only managed another half an hour of sleep before I jerked awake with the terrifying sensation of falling. Tired of lying worrying in bed, I dragged a reluctant Hilda out for an early morning run. Well, I was running, she was lolloping along at a comfortable trot, not having to put any effort in to keep up with me thanks to her long legs. Instead of doing our usual Jericho circuit, we turned towards the centre of the city, jogging up past the train station, along Broad Street and turning down Turl Street. I needed to get away from the bubble of the canal area where everything seemed so intense. I hoped running among the dreaming spires would help put things into perspective and remind me that despite the challenges I faced, my bookshop dream was not over yet.

The streets were practically empty, just a few students in bedraggled black tie wandering home after a long night at one of the college's summer balls. I envied them with their carefree demeanours, although I reminded myself that a cheery exterior was no guarantee they weren't also battling with interior demons. I pounded down Brasenose Lane, then slowed my pace as we reached Radcliffe Square, taking care not to trip on the cobbles. It was exactly the kind of challenge I needed to distract me from last night which was playing on a loop in my head. Each time I thought about it, I cringed harder, fluctuating between righteous indignation at Jack's behaviour and an ever-growing doubt that he'd done any of the things I'd accused him of. I was cross with myself for being influenced by his offended innocent act, yet it had seemed so genuine, his expression one of confusion and hurt, rather than frustration that he'd been called out. He was either an amazing actor, or I had got things very wrong.

I stopped in front of the gilded gates of All Souls College and let out a growl of frustration which startled the pigeons. In truth, I didn't know what to think anymore. I wondered if the academics behind those grand stone walls got caught up in similar predicaments, torn between conflicting gut feelings, or whether their minds worked on a higher plane. I smiled to myself. There was probably drama to be found in every environment. It was how you dealt with it that mattered. And if I was being completely honest with myself, I knew I should have dealt with the Jack situation better, waiting until I was totally sure of his guilt on my own account, rather than allowing Liam to persuade me of it.

I tried to cheer myself up by purchasing a breakfast bagel from a shop on the High, then took a roundabout route back, putting off the inevitable moment of returning home to do my accounts. I knew that it would be touch and go whether last night had made a profit. I could lay the blame at Jack's door or admit that I'd taken my eye off the ball because I'd allowed myself to get distracted.

Hilda and I wandered along Longwall Street, the majestic walls of Magdalen College on the right, then I let her lead me down Holywell Street. She paused to have a good sniff around the steps of a building which had been boarded up for ages, but which now had a red banner across the door decorated with a picture of a pile of books and a big 'Coming soon' sign. My heart sank at the sight. I really hoped it wasn't another bookshop about to open in the city. The last thing I needed right now was yet another competitor. I tried to peer between a slight gap in the boards over a window at street level, but it was too bright for me to be able to see what was going on in the gloom inside.

The rest of the world was starting to wake up now, doors banging as students emerged from their lodgings to head to the library, or more likely, to get to the park and bag a prime spot by the river. I checked my watch and picked up my pace. The Bookship operated with reduced hours on a Sunday, but I needed to get back soon to open up.

Hilda and I trotted past the Ashmolean, gave a little wave to the books in the Oxford Community Library, then we cut through a few sneaky side streets, weaving our way back to Jericho and home. As we reached the towpath, I spotted a shadowy figure stepping from the foredeck of the Oxford Bookship back onto the bank.

'Oi, what do you think you're doing?' I yelled across the water, but the unwanted visitor showed no sign of having heard me. They headed along the path in the direction of the city centre and were soon out of view. I broke into a run, instantly regretting the breakfast bagel, as I attempted to catch up with the mystery intruder and get a look at their face, but I didn't get very far. Hilda had had enough of the morning's excessive exercise regime and refused to indulge me, her weary plod effectively slamming the brakes on. I tried to offer words of encouragement, but my breathing was so ragged that she couldn't or wouldn't follow my instructions.

I gave up and turned back towards the Oxford Bookship, my heart pounding equally from the exertion and from the anxiety over what I might be about to discover. I let Hilda off the lead, and she instantly flumped down on the cool grass, watching me balefully as I gave the boat a quick visual check from the opposite bank. Aside from the damage which the Jericho Wine Barge had inflicted, everything looked neat and shipshape. But I needed to be closer to be sure, and I was still on the wrong side of the canal.

'Come on, Hildy-girl, nearly there. Just this final push then no more running today, I promise,' I pleaded.

With a show of great reluctance, she heaved herself back up and grudgingly conceded to match my jog as we made our way back over the footbridge and along the bank to the Oxford Bookship's mooring. I checked the ropes and cast my eye over the roof and deck areas. Everything appeared as it should, much to my relief. Everything that was aside from a large object wrapped in brown paper which was now cluttering up the well deck.

'Great, that's all I need, some lazy passer-by dumping their rubbish on my boat because they can't be bothered to carry it to the bins.'

I left Hilda having a sniff around the towpath garden while I clambered aboard, checking carefully around for any clues about who might be responsible. I tried the cabin door and was relieved to find it was still securely locked. Then I turned my attention to the item on the deck and realised it wasn't rubbish at all but a carefully wrapped parcel, affixed to which was an envelope with 'Molly Bramble' written on it in neat, confident cursive. I traced my finger over the lettering. The ink seemed strangely old-fashioned, possibly from a fountain pen. It definitely wasn't a biro at any rate. The stationery was also of a high quality, although not quite as fancy as that used by the Oxford Boating Association. But who else would personally deliver something to my boat?

I lifted the parcel, weighing it in my hands, apprehensive about what it might contain. Should I open it or the envelope first? The envelope might be more likely to provide me with answers. But Hilda had other ideas, answering my dilemma by jumping on board and catching the parcel with her claw, making a rip in the brown paper.

'Very well, the parcel it is,' I said.

I continued Hilda's work and removed the rest of the wrapping, then gasped. There in front of me was something I'd never expected to see again. The sign for the Oxford Bookship, the one which had stood resplendent on the roof of the boat, or had done, until Jack had come along and knocked it into the water. I ran my fingers over its surface. The wood had swelled from its dunking, but the varnished paintwork seemed to have survived the immersion, and the gold outline of the lettering still sparkled as I moved it in the sunlight. I felt a burst of positivity. This had to be a sign that things were going to work out okay. I smiled to myself at the unintended pun. Putting the shop sign back in its rightful place on the roof would indicate to the world that the Oxford Bookship was here to stay.

I climbed up and fixed the sign back into position. It would probably be a good idea to create a more permanent fitting for it to prevent a repeat of what had happened before, but that could be easily sorted later with a power tool and a few bits of woods. However, before I did that, I needed to open the envelope to find out who had retrieved this precious object from the canal for me, and more importantly, why.

I slid back down into the well deck just in time to retrieve the envelope from Hilda's mouth.

'It's paper, you daft doggy. Why don't you go and play in the garden with your ball instead?'

She huffed at me, disappointed that I'd spoilt her fun, and instead flumped down on my feet, effectively pinning me in position. Within seconds she'd started snoring. I was pretty sure she was putting it on for effect, but I wasn't heartless enough to move a snoozing pooch, even if she was only pretending to be asleep, so I stayed where I was and opened the now slightly slobbery envelope. I immediately scanned through the thick sheaf of papers and spotted the signature at the bottom of the letter. Jack. Had that splash I thought I imagined this morning been him retrieving the sign? And what did he have to say in his letter? I leaned back against the bookshop door and started reading.

# Chapter Twenty-Four

*Dear Molly,*

*Please accept the return of the Oxford Bookship sign with my apologies once again. The poor steering which led to its unhappy dunking was unforgivable. As you rightly pointed out, I should not have been let loose alone on the barge when my canal experience was so limited. It may be too little too late in your eyes, but I would like to reassure you I have signed up to the 'Beginner Boating' course offered by the Oxford Boating Association, and until I have successfully completed that training, I promise not to attempt to take the Jericho Wine Barge away from its moorings.*

*Speaking of moorings, I feel this is an issue which should be addressed. If you'll forgive me, I will get to it in a bit, but first it's important for me to explain something else – my history with Liam Crawford. What I'm about to share with you is not something I widely discuss. It was a painful time for the parties involved and it's not solely my story, but I want you to be aware of it. Whether you choose to believe me is your decision, but I hope that you do. You should be aware of the true nature of the man. However, I trust that whether you take my word or not, you will respect my confidence.*

'The true nature of the man?' That sounded ominous. And yet given what I'd discovered yesterday, I wasn't surprised there were further revelations to be had. I patted Hilda and carried on reading.

*Liam and I were once the closest of colleagues. I'm sure he's told you I was what's widely termed a 'Nepo Baby'. My father and grandfather before him worked at the same firm, and it was always expected I would join the family profession and follow in their footsteps, whether that was what I wanted or not. I hope you appreciate I say this not as an attempt to elicit sympathy or pity from you, but because it is the truth. That weight of expectation was a burden from day one of me starting the job. Not wishing to let down my family, I'd dismissed my own, very different, dreams as frivolities and was intent on living up to the Siddall name. But the Siddall name was both a virtue and a disadvantage. People expected more from me because of it, but they also dismissed any actual achievements as being the result of family influence. I was never sure whether people were friends with me because of who I was as a person, or because of my surname.*

*Liam seemed to be different. He treated me as plain old Jack, rather than Jack Siddall the boss's son. I learnt something from his confidence and his easy way with people, and I like to think he gained too by picking up some of my business acumen. As you may have realised, I'm not always the best at social interaction. I was abominably rude when we first met and you were quite right to call me out for my 'pretentious' Greek. I can only explain it by telling you I was horribly nervous attending a dating event and every time I opened my mouth, things came out wrong. But nerves are no excuse, and I'm genuinely sorry for my appalling attitude. I can hear you expressing surprise that someone who isn't naturally at ease in social situations is running a bar, but that's part of the point. I wanted to challenge myself, but more importantly I wanted to create an environment where everyone feels welcomed and accepted, whatever their quirks.*

*Anyway, I should get back to what I was trying to tell you. Liam and I were the closest of colleagues, and friends too, or so I thought. I knew he was ambitious, but it wasn't until it was too late that I realised just what lengths he would go to in order to achieve his ambitions. I was asked to work on a project researching a potential investment for a long-term client of the company, and I invited Liam to join me on the team. The information we were uncovering was financially sensitive and it was a big deal to be trusted to take on the assignment. We were close to reporting back to the client when I discovered that Liam had been using the information we'd discovered for his own personal gain. I'm sure you'll have heard the term 'insider trading'. That's exactly what Liam was setting out to do. If he'd gone through with it, he would have made a fortune. As soon as I worked out what he was playing at, I confronted him, feeling incredibly betrayed by his behaviour. He didn't deny it and actually laughed at my indignation. He couldn't understand (or maybe didn't care) why it would be wrong to profit from the confidential information we'd been party to. But if he'd done that, he would have been breaking the law, and sooner or later, he would have been found out by the authorities and the repercussions of that had the potential to destroy the business, and worst of all, my dad's reputation as he was the CEO with ultimate responsibility for everything that happened. I tried to explain everything to Liam, but he was unmoved by my fears. What I'd thought had been a real friendship actually counted for nothing.*

*And so, I followed protocol and reported his actions. Liam was allowed to write a letter of resignation rather than being fired on the spot, a generous gesture that I'd had to plead with my father to offer. We should really have gone to the police about what had happened and sometimes I still wonder whether the decision not to do so was the right one. But that was the decision we made, and we will have to live with the consequences.*

*After that episode, I started to question my own path. It awakened me to the cut-throat nature of the corporate world and how it could lead some people to ruthless behaviour in the pursuit of coming out on top. I knew in my heart it wasn't the right world for me. I wanted to prove myself on my own terms, striking out without the safety net of being part of the family firm, hence my wine bar endeavour.*

*I can't offer you any physical evidence proving what I've written in this letter is the truth. I can only offer you my word. It is your choice whether to accept it or not. But I hope you consider it when it comes to your future dealings with Liam Crawford. He can be a plausible and entertaining individual. However, in my experience, there is only one person that Liam cares about, and that's himself, never mind the cost to others.*

As I'd been reading, I'd gradually sunk down to sit on the deck, gently squeezing a space for myself beside Hilda, although she was still pinning my feet underneath her. I looked up from the letter, half expecting Liam to be lurking nearby having had some kind of sixth sense knowledge of what I was reading. Jack's version of events wasn't that different from Liam's apart from the obvious – who had been in the wrong. If I were to challenge Liam, I had no doubt he'd come up with a plausible alternative explanation in that charming manner of his. Given what I'd discovered with my own detective work and his crappy behaviour towards Flick, I was more inclined to accept Jack's account, but I needed to read the rest of the letter before I made up my mind about that. I'd made the mistake of jumping too quickly to conclusions before.

*Now I've explained what happened with Liam, I'd like to move on to addressing the mooring situation. You keep suggesting I'm trying to take possession of the Oxford Bookship's mooring. I want to put your mind at rest and assure you again that I am not. While I am keen for the Jericho Wine Barge to thrive, I have no intention of developing it to encompass two boats at this stage, or down the line. For me, the charm of the venue will be in its intimate size. I had initially thought I might expand at some point by moving ashore and converting my living space into an extension of the bar, but now I've got a taste of canal life, I'm hooked, so any future growth in the business will be through opening an additional bar in another unique location. That is a way off, however.*

*I very much hope that the Oxford Bookship and the Jericho Wine Barge will co-exist happily beside each other, with customers moving between the two boats. We had a taster of that last night during our respective events, and I am confident that with a little collaboration between us, our businesses could benefit each other. But perhaps I'm getting ahead of myself. I mentioned earlier you would have to trust my account of what happened with Liam. However, when it comes to my plans for the Jericho Wine Barge, you don't merely have to take my word for it. I enclose the complete paperwork of my agreement with the Oxford Boating Association, which details the extent of my plans. As you will read in that, the Wine Barge will only ever be one mooring space big.*

*As to the misfortunes you mentioned, I'm sincerely sorry you've been experiencing such problems. You obviously feel strongly they are more than coincidental. I can't speak to that, but I would like to assure you I am not the man responsible. I'm afraid this is another area where I can offer no proof, but I hope my transparency elsewhere in this letter will help you to trust me.*

*I didn't expect to spend most of the night following my launch staying up to write this letter, but it's important for me to set the record straight. We've not had the chance to get to know each other very well, and yet I find that your good opinion matters to me a great deal. I'm happy to discuss any of this with you, and I hope going forward we can develop a more amicable neighbourly relationship.*

*Yours,*

*Jack Siddall*

I read the letter a second time to make sure I hadn't missed anything. It was a strange mix of formal and friendly, but it was that combination which made it sound so sincere. I could hear Jack's voice in every word, both earnest and slightly awkward, a normally private man I'd struggled to get a read on from the beginning who had chosen to open up to me, not because he was obliged to, but because he wanted to – and believed – it was the right thing to do. He was embarrassed by his social unease which had manifested as rudeness, and I felt equally ashamed of the way I had acted in return, repeatedly lashing out at him instead of showing the compassion and understanding I normally prided myself on. My behaviour towards him so far had not been deserving of his honesty, but I was grateful he had gifted it to me.

I turned to the photocopied pages and scanned through them. There it was in black and white, the Oxford Boating Association agreement with the Jericho Wine Barge, for a single mooring position, exactly as Jack had said in the letter. I felt myself grow hot with embarrassment at how wrong I'd got it. I could blame Liam for playing on my fears, but it had been my prejudice against Jack which had made it easy for him to do so. I had been so easily taken in by Boaty Liam, my star-struck gratitude for his help in advertising my first Blind Date with a Book night blinding me to his duplicity.

And then there was the matter of the mishaps which had beset me of late. Although Jack could offer no proof of not being involved, my gut told me his denial rang true. They were either coincidences, or somebody else was behind them.

I considered the issue as dispassionately as I could. Unless some kind of magic had occurred, in which case presumably my invitation to join Hogwarts was on its way, there was no denying that my power cable had been stolen by someone. But Liam had gone out of his way to lend me his spare and had seemed as shocked as I was about the incident. I could see no benefit to him in stealing it. And just because Nana Rose had never experienced a snap inspection, it didn't mean they never happened. The Oxford Boating Association had many members, any of whom could have demanded the inspection. In fact, now I thought about it, wasn't there a good chance the reason for Eric's caginess was that he didn't want to admit he'd been the one to instigate it? The Oxford Canal had always been his main love, and keeping its residents in line was a responsibility he took very seriously. If he had concerns about the Bookship and the way it reflected on the Oxford Boating Association, then it would make sense for him to apply pressure on me to bring my boat up to the standard he expected from businesses along the canal.

My brain was throbbing with it all. But I'd rushed to

conclusions about Jack and look where that had got me. I rubbed my eyes, which felt tired and achy after my disturbed night followed by the long period of deciphering Jack's handwriting and poring over the tiny print of the documents he'd included. I felt confused and upset, let down by Liam, and embarrassed by my behaviour concerning Jack. Having read *Pride and Prejudice* at least once a year from the age of seven, I thought I'd learnt the lesson about not being charmed by Wickham types. Not that I was likening Jack to Mr Darcy, although I reckoned the pair of them would probably get on famously with their similar awkwardness.

'You were right all along, Hilda, and I was wrong,' I said, scratching her between the ears. 'You immediately clocked Jack as being a decent sort and wanted to spend time with him, while you either ignored Liam or were grumpy whenever you saw him. I promise to pay more attention to your character assessments in the future.'

She grunted and rolled on her back, inviting me to tickle her tummy in recompense.

'The question is, what do I do with this information now I have it?' I wondered aloud.

Thinking about Liam was easier than considering how I was going to interact with Jack in the future. It wasn't like I could do the ultra-mature thing of avoiding him until he forgot all about me. The man was going to be living next door for the foreseeable future. And I was going to have to thank him for retrieving my Oxford Bookship sign from the canal.

Jack had written to me, so I could take the coward's way

out and write a letter in response, but I knew I wouldn't do that. I was a big enough person to admit to my mistakes in person, and I would do it. Only perhaps not today. I'd experienced enough emotional turbulence in the last twenty-four hours.

# Chapter Twenty-Five

Hilda bounded ahead of me and leapt onto the Jericho Wine Barge before I could stop her, sabotaging my attempt to delay the inevitable. I'd not slept well yet again last night, going over and over in my mind what Jack had said in his letter, cringing at the assumptions I'd made and dreading the prospect of having to face him. But I knew I had to do it. I owed him an apology, however uncomfortable a prospect that was. While I might initially shy away from dealing with some challenging situations, I always got round to facing them eventually, the voice of wisdom in my head, which incidentally sounded suspiciously like Nana Rose, reminding me that problems always ended up bigger in the imagination than they actually were in reality.

I waited for the Jericho Wine Barge to stop rocking, half expecting Jack to emerge from the cabin at any moment, then realised there was no point as Hilda started spinning joyfully around on the well deck like a boy racer doing doughnuts in a car park. With a growing sense of trepidation, I jumped on board myself, only just managing to stay upright due to the Irish wolfhound-induced waves.

'Here goes,' I muttered under my breath, and knocked smartly on the door of the wine bar cabin, my nerves jangling.

I stepped back, waiting for the door to open and trying to practise in my head what I would say when it did. Sorry for making the wrong assumptions would be the best place to start, but then what? Carry on and pretend everything was going to be completely normal? But having never experienced 'normal' with my neighbour, I wasn't sure what that would look like. Although judging by the fact that the door was still shut tight, it didn't seem as if I was going to get the opportunity to find out any time soon. Maybe I should try the other cabin door. There was a chance he was ignoring my knock in case it was an overly keen customer clamouring for him to open up. With Hilda thundering around on the deck, it would be a natural conclusion to jump to.

I hopped back onto land and walked slowly along the towpath towards the stern of the Jericho Wine Barge, still rehearsing what I was going to say. Unfortunately, Hilda decided against following in my footsteps. With a graceful leap, she took off from a chair on the deck and jumped onto the roof of the boat, bounding along parallel to me.

'Hilda, get down, now,' I said, torn between laughter and horror at her new-found boldness. She'd never jumped up like that on the Oxford Bookship and it was typical that she'd decided to do it for the first time on someone else's vessel. I really hoped the roof was in a better condition than the boat's engine.

As I approached the stern, a tousled head poked out of the rear cabin door.

'What—' started Jack, but before he could get the rest of his sentence out, Hilda arrived at the end of the roof and came to a sudden realisation that she very much did not want to make the leap down onto the deck, even though it was no further than the height she'd already scaled at the other end of the boat. Her eyes widened, her tail went between her legs, and she did the doggy equivalent of digging her heels in as she started to quiver.

'It's alright, Hilda-girl. You're okay,' I called out, in as reassuring a tone as I could muster. 'Do you mind?' I asked Jack, gesturing to the deck.

He emerged fully from the cabin and did a double take as he looked up and saw Hilda looming above him.

'Stay,' I shouted, in case Hilda decided to use him as a staging post on her way back down onto the deck.

Jack stopped right where he was, one pyjama-clad leg in front of the other. The flaps of his pyjama shirt fluttered in the breeze, and I was irritated with myself for noticing the top three buttons were undone, similar to my daydream. He was actually more dressed than he had been when I'd interrupted his DIY, but the just-out-of-bed look somehow seemed more revealing.

'That was for the pooch by the way, but nice to see that you take direction,' I said, trying to make a light-hearted comment to dispel any awkwardness between us. Jack looked at me and raised a questioning eyebrow. I felt my features flood with heat as I realised I'd achieved the exact opposite of my intention. There was nothing to do but style it out.

'I'm coming aboard,' I said.

'I'll get the gangplank,' said Jack, but I didn't want to wait. I clambered somewhat inelegantly onto the deck, scraping my shin against the gunwale on the way and winced.

'Are you alright?' he asked.

'I will be once we've got Hilda back where she belongs,' I replied. Bruises were a small price to pay as long as my dog was safe. Jack reached out and briefly took my hand, helping me to stand up straight.

'Are you okay?' he asked again.

'I'm fine,' I reiterated. 'Sorry for all this.' I gestured towards Hilda and then back towards myself.

His expression brightened. 'You read my letter then?'

I realised he thought the apology was because of that and hurried to correct him.

'Yes, but the sorry was about Hilda's and my intrusion.'

'Oh.' His face fell again.

I shook my head. 'This is coming out completely wrong.' I took a deep breath and looked directly at him. 'I'm sorry my dog is currently cowering on your roof, and I'm sorry I've invaded your space so early on a Monday morning. But what I'm most sorry about is that I leapt to conclusions about you. They were wrong conclusions, and I'm ashamed I allowed my own fears and a chunk of malicious towpath gossip to prejudice me against you. I'm not proud of how I've acted.' It was hard to tell from his expression what he was thinking, but I ploughed ahead anyway. 'You shared something really personal with me, so in turn, I'll admit I'm a worrier at heart, and you unfortunately happened to turn up when I was already pretty anxious about my position on the Oxford Canal. I jumped to the worst-case scenario about your business, and I was helped into continuing to think that way by Liam, for reasons of his own. To be honest, I'm really ashamed of myself for allowing someone else to affect my judgement, and I'm a big enough person to admit it.'

Jack had been leaning against the stern rail throughout my speech, but how he stood up and nodded. 'Thank you. I appreciate your candour.'

'What...' I started to ask. I'm not sure what I'd been expecting, but this understated response wasn't it. I realised I wanted, no needed, to hear more about what was going through his head, to know whether he really accepted my apology, and what he thought about me now. He must have read that in my features because he added, 'I'm glad we've had this chat and I'm sure there's more we could discuss at a later date, but at the moment, I'm more worried about the fact that your dog is apparently trapped on my roof, and she might start to panic properly if we don't get her down soon.'

'Right. Yes, absolutely.' I felt stupid for my neediness, thrown off balance by his dignity and matter-of-fact attitude.

But then he reached out and gently touched my shoulder. It was the briefest of brushes, but there was something simultaneously reassuring and yet unsettling about it. Reassuring in that it demonstrated that yes, my sincere apology had been accepted, and unsettling because I felt the tender absence of it as soon as his hand had moved away, and I didn't know how to react to that.

Thankfully, Jack seemed oblivious to my confusion. He turned and gave his full attention to Hilda who was still quivering on the edge of the roof.

'How did you get up there, old girl?' he asked, his voice hypnotically soft. He reached up and held his palm out towards her. After a moment's hesitation, she bent her nose down towards him and tentatively sniffed. He let her carry out her inspection, then ever so gently stroked her muzzle, tracing along the line of her jaw up towards her ears.

'I read in an article that this reminds dogs of their mothers licking their faces when they were puppies,' he explained softly.

'She seems to like it,' I replied quietly, as Hilda let out a whimper.

'If you come down here, I'll give you a tummy rub,' he promised her.

Hilda's tail twitched as if she was considering his offer, but as he slowly reached towards her again, she backed up, one paw slipping off the edge of the roof.

'Whoa,' I said firmly. 'Stay right where you are, girly girl. I do not want you tumbling into that smelly canal water.'

'It's actually quite clean, like you said when you leapt aboard after the crash. In fact, I rather enjoyed taking a dip to retrieve your sign,' said Jack, a glimmer of amusement in his eyes.

'About that...'

He shook his head. 'Before you say anything, I was responsible for it falling in, so it was right I should sort it out. I'm only sorry I didn't do it straight away. And I am still good for my promise to sort out the damage to the hull.'

'Thank you,' I repeated, feeling bad all over again about how rude I'd been to him since he arrived, but another whimper from Hilda soon concentrated my mind.

For the next couple of minutes, we both tried to coax her down, our tones ranging from wheedling to extreme excitement in case her desire not to miss out gave her the courage to put aside her fear.

'Short of clambering up there and lifting her down, which I don't reckon would be a pleasant experience for any of us, I think we're going to have to get the big guns out,' I said eventually. 'Do you happen to have any cheese on board?'

Jack frowned. 'Let me go and check. There might be some left over from the opening night. Other than that, I've not really had the time to do much catering for myself of late.'

'I remember what it was like when I was trying to get the Oxford Bookship ready to launch,' I said. 'If it hadn't been for Nana Rose forcing me to join her at the care home for lunch every day, I think I'd have ended up pushing through without a break, which probably wouldn't have helped me be my most efficient.'

Jack grinned. 'Yep, I've certainly been guilty of that. I've actually been really missing cooking. I won't pretend I'm particularly talented at it, but preparing food is always a good opportunity to find some head space. Picnicking on scraps in the middle of doing work isn't the same, although at least it's not as bad as eating cold takeaway at my desk, like I used to do all the time in my corporate life. Give me two secs, I'll take a look and see what I can find.'

He retreated into the cabin and emerged a short while later with a small block of cheddar.

'Will this do?' he asked.

'Hilda's favourite,' I said with satisfaction. 'If that doesn't work, I don't know what will.'

Jack broke off a chunk and held it up to Hilda, who was now lying down, the tips of her front paws hanging over the edge of the roof, while she looked sadly at us with a mournful expression which said, 'Save yourselves, leave me to my fate.'

Her nose twitched as she smelt the cheese, and she shuffled forward an inch or two, opening her mouth for the treat.

'That's it, good girl, if you come down here, you can have this yummy snack,' coaxed Jack.

'You might want to take a step back…' I started to say, but it was too late. Hilda had delicately snaffled the cheese from his grasp and then quickly shuffled out of reach to polish it off.

'Schoolboy error,' said Jack with a shamefaced grin. 'You'd think I'd know better. Do you reckon we should try again, or will the appeal of the cheese have worn off now she's had a chunk?'

I raised an eyebrow, and he laughed. 'You're right, what

am I saying? Dog Husbandry 101, cheese will never be boring. Here, you'll probably have better luck with her.'

He broke off a few more chunks of the cheddar, snaffling one himself, then passing the rest to me.

'Don't mind if I do,' I said, following his example. 'One for Jack, one for me, but what am I going to do with all this leftover cheese?' I added in a sing-song voice which I knew would attract Hilda's attention.

She raised her head and put it on one side, tilting a giant ear in my direction, listening closely. I pretended to be debating my options.

'Hmm, maybe I should throw it in the bin.' I took a couple of steps closer to the gunwale, and Hilda sat up. 'Actually no, that would be a waste, wouldn't it, Jack? Perhaps I should feed it to the ducks?'

I walked slowly to the other side of the boat, moving the cheese from hand to hand as if I was warming up for throwing it into the water. Hilda let out a whuffle of disapproval.

I stopped just out of her reach. 'Maybe Hilda would like it. What do you think, girly? Would you like some cheese?'

She stood up and leaned forward, trying to get it from my hand. I took a step backwards and trod on Jack's foot.

'Oh gosh, sorry, I didn't realise you'd moved there.' I twisted round to address him, which turned out to be a mistake. Because Hilda decided it would be the perfect moment to get over her fear of the not very big distance between the roof and the deck and jumped down. Only in classic Hilda fashion, she overestimated the amount of effort she needed to put into the jump and overshot, colliding squarely with my back, sending me tumbling forward in a domino effect. Thankfully my fall was broken, although as it was Jack who broke it, he'd probably disagree with that assessment.

'Ooooffff,' came his muffled cry from under me. I felt the movement of his chest where it was compressed beneath mine.

'I'm so sorry, are you okay?' I forgot that I was still holding the cheese and instinctively reached my hand up next to Jack's head, trying to get some leverage to push myself back up. Hilda took the movement as invitation to join in the game on the deck and flumped down on top of me, the front half of her body sprawled across my shoulder blades as she swiped the cheese from my hand and started chomping on it.

I normally liked to think my upper body strength was fairly decent, honed by regular weightlifting, otherwise known as shelving books in the shop and carrying supplies along the towpath. But doing a press up with a fully grown Irish wolfhound casually hanging off my shoulders was another thing altogether.

'Hilda, move,' I tried to say, but it was difficult getting the words out given that I was the human filling to the Jack-Hilda sandwich. I was also super conscious that every movement I made brought me even more tightly against the firm planes of Jack's body. I closed my eyes, not daring to catch his gaze, trapped as we were in a position which would have required an intimacy coordinator on a film set. This was so not how I'd seen my apology going.

'May I?' he asked politely. His words reverberated from his chest to mine.

'What?' I asked, my pulse suddenly racing as my fiction-fuelled brain leapt to all kinds of wrong conclusions.

He whistled two cheery notes, the first higher than the second, his breath tickling the left corner of my lips. Hilda thumped her tail. He repeated the whistle, and at last I felt her sit up and remove her paws from my shoulders.

I rolled away from Jack and took a couple of deep breaths, hoping he'd assume that my need to suck in extra oxygen was due to my lungs being compressed by a massive dog. Embarrassed didn't even come close to how I was feeling right now.

And then I heard Jack laughing. It started as a low rumble, then bubbled up into a full-on roar of infectious humour, which I found myself joining in with, my awkwardness slowly seeping away to be replaced by a tension of a different kind.

'There's certainly never a dull moment when you're around,' he managed to stutter out eventually. Hilda thumped her tail against the deck as if agreeing with his words.

'I shall take that as a compliment,' I responded with as much dignity as I could muster, which wasn't a lot.

'It most certainly is,' he said, his voice suddenly serious.

It would have been very easy to allow myself to get caught up in the moment and continue lying companionably next to him. But then I heard a voice calling my name from the bank.

'Molls, are you alright? What are you doing?' demanded Liam.

I sat up straight, automatically trying to smooth my hair down, which probably made me look even more suspicious.

'Ignore him,' said Jack softly. 'You don't have to justify yourself to anyone.'

'I know,' I said under my breath in a defensive tone which unfortunately came out as snappy. 'I'm just leaving,' I raised my voice to address Liam, hoping he would carry on his way.

'You're very welcome to stay,' said Jack as he also sat up.

I quickly glanced towards the towpath and realised that Liam was hovering around waiting for me. I was stuck now. I wasn't prepared to answer the questions he'd inevitably ask if I started showing him the cold shoulder and stayed on Jack's boat having just said I was going. But I knew how it might look to Jack if I walked off accompanied by Liam. I wanted to explain that by leaving the Jericho Wine Barge I wasn't making a choice or demonstrating loyalty to one particular party. But as Jack himself had said, I didn't have to justify myself to anyone, and right now I wanted minimum towpath drama.

'I've got things to do,' I said. 'Thanks for your help and everything else,' I added sincerely, keeping my words vague, aware Liam was listening intently from the bank.

Jack's expression was studiously neutral. 'It's not a problem. Goodbye,' he said, a stiff finality to his farewell that made me question where the relaxed, laughing guy of the last few minutes had disappeared to.

Before I could say anything else, he retreated to his cabin and shut the door, leaving Hilda and me alone on the deck.

'What was all that about?' asked Liam, his eagerness for gossip evident by the relish in his tone.

'I was letting him know the date of my next event out of courtesy when Hilda jumped on the roof,' I improvised quickly. 'He helped me get her back down again, that's all, no big deal.' I shrugged indifferently as if my insides hadn't been tingling in a manner which I'd thought would never happen again.

Liam reached out, offering his hand to help me back across to shore. I cursed the ingrained aversion to causing offence which made me accept his assistance. A man probably wouldn't have thought twice about brushing him aside, I reminded myself. Still, I used the excuse of feigning a sudden need to scratch my neck to break free from him once I reached the shore rather than merely letting go. Hilda trotted on happily ahead, as if she hadn't just been at the centre of a drama.

'I'd better get to work. Monday mornings wait for no woman,' I said, hoping Liam would take the hint and leave me to it.

He did not.

'Can I film you opening the shop up?' he asked, still hovering by my side as we reached the Oxford Bookship. 'Could be great for boosting custom,' he wheedled.

'Not this time,' I said.

Liam pouted with disappointment. 'If that's what you want. I'll be looking out for you, Molls, don't you worry.'

I forced a smile, trying to ignore the chill I felt run down my back. Liam's words had sounded more like a threat than a promise.

<h1 style="text-align:center">Chapter Twenty-Six</h1>

I'd hoped that my conversation with Jack following the letter would wipe the slate clean or at least reduce the hyper awareness I'd felt ever since he moved into the berth next door. But that awareness had morphed into something else, something even more acute, which I didn't want to examine too closely. And now I had the added problem that I actually cared about the way I interacted with my new neighbour. Although that proved to be less of a problem than I'd anticipated because Jack seemed to be actively avoiding me, which was quite the feat given how closely moored our respective boats were. It was like we were strangers all over again, as if that shared moment of laughter and closeness on the Jericho Wine Barge had never happened.

While Jack was avoiding me, I was trying to keep my distance from Liam, although he seemed determined to do the opposite. He was obviously worried after having seen Jack and me in what would have appeared to be a compromising position, so he was playing up his hard-done-by routine. It was growing increasingly hard not to challenge him, but Jack had asked for my discretion, and I didn't want to betray his confidence. I was also dying to have a go at him about his treatment of Flick, but she kept on insisting she didn't want me to get involved, so I was having to bite my tongue about that too.

Instead, I tried to focus on planning my next event, the Oxford Bookship's unique interpretation of an afternoon tea which I'd promised my best customers Kat and Leo I would hold. In an ideal world, I would have had some recovery time from the Blind Date with a Book evening, but September would be here sooner than I would like, and my latest review of the accounts had impressed upon me the need to be proactive. My profits were undoubtedly increasing which demonstrated the success of my business strategy, which I was proud of, but unfortunately they weren't increasing fast enough. By my calculations, it would take me until at least Christmas to have the amount I needed for the mooring fees, which would of course be far too late.

I toyed with approaching Jack to see if he would consider making my 'Food and Fiction' afternoon a joint event. I told myself that being able to offer alcoholic drinks would be an added selling point, although I was self-aware enough to accept I was actually looking for an excuse to talk to him again. But after loitering outside his boat for two afternoons on the trot in the hope of accidentally on purpose bumping into him, I gave up and decided to stick with my original plan, remaining completely independent.

Given that I'd only allowed a few days for selling tickets, they'd all been snapped up remarkably quickly, with four going to two new couples from my first Blind Date with a Book night, which had given me a particular glow of achievement. I had created list upon list of things I needed to do, and when Saturday – the big day – dawned, I was already up and about long before my alarm clock, trying to get everything ready to my exacting standards. I bustled in and out of the Oxford Bookship, setting up picnic blankets and cushions in the towpath garden, hoping that my customers would embrace the informality.

Hilda dutifully trailed my every footstep, occasionally pinching a cushion or two, which I generously tried to interpret as her version of helping. By theft incident number four, however, I had rather lost patience.

'Hilda, stop that right now, or you'll have to go inside,' I warned her. She blinked innocently at me wagging her tail, pleased at having drawn my attention away from my task and back towards where it should be – on her.

Five minutes later, she galloped past triumphantly trailing a picnic blanket on the ground.

'Right, that's it, young lady, you're in big trouble,' I said, doing my very best to keep the amusement out of my voice at the sight of her lolloping around with a daft grin on her face. She darted to one side, lowering her front legs, inviting me to chase her. I deliberately turned my back, feigning disinterest. She decided to do another fly-past to attract my attention, only this time, I managed to grab hold of her collar and relieve her of the picnic blanket.

'Are you going to leave things alone now?'

She gave her answer in the form of an excitable whuff.

'I reckon it's time you put your paws up and had a nap, my girl. Come on, let's go.'

I escorted her reluctantly back on board. Just as I was closing the cabin door, my phone went off.

'Hello,' I answered, moving towards the tiller where I could hear more clearly over the sounds of Hilda dramatically flopping down onto her bed in protest.

'Hi, it's Becki from the Covered Market. I've got your food delivery. Are you okay to come and fetch it as we agreed? I'm parked up on Canal Street.'

'Sure, no problem, I'll be with you in ten minutes,' I said, already leaping off the boat and hurrying down the towpath, forgetting to take my collapsible trolley in my haste. The downside of canal life was the difficulty of getting stock and other supplies on board. At least today I wouldn't be ferrying heavy books, but carrying the bags of cakes and other delicacies I'd ordered during my shopping spree at the Covered Market yesterday would present no less of a challenge, especially as I'd gone overboard and chosen more dishes than I could possibly need. Everything I'd bought was home-made and freshly prepared, and as I hurried along to Canal Street, my mouth watered at the thought of the melt in the mouth treats which would complement the books I had for sale on board. I'd selected trays of the shiniest artisan chocolates on offer as a nod to Joanne Harris's book *Chocolat*, had gone for a giant baklava as an admittedly somewhat tenuous reference to the Greek setting of Victoria Hislop's novel *The Island*, and of course there was plenty of carrot cake in honour of *Anne of Green*

*Gables*. For those who fancied something savoury, I'd ordered two large lasagne, one meat, one veggie, both inspired by Elizabeth Zott's determination to find the dish's perfect iteration in a favourite book of mine, *Lessons in Chemistry*. I hoped the fictional characters would approve of the selections I'd made, but more importantly, I hoped the very real people who'd forked out for tickets would deem them worthy of the entry price and be inspired enough to buy the books the food was linked to.

'Thanks for bringing these,' I said to Becki as I arrived at her brightly coloured van.

'No problem. I wish I could help carry them back to the boat for you, but...' She gestured at her pregnant belly apologetically.

'Gosh no, you've done more than enough already. I'm sorry for dragging you down here in the first place.'

'To be honest I leapt at the chance to have a break. It's been non-stop in the market today. The tourists are out in force.'

'Feel free to send some of them my way,' I said with a smile. 'I've definitely been getting more of them down, but I'm always happy to welcome even more.'

'I'd be glad to,' she said. 'Which reminds me, we've nearly run out of your promotional bookmarks. Drop some extra ones by whenever you like.'

'Thanks, you're a star. This lot smells delicious by the way.'

'It took every bit of will power I possess not to tuck into those chocolates.' She grinned. 'On to the important details. I took the liberty of packing everything into cool bags.

The boxes are all lying flat at the moment but be careful if you put them down on the way back to the boat. The lasagne will take about thirty minutes to reheat, and the chocolates could probably do with going in the fridge until you serve them. It's pretty stuffy today, despite the breeze.'

'As long as it doesn't rain, I'm happy. That sounds good, I'll stow them away as soon as possible. Thanks again, and I'll stop by tomorrow to drop off those bookmarks.'

I waved as Becki drove off down the street, then loaded myself up with the bags, balancing myself up as best I could. It would have been better to carry them in two loads, but there wasn't anywhere I could safely leave them without risking the food being snaffled by hungry dogs and/or students.

I set off at a good pace, but before long the straps of the heavy cool bags started to dig into my hands. Why had I bought so much stuff? I wasn't even sure there'd be enough room to store it in my tiny galley area. It took at least twice as long as it should have to reach the canal. I decided to set the bags down on the ground for a moment and stretched my fingers out, wincing at the deep red lines on my palms from where the canvas of the handles had been pressing into my skin.

'No Hilda this morning?' asked a familiar voice. I looked up and saw Jack strolling into view from the direction of the moorings, all cool, calm and collected in a pale blue shirt and light-coloured jeans, while I sweated messily on the towpath. Brilliant. He'd been avoiding me for days then chose the moment I looked like I'd been weightlifting in a sauna to strike up a conversation again.

I tried to look nonchalant as I felt a trickle of moisture trace its way down my spine. 'She's chilling out at home.'

'Sensible creature.'

We stood awkwardly for a moment. I'd rehearsed this conversation in my head ever since I'd left Jack on the Jericho Wine Barge and walked off with Liam, but now I was standing in front of him, I was scared it would come out wrong. But I reminded myself that not talking about what was on my mind hadn't helped me much in the past.

'Jack—'

'Molly—'

We both spoke at the same time.

'You go first,' I said.

'No, you,' he replied, ever the gentleman. 'In fact, how about we stand in the shade for a moment? I'll bring your bags.'

He scooped them up and carefully placed them in the shadow of a tree trunk then returned to my side.

'Shall we?' he said. For a moment I thought he was going to offer me his arm, as if he was about to escort me onto a dance floor, but instead he did one of his funny little half bows and held his hand so it was hovering behind the small of my back as he indicated a cooler spot for us to stand. My skin tingled as if he had touched me. We moved under the canopy of leaves. I stood so I was facing the canal rather than Jack, feeling his quiet gaze on me as I tried to gather my thoughts.

'I'm sorry. I believe you, not Liam. I'd much rather have stayed on the Jericho Wine Barge with you when he appeared the other day, but I was worried about what he might do, so I went off with him which upset you, then you didn't want to see me at all—'

My words came to a halt because Jack had reached out and was now lightly resting his palm on my forearm. I turned towards him, his hazel eyes locking with mine.

'You don't have to explain yourself to me or anyone else,' he said softly. 'It was an awkward situation, and you handled it just fine. You haven't upset me at all. I'm the one who should apologise. When I wasn't working, I was actually steering clear of Liam, not you. It wasn't exactly a mature way of handling things. I'm sorry I gave you the impression I didn't want to see you.' He glanced down for a second, then fixed me again with his steady gaze. 'It was quite the opposite in fact. I was hoping that we could become friends.'

'Friends. Yes. Of course,' I stammered, taken aback by the pang of disappointment I felt. I tried to cover it by clearing my throat. 'I should really get the food in the fridge.'

'Let me help you,' offered Jack.

'I'm fine, thanks. You're going in the opposite direction, and it won't take me two minutes.'

'It really wouldn't be—'

'No honestly, it's not a problem,' I insisted, 'Enjoy your walk.'

'Only if you're sure.' He paused, giving me another chance to accept his assistance. I tried to assume the expression of a strong and independent woman.

Jack shrugged, finally admitting defeat. 'I guess I shall carry on my way. See you back at the boats in about half an hour I calculate, at your current rate,' he added with a provocative grin, and marched off down the path whistling cheerfully before I could think of an appropriate retort.

And if I stood there watching his narrow-hipped, long-limbed, easy stride for a little longer, it was only because the pins and needles were finally going from my hands, something which I attributed entirely to the rest I'd given myself, rather than acknowledging as being a handy by-product of my slightly elevated heart rate. Which was most definitely exertion related. One hundred per cent exertion related.

# Chapter Twenty-Seven

The walk back took less than the half an hour Jack had teasingly predicated, but as I approached my mooring position, I stumbled and came to an abrupt halt. There was something very wrong about the scene in front of me, but for a moment some kind of protective force in my brain prevented me from realising what it was. The flowers in my little towpath garden were dancing in the breeze, their bright colours as cheerful as ever. The ship's bell used by Jack to signal last orders on the Jericho Wine Barge was sparkling in the sunshine, and the bar furniture was set out on the deck. By the towpath, my neighbour's mooring ropes were neatly tied and everything looked shipshape. My gaze continued on to the Oxford Bookship and that was where my mind stuttered, because the Oxford Bookship wasn't there. Or rather, she was, but she wasn't where she should be, safely secured to the mooring rings on the towpath with the sturdy ropes which I checked religiously every time I stepped foot on shore. The rope at the stern of the boat was still looped through the ring, just about, but it was slack instead of taunt, trailing loosely into the watery gap between the boat and the shore, a watery gap that was far bigger than normal and growing greater by the second.

I dropped my bags onto the towpath, not even pausing at the ominous smashing sound which came from within them. Heart pounding with terror, I ran forwards. Now I could see the bow more clearly too, facing diagonally out towards the centre of the canal, the mooring rope floating on the surface of the greenish-brown water, nowhere near the ring it was meant to be secured to.

'No, no, no,' I said, each horrified 'no' getting progressively louder.

I lunged at the stern mooring rope, trying to trap it under my foot, but it was too late. The rope plopped into the water as a gust of breeze blew the Oxford Bookship away from the bank.

'Don't panic, Hilda,' I yelled, imagining her cowering in fear in the cabin, wondering why her world was moving without me on board to reassure her. She'd never travelled on the boat without me at her side and I couldn't bear to imagine how much it might freak her out to see the landscape changing and have no idea where she was going.

What could I do? Although the canal wasn't that wide, the rope was already too far away to reach, even supposing I had a boat hook or a long stick to hand. I knew my neighbour was out for a walk, and there was no sign of anyone else around who might be able to help me. I did some rapid calculations. The next nearest neighbours were Bill and Rozina, but it would take them at least five minutes to get here, even supposing they weren't at work. Or I could run to the Oxford Boating Association headquarters to raise the alarm and borrow one of their dinghies to regain control of my canal boat. That could be a sensible option. After all, the breeze wasn't that strong. The Oxford Bookship wasn't going to drift away and never be seen again.

But on the other hand, the breeze was powerful enough to send my beloved boat into the opposite bank within minutes, where the already-damaged hull could be further impacted. And there were no guarantees that someone would be around at the Boating Association to help. What if another boat came puttering along the canal in the meantime? An untethered boat the size of the Oxford Bookship could cause some serious damage, both to property, and more importantly, to people or animals. No, I couldn't afford to risk it. I needed to get hold of the Bookship as soon as possible. And there was only one way I was going to manage to do that.

I removed my shoes then stripped off my t-shirt and skirt, wary of the risk which could be posed by the extra fabric dragging me down, then made my way to the edge of the bank.

'Molly, wait...'

'Molls, what...'

Two male voices tried to stop me, two guys appearing out of nowhere as if some flash alert had gone round the Man Network saying, 'Woman in mismatched undies about to jump into slightly mucky canal'.

I ignored them and lowered myself into the tepid water. Despite my panic at the situation, I wasn't daft enough to dive in without knowing what I might encounter, especially given that the water level was slightly lower than normal due to the summer weather. Although I'd claimed otherwise to Jack, in reality anything could be lurking under the surface of the canal, and impaling myself on a rusty shopping trolley wasn't going to help save the Oxford Bookship.

Somebody else had no such qualms, because as I started a steady breaststroke towards my boat, there was a loud splash behind me. Somehow I knew who it was without having to turn back to check.

'You go for the bow rope. I'll keep swimming for the stern one,' I shouted to Jack.

'On it,' he said, his confident tone a reassurance.

I pushed on, finally grabbing the rope and hauling it over my shoulder. I trod water for a few seconds to check Jack had managed to get the bow rope before I turned back and set off for the shore again. It was harder work on the way back as I was terrified of losing the rope again, plus I was effectively dragging the barge behind me. The boat's buoyancy could only help me so much and I was hyper conscious of all the ways in which this manoeuvre could go horribly wrong. If another boat was to arrive and its helm wasn't concentrating on what they were doing, it didn't bear thinking about what could happen.

It was a relief to reach the shore again. I grabbed hold of a tuft of grass, before quickly transferring my grip to a more solid looking tree root. Now I needed to work out how to get out of the water without letting go of the rope. A pair of Nike trainers appeared in my eyeline.

'Lovely day for a dip,' said Liam, who I'd already identified as being the owner of the other male voice.

I was not in the mood for banter.

'Can you help?' I asked brusquely.

'What can I do?' he asked in a rather hurt voice, clearly disappointed I wasn't engaging.

'Could you take the rope off me?' I instructed, adding in a conciliatory please as an afterthought. 'I'd rather not be holding it as I get out, in case I slip and catch myself on it. Rope burn or worse is not the next challenge I want to be dealing with today.'

Liam bent down and grabbed it, wrinkling his nose.

'Eurgh, grim. It's a bit slimy,' he said as he immediately started hauling on it.

'Wait a moment,' I said, deploying my best dog disciplining tone. 'I need to get out first. If you pull the boat in, I'm in danger of getting caught between it and the bank.'

'Heck, sorry, what an idiot move to make. Do you want a hand?' He dropped the rope and reached out for me, seemingly oblivious to the more important role he was meant to be playing.

'Blimey, Liam, don't let go after I went to such efforts to get it,' I rebuked him. 'The best way you can help me is by picking the rope back up and keeping a tight hold while I get out myself.'

'Sorry, Molls,' he said sheepishly. As he leaned forward to pick the rope up again, his denim jacket flapped open, and I spotted a red blinking light on a small camera strapped to his chest. Yet another boat drama involving me that he'd managed to get on film.

'Turn that off before I get out,' I said, not bothering with a please this time. I was beyond tired of him recording my every move for posterity, plus I had no desire to appear on the internet in my current state of undress.

'I happened to be filming in the area when I heard your cry for help,' he responded defensively. 'I started running, knowing something bad must have happened. To be honest, I forgot it was still recording,' he added, covering the lens, which in my mind wasn't the same as turning the thing off. I also noticed that he didn't bother looking away himself as I started to scramble out of the canal, but by that stage I was too shocked and tired to make a fuss about it. The cold of the water was catching up with me, and my teeth were starting to chatter.

I slowly hauled myself out of the canal, which took a lot more effort than I would have liked. I could comfortably swim for hours in the public pool, so it was embarrassing that just a few metres in the canal had taken it out of me like this. I decided to blame it on shock. I dragged myself onto the grass and flopped down trying to get my breath back, undoubtedly looking like a creature that had been washed ashore.

There was a pounding of footsteps, and a pair of sodden deck shoes arrived at my side. I rolled over and looked up. For a moment I thought I was hallucinating and that Colin Firth aka Mr Darcy, wet shirt and all, had arrived to rescue me from my watery doom. I blinked and wiped my eyes, my pulse quickening for reasons that had nothing to do with my recent immersion.

'I grabbed the bow rope and tied it back to the mooring

ring with a bowline. Liam, can you go and do the same with that stern rope?' said Jack.

Liam did as he was told, although the thunderous expression on his face made it very clear that he wasn't pleased about taking orders from Jack.

While Liam made a meal out of looping the rope through the mooring ring and tying it off, Jack squatted down at my side, his gaze as dispassionate as a paramedic's as he quickly glanced over me, checking for injuries. I knew I should sit up and act like a normal person, but I was transfixed by the drips from his wet hair winding their way down his neck and pooling in the hollow of his collarbone. I'd never considered that particular part of the male body as being especially erotic, but an unexpected image of my fingers tracing along it flashed into my mind. I rubbed my eyes again, trying to pull myself together.

'Let's stay here for a second while you get your breath back,' Jack suggested. 'Once you've recovered, we can secure both ropes more tightly and you can check them out for yourself. But first things first, are you alright, sweetheart?'

I registered several things about this statement, although it took my brain a little while to process them given its water-soaked/Mr Darcy delusional state. First, Jack had thrown himself into the canal without hesitation to save my boat. Second, he'd picked up an impressive amount of boating lingo with his talk of bowlines and the like, so he must have been paying attention to some of what I'd been saying to him over the last few weeks. And third, he'd called me sweetheart. It was this third thing which I found myself fixating on. I mean sweetheart was a common enough term of endearment. Heck, I'd encountered more than a few tradespeople who dished it out like jelly babies to marathon runners. But Jack wasn't the type of person to use such a word lightly. And it wasn't just the use of the word which had struck me. It was the way he'd delivered it, tentatively, and … tender? I must have caught something from the canal water because I was seriously confused now.

'Why?' I asked.

Thankfully Jack took my choked question at face value.

'I heard you shout as I was walking back along the towpath and saw the Oxford Bookship drifting,' said Jack. 'I ran as fast as I could. Liam arrived from the other direction only moments later.' He nodded towards Liam, scrupulously fair in making sure he got the credit for helping me as well. 'How on earth do you think the boat came free? It can't have been an accident. I know how meticulous you are when it comes to checking your mooring ropes.'

I managed a spluttered 'Thanks' in response to his compliment of my boat-sense, before I succumbed to another bout of coughing.

'Do you think you can sit up a bit?' suggested Jack. 'That might help get some more air into your lungs.'

'I'm fine, honestly I am,' I choked as I moved into more of a curled-up crouch position.

Jack patted me between the shoulder blades. 'You've not swallowed any water, have you? Do you think we should call a doctor?' he asked Liam who seemed to have finally finished fiddling around with the stern rope. Unfortunately, the length of time he'd spent faffing with it didn't reassure me about how secure it might be.

'Thanks for your concern, but I'm okay, I promise. Plus, there isn't a doctor in Oxford who would come out here on a call, especially on a Saturday. I'd have to be at death's door, and I can assure you that I'm not. I'm absolutely fine.'

As if to prove it, I tried to push myself up to standing, realising too late that I should have taken it more steadily. For a couple of moments, there was a roaring in my ears and the world darkened around me as shock and my recent exertion conspired to send a wave of dizziness over me. Then I felt a strong grip on each elbow and realised that I had a man on each arm holding me steady. Flick would be green with envy, I thought, and giggled as I imagined her expression.

'Come and sit back down,' said Jack slowly and gently.

'Don't worry, Darcy, I'm not going to swoon,' I responded. Shit. Had I just called him Darcy? I feigned more coughing to cover my embarrassment.

'Better out than in,' said Jack, patting me lightly on the back again. 'You're shivering like mad. We need to get you warm. Perhaps you'd like to offer Molly your jacket, Liam? My clothes are unfortunately soaking.'

My befuddled brain didn't quite agree with all of that statement. There was nothing unfortunate about Jack being in a wet shirt which clung to every contour of his chest. I realised there was a double standard at play in me lusting after Jack and being offended by Liam checking me out because of a similar wet clothing predicament, but I hoped I was being more subtle about it. Besides, Jack still had proper clothes on whereas I was much more vulnerable in my underwear, plus I had just nearly drowned. Kind of. Actually, that was probably why my mind was acting so frisky. That sort of experience was bound to make a person seek out something to make them feel alive again.

I shivered again, although my overactive brain was doing a good job of warming me up.

Jack didn't wait for Liam to do as he'd asked. He quickly scooped up my pile of clothing and passed it across to me.

'I realise there's no point in suggesting you dry off properly. I know you'll want to make sure that the Oxford Bookship is okay before you do anything else,' he said.

Jack turned away as I pulled my clothes back on, a pointless courtesy given the state of undress I'd been in for a while, but one I appreciated. Liam meanwhile seemed to have malfunctioned somewhere along the way and was staring at me as if he'd never seen a woman in mismatched underwear before. His jacket had fallen back in place so I couldn't see whether he'd stuck to his word and turned the camera off, but I still felt uncomfortable under his gaze, and got dressed as quickly as I could.

Feeling slightly more dignified now that I was at less of a disadvantage on the clothing front, I pulled my shoes on then hurried to check the ropes at both ends of the boat. The one which Jack had sorted needed no adjustment, but I refastened Liam's messy knot to be on the safe side.

'Good bowline,' I complimented Jack when I returned to his side.

He looked surprised at my comment, and then to my

astonishment his cheeks reddened as he smiled back at me. Had my praise made him blush?

'I've been practising,' he admitted. 'In fact, this will probably make you think I'm a complete geek, but I've discovered that I find learning different nautical knots rather relaxing.'

'Well, for someone living on the water, that's a very good thing. Anyway, geeks make the world go round. We're people who care passionately about what we do. What's not to like about that? It's time we reclaimed the word and celebrated it rather than using it to dismiss ourselves.'

'You're not wrong,' said Jack, looking somewhat surprised at my impassioned lecture.

'In fact, I have exactly the book on board which will help you expand your nautical knot knowledge even further,' I said. 'It's actually got over three thousand knots to learn in it, which will keep you going for a while.'

'Sounds fascinating, I'd love to buy that,' he said without hesitation.

I replied equally as quickly. 'Out of the question. I'm hoping you'll accept it as a gift to thank you for your help in saving my home and business today.'

'Anyone would have done it,' he said. 'But I'm touched by the gesture, thank you.' The sincerity in his voice was more effective at warming me up than putting my clothes back on.

Liam cleared his throat. 'It looks like you've got everything in hand, so I guess I'd better be off. Unless you'd like me to stay that is, Molls?' He glanced significantly at

Jack and then raised a questioning eyebrow at me, signalling his opinion that I should be on my guard.

'Thanks for your help, Liam. We've got it from here,' I said. A shadow passed his face at my use of the word 'we' rather than 'I'. He hesitated, as if trying to come up with an excuse to hang around longer, but then he shrugged and turned on his heel.

'You know where to find me if you need me,' he called over his shoulder before stomping down the path and out of sight.

Now I was confident the Oxford Bookship was moored securely again, my attention turned to my next concern.

'Time to check on Hilda,' I said. 'She'll be wondering what on earth was going on. In fact, I'm surprised she didn't even bark. Perhaps she slept through the whole thing. And then I need to get the food and see how much of it survived its bad treatment.'

'I guess I'd better...' Jack gestured towards the Jericho Wine Barge.

I wracked my brains for an excuse to ask him to stay, but the guy was soaking wet. He'd probably agree to help me bring the food in were I to ask, but it wasn't fair to make him hang around when he was still dripping.

'Thanks again for your help, I don't know what I'd have done without it,' I said.

He smiled. 'I'm sure you'd have managed fine. But I'm glad I was there to do what I could.'

He started heading back towards the Jericho Wine Barge, but before he climbed on board he turned towards me again.

'By the way, I'm truly honoured.'

I frowned in confusion.

'You called me Darcy earlier. I know that's the highest of praise coming from you.' His expression was mischievous, but there was something slightly different about his tone, which I couldn't quite put my finger on.

I pulled a face. The only way I could style this out was by making a joke of it. 'I was half drowning. I have no idea what I said.'

Jack winced in an exaggerated fashion. 'Ouch. That's put me in my place. But whatever you claim, you can't take that memory away from me.' He tapped the side of his head. 'I'll stow it up here for the next time you have a go at me about something.' He winked at me.

'Me? Have a go? I have no idea what you're talking about,' I said with a laugh, allowing him the dig.

I was still laughing as I climbed on the stern deck of the Oxford Bookship. But as soon as I saw the cabin door, the laughter died, and my stomach turned over as a shot of panic surged through me.

# Chapter Twenty-Eight

'Oh my God.' I rushed forward, hoping I was mistaken and that the cabin door wasn't cracked open.

'Molly? What's the matter?' I heard Jack's question. By the sound of it, he'd jumped ashore and was heading back towards the Oxford Bookship, but I couldn't give him an answer. Steeling myself for the worst, I tentatively pulled the cabin door wider and stared into my living quarters. The boat being released into the middle of the waterway could have been a badly thought-out prank, but the open door suggested much more sinister forces were at work. I'd heard cases from elsewhere in the country where boat owners had returned to find their vessels broken into and sunk in the middle of the canal, their interiors entirely stripped by ruthless thieves who didn't give a toss about the impact their actions would have on the individuals whose pride and joy they'd violated and destroyed. Had the Oxford Bookship been similarly targeted?

It took my eyes a couple of seconds to adjust to the shadows in the cabin compared to the sunshine outside, but it felt like endless minutes, during which I fought to control my sense of dread. I imagined books shredded, their ruined pages heartlessly tossed around the floor, graffiti on every surface, drawers wrenched open, their contents trashed. It would break my heart. And worse, the desecration of her beloved former home might just kill Nana Rose.

But as my gaze grew clearer, I realised the cabin was apparently untouched, my personal collection of books still neatly lined up on their shelves, the washing up still on the draining board, the cushions plumped on the bench. Everything was as it should. Or nearly everything. The dog bed was empty.

'Hilda?' I called, my voice cracking. I cleared my throat and repeated my summons, hoping against hope that the reason I wasn't hearing the reassuring tip tap of her claws clattering across the cabin floor was because I'd struggled to get her name out. My senses were on red alert, every step I made thudding noisily in my brain as I walked across my cabin, through the bathroom and into the shop, examining each nook and cranny on my way. Logically I knew there were no hiding places in the boat which would be big enough for Hilda to tuck herself into, but I checked them anyway, because the alternative was too hard to consider.

There were footsteps behind me, and I turned, cruel hope trying to convince me that the confident tread could actually be Hilda's paws instead.

'She's gone, Jack.' My words were matter of fact and

emotionless, but the heaving sob which followed them was anything but.

He didn't say anything but reached for me, wrapping me in an embrace which felt strong enough to keep the rest of the world temporarily at bay and let me cry into his shoulder. I was grateful he didn't try to comfort me with reassurances which he couldn't guarantee. Nothing would be okay again until I found Hilda.

After a few minutes, Jack gently rubbed a circle on the small of my back. 'Do you feel ready for us to talk about next steps?' he asked softly.

I swallowed hard, my hands trembling with the effort of trying to stop the tears.

'It's a good thing I haven't changed out of my wet gear yet what with all the snot you're depositing on my shoulder,' he added. It was exactly the kind of deliberately ridiculous statement that I needed to pull myself together and snap into action.

'Every cloud and all that,' I said, my voice wobbly. I managed to nod at him, grateful for his practical approach. He was right. I couldn't afford to indulge in wallowing.

'Tell me everything you can about her last known movements,' he said. I nearly laughed in a strange kind of reflex response. He sounded so like a police officer from one of my favourite crime series, an Adam Dalgliesh or a Harry Nelson. A dependable sort, the kind of man who would seek answers and find a solution no matter how challenging a problem he faced.

'She was messing around while I was setting up the

afternoon tea. Oh heck, the afternoon tea. How on earth will I be able to host all those guests?'

'Don't worry about that. We'll ask for their help in searching for Hilda,' said Jack decisively. 'They're book people. I'd say that means they're probably a pretty empathetic lot. I'd imagine most of them will be more than happy to step up.'

'They might be nice people, but will they be nice enough to spend their time searching for a missing Irish wolfhound, having paid twenty-five quid for a Food and Fiction event?'

'Where's your optimism, Bramble?' That bolstering tone was back. 'We'll explain they can take a rain check and you'll run the event on another occasion. Also, we've got a couple of hours before they're due to arrive. Anything could happen in that time. Hopefully she'll turn up long before that. Right?'

I nodded miserably.

'Okay, think back to when you last saw Hilda.'

I frowned, trying to picture every moment, but it had been so ordinary, so mundane that it hadn't really registered with me. If I'd known what was to come, it would have been ingrained into my mind.

'She was mucking around with a cushion while I was trying to get ready for the afternoon tea, so I chased her round trying to get it off her. Then I managed to persuade her to go into the cabin, and she was settling down in her bed when Becki from the Covered Market rang to say my delivery was waiting for me.'

Jack nodded. 'Good. So, you locked up and then…'

A sudden thought filled me with horror. 'I'm not sure I

did lock up. I can't remember doing it.' I knew my keys were in the pocket of my skirt; I could feel the bunch heavy against my thigh. I searched my memory, trying to picture the moment of putting the key in the lock and fastening it, but I couldn't summon it.

'That doesn't mean anything,' said Jack in a reassuring tone. 'It's one of those completely routine things that your brain has probably filed away as unimportant. I can't generally picture myself pulling on my underwear, but I've never found myself not wearing it beneath my clothes.' He grimaced. 'Sorry, that was a very inappropriate example. I was trying to think of something mundane and every day, but it was a weird analogy to make.'

'No need to apologise, I get the point. The trouble is, I was so distracted. I knew that Becki wouldn't be able to wait for long, and I rushed off to get there as soon as possible. I usually always check the door is locked behind me. But the more I think about it, the more I have a horrible feeling I left it open. This is all my fault. How could I be so irresponsible?'

Jack squeezed my shoulder bracingly. 'There's no point in beating yourself up about something that might not even be true. There's the fact that the Oxford Bookship was adrift to consider. Doesn't it make more sense that whoever was responsible for that also broke into the cabin?'

I shuddered at the thought. 'The door doesn't look like it's been forced. And if someone had broken in, wouldn't they have nicked other stuff while they were at it? Admittedly there's not much in the cash box, and I certainly don't have any super expensive jewellery, but the diamond stud which Nana Rose got me for my twenty-first birthday is still there in the tray with my other bits and bobs.'

'But it's still a fact that Hilda is missing. Sorry, I'm stating the obvious yet again and making things much worse,' he added, no doubt seeing that my face was about to crumple once more.

'You're seriously suggesting someone might have broken into the boat to steal my gorgeous girl?'

Jack sighed. 'I hate to say it, but I reckon it's a possibility we should consider. There are some very unscrupulous people out there.'

'But I thought dognappers went after the cockapoos and other designer dogs. I love Hilda to pieces but she's not exactly the cutesy handbag dog that someone would pay thousands to acquire.' I put my hand over my mouth. 'And now I feel like even more of a bad pet parent because I'm making out that she's some scruffy beast, which she is, but she's my scruffy beast and I love every part of her.'

'Of course you do. Don't be so hard on yourself. You're an excellent dog parent. I knew within five seconds of meeting Hilda that she was an extremely well loved and well-adjusted pooch.'

'You accused her of being a horse,' I said contrarily.

'And in this instance, I think her size will play well for us. She'll stand out wherever she's got to, whether someone's persuaded her to go for an adventure with them, or she's wandered off on her own accord.'

I sniffed. 'That's true. There aren't many Irish wolfhounds in Oxford.'

'Exactly. She's very recognisable. Everyone on the

Oxford Canal will know instantly who she is if they come across her. Have you checked your phone? Someone might have already sent you a message saying they've found her.'

My burst of optimism was short lived as I checked every messaging service. 'Nothing. I think we should start searching along the towpath,' I said, trying to focus on practical actions rather than letting another wave of helplessness paralyse me.

'Good idea. Perhaps we should follow the route of your usual walk. There's a good chance she'll have stuck to familiar places if she has just wandered off. Sorry, I'm taking over again,' he added. 'Feel free to tell me what you'd like me to do.'

I squeezed his forearm. 'You're not taking over. I'm grateful for your support. But I'm not so heartless as to make you search while you're still dripping wet. You go and get changed while I bring the food from the Covered Market delivery on board before I add a littering complaint to my problems. By the time I've dug out a selection of Hilda's favourite treats, I'm sure you'll be ready, and we can get going.'

'Good plan. I'll be back in two ticks.'

I stuffed the surviving food in the fridge as best I could and shoved a load of dog treats into a bag, along with Hilda's favourite soft toy, the sight of which brought tears to my eyes all over again. I was just changing into a sturdier pair of shoes when there was a tap on the cabin door.

'Come in, you don't need to knock,' I called out. 'Are you feeling more civilised now you've dried—Oh,' I broke off, as I turned round and realised there was a complete stranger standing in my cabin.

'You're not Jack,' I said stupidly.

A line appeared between the man's thickset brows. 'Who's Jack?'

I shook my head. 'Never mind that. Who are you, if you don't mind me asking?' I wondered why I was being so polite about it. This was my boat. I was entitled to expect any visitor to the private side of the Oxford Bookship to identify themself.

'I've been appointed on behalf of the Oxford Boating Association to carry out a snap inspection of this vessel. You can check my identification.'

He held up an ID card in a leather case as if he was a police officer on official business, which he might as well have been, given the authority which I knew this Mr Fred Zimmer, as the card named him, would hold over my affairs.

'Thank you. But now's really not a good time.' I was about to explain about the Hilda situation, but he cut me off.

'I apologise, Ms Bramble, but that's the nature of a snap inspection. It happens when it happens. I appreciate it's rarely a good time for boaters, but when you signed the lease for the mooring position, this is one of the terms which you agreed to.'

'I'm in the middle of a family crisis at the moment,' I tried to explain. 'I promise you can come at any other time, but I really need—'

'Family crisis?' asked Mr Zimmer. 'According to my

records you are the sole occupier of the Oxford Bookship. You don't have any family.'

If I wasn't so distressed about Hilda and wary of exacerbating an already tense situation, I would have given him a piece of my mind, livid at the suggestion that just because I was single it meant I didn't have family. There was Nana Rose, my parents, Hilda herself, not to mention my close friends like Flick. I had family in abundance, even if it didn't look like the cookie cutter version that society expected for women.

'My dog is missing,' I said.

'I'm sorry to hear that,' he responded in a tone which didn't reflect the sympathy of his words, 'but I've got a job to do. I should warn you that if you refuse the inspection without appropriate cause, it will put you in contravention of your licence terms. See here, it's stated on this document.'

He wafted a piece of paper covered in type towards me.

I was about to reply saying he could stuff his document, when Jack returned to the cabin. It had been less than five minutes since his departure, but this patrician individual with slicked back hair and a power stance couldn't be more different from the dripping wet man who'd let me blub on his shoulder.

'Hello, Mr Zimmer, isn't it? I recognise you from your profile on the Oxford Boating Association's website.' He held out his hand expectantly, forcing the inspector to juggle his paperwork in order to respond to the gesture. 'I'm Jack Siddall, owner and proprietor of the Jericho Wine Barge next door. Perhaps if Ms Bramble is in agreement, I can assist you with your endeavours while she continues the search for her dog. It is after all most important that you are able to fulfil your duty.'

Fred Zimmer looked ready to salute in grateful obedience, swept up in the easy authority of Jack's manner.

'That would seem to be a sensible solution,' he said.

'Excellent, where shall we start? How about in the bookshop?' suggested Jack heartily, clapping the man on the shoulders and steering him in that direction without giving him the chance to disagree. As they left the cabin, Jack sent the ghost of a wink over his shoulder towards me and mouthed, 'Good luck.'

I scurried off the Oxford Bookship as fast as I could before the inspector changed his mind. I had to trust that Jack would keep a careful eye on him in my absence. After all, if I failed the inspection, Hilda might not have a home to come back to.

# Chapter Twenty-Nine

I searched every inch of the towpath, tracing the steps of our favourite walks, calling Hilda's name and asking passers-by whether they'd seen her. I tried to work as methodically as possible, but I was only one person, and while I tramped back towards Jericho, Hilda could easily be lolloping in the opposite direction heading towards the train station and the centre of the city. I flinched at the thought of her wandering towards the more populated areas, where impatient drivers and thoughtless cyclists would be extra hazards. When I first brought her home from the rescue centre, she was skittish and unpredictable when surrounded by crowds. We'd worked hard together to make her feel more comfortable in those situations, but I didn't know how she might react when I wasn't around to place a comforting hand on her haunches.

I shook my head, physically trying to push away the intrusive thoughts.

I let out a piercing whistle, followed by another shout of

'Hilda', then looked at my watch. Just half an hour to go until the guests were due to arrive at the afternoon tea. I decided to do a quick check along the banks of Castle Mill Stream, still hoping she'd emerge from the undergrowth, wagging her tail and looking expectantly at me in anticipation of getting a treat.

I hurried up towards Isis Lock, aiming for the footbridge, when I bumped into Liam.

'Is everything alright? Why are you shouting for Hilda?' he asked.

I started to explain the situation.

'Hold on a second, I need to get this on camera. I'll post it on all my channels and ask people to share. Hashtag Find Hilda. The more people we get looking, the better, right?'

'I'll take any help I can get,' I said, crushing the stirring of anxiety at the thought of my personal tragedy being made so public.

I have no idea what I said to the camera, but Liam seemed satisfied, tapping busily on his phone.

'There we go. It's posted on all my channels. Hilda will be trending in no time. I've tagged the Oxford Bookship as well, so when people reply, their comments should pop up in your feeds too.'

'Thank you, I really appreciate your help,' I said. Whatever he may have done in the past, at least he was showing up now.

Liam's phone was buzzing away.

'Listen to that,' he said with a pleased grin. 'The notifications are rolling in.'

I glanced at my watch. 'How is that the time already?

I need to check Castle Mill Stream, but in about five minutes a load of guests will be arriving at the Oxford Bookship expecting afternoon tea, and I've got to tell them it's cancelled.'

Liam pulled a sympathetic face. 'Tough one. Don't worry, I'll have a good nose around there for you. In fact, I was planning on taking the *Lydia* for a spin to keep her engine ticking over, so I'll keep my eyes peeled for Hilda while I do that. I'll call you if I get any good leads. Ha, did you see what I did there?'

I forced a smile. 'Thanks, Liam, I'll be waiting to hear from you.'

'I'll keep you posted,' he promised as he headed back towards his boat.

I hesitated, wishing I had time to go and search the area around the stream myself. But another check of my watch forced me to move in the opposite direction. I'd have to trust Liam would be thorough.

Jack was waiting on the stern deck of the Oxford Bookship when I arrived back.

'Good news,' he said as soon as he saw me.

I felt a huge surge of relief. 'She's come home,' I said.

Jack's face fell. 'Oh, Molly, I'm really sorry, that's not what I meant.' He held out a piece of paper. 'The Oxford Bookship passed the inspection with flying colours. In fact, Mr Zimmer was so impressed that he left his details so you could sign him up to your book subscription service.'

'That's something I suppose,' I said, trying to put on a brave face. Hilda had been gone for at least three hours now. Every additional minute of separation was a minute too much to endure.

'Hello, it's only us.' A cheery voice called from the towpath. 'Leo and I thought we'd arrive early in case you needed a hand and—Oh, Molly, whatever's the matter?' Kat's happy expression fell as soon as she caught sight of me.

Kat was a good friend, but I couldn't face the prospect of explaining about Hilda's disappearance all over again. I opened up Liam's post on my phone and passed it across to her. Leo leaned over her shoulder so he could see it too.

'Where have you searched so far?' he asked. 'We'll organise groups of people armed with dog treats. I'll drop a line to my old contacts at the police as well. You never know, someone might have handed her into the station.'

The next few hours passed in a blur. One by one the guests arrived for the afternoon tea to be greeted by Kat or Leo. I don't know what they said to them, but I didn't receive a single demand for a refund and the majority stayed on to join the search parties which Leo organised in an efficient manner. By the time darkness fell late that night, I was confident that every inch of the towpath had been thoroughly searched, along with many of the adjoining gardens, and several of the streets in the wider Jericho area. It was as if Hilda had vanished off the face of the planet.

Jack had stuck with me throughout, quietly supportive and full of good suggestions. As time wore on, I felt it was more important for me to stay at the Oxford Bookship. Hilda had a strong sense of home, and I knew that even if she'd decided to have an out of character adventure further afield, she would eventually return here when hunger and tiredness caught up with her. The longer she was away, the more convinced I became that something else must have happened.

'I'm going to start ringing around the rescue centres and vet practices,' I said. I forced myself to sound matter of fact about it, but my stomach was in knots.

'Sensible plan,' said Jack, squeezing my hand reassuringly. 'Let's divide the list up between us.'

One by one, the searchers made their apologies and left, promising to keep their eyes open for Hilda. Kat and Leo stayed long after the time I knew their last bus home departed, but eventually even they admitted defeat.

'I'm so sorry. I wish there was more we could do,' Kat kept repeating as she fought to contain yet another yawn. She looked exhausted.

'You've both been a huge help, thank you,' I said.

'I'll put posters up in the library,' she said.

'And I'll keep pestering my police contacts,' added Leo.

'Honestly, guys, you couldn't have done any more. I'll let you know when she turns up,' I said. When. It was going to happen.

And then it was just Jack. The distant sound of a college bell tower striking eleven o'clock was carried on the breeze towards us. Closing time.

'You didn't open the Jericho Wine Barge this evening,' I said with a sudden realisation.

'There were more important things to do,' he said.

'Thank you.'

He shook his head and fixed me with a firm expression.

'No. You don't have to say that. It's what any neighbour would do. What any friend would do.'

He hesitated slightly before he used the word 'friend', as if he was uncertain of his right to use the term.

'You're the best kind of friend,' I replied simply. We'd had our ups and downs since he'd moved in next door, a lot of downs in fact, but it was this kind of situation which demonstrated the truth of a person. And Jack's truth was that he was a good man.

'Well, as a friend, may I suggest that you try to get some sleep?' He pulled a face in anticipation of my obvious response. 'I know it's the last thing you feel like doing, but it's important to keep your strength up. You owe it to Hilda to be on top form so you can do your best for her.'

He'd got me there. But even though I accepted the logic of his suggestion it still seemed like an impossibility. I couldn't imagine my brain quietening enough from my worries to allow me to go to sleep.

He read my response in my expression.

'Okay, how about this? Why don't I set up some cushions and blankets for you in the well deck? I know it's one of Hilda's favourite places, so you can keep watch for her there, but at least you'll be comfortable while you do it.'

'Than—That would be kind,' I said, cutting off the thanks I knew he didn't want. While he bustled around on the deck, I retreated into the cabin, trying not to stare at the empty dog bed as I forced my aching limbs into a set of warm jogging bottoms and a hoody. Then I put the kettle on and made a couple of hot chocolates. There was a chill in the air, but my terror was making me feel even colder.

I emerged onto the well deck, a mug in each hand, to see it transformed into a cosy nest. Jack had even strung a set of fairy lights over the arch of the doorway.

'I thought they might help ward off the darkness in both senses,' he said, nodding his head towards them. 'They're dim enough that you'll still have good night vision to keep an eye out for our girl.'

'That's very thoughtful.'

'I should—'

'Would you—'

Again, we started speaking at the same time.

'You go first,' he said.

I held a mug of hot chocolate out to him. 'I know I've asked a lot of you today, but I was hoping I could impose on you a little longer. Would you mind staying for a bit? It's so quiet without Hilda.' I swallowed. 'I made hot chocolate, if that helps,' I added, forcing a brightness I didn't feel into my voice.

Jack chuckled softly. 'It's no imposition when there's hot chocolate on offer. Of course I'll stay.' He accepted the mug and took a sip. 'Delicious. I might have to enlist your help creating hot beverages for the bar when winter comes.'

I wrapped myself in a blanket and snuggled down among the cushions. Jack meanwhile perched somewhat precariously on the gunwale.

After a few minutes, I said, 'You must be as exhausted as I am, and that looks far from comfortable. Come and join me here. There's plenty of room for both of us.'

'I'm not sure…'

'No excuses. Besides, I'm not convinced you've got

enough boat sense yet to maintain that position. I'd prefer not to add you falling into the water to my list of concerns.'

'Well, if you insist,' he said, the note of reluctance in his voice provoking a hurt that I couldn't cope with examining too closely at this point in time.

He lowered himself onto the cushions, sitting rigidly upright, looking more uncomfortable than he had been on the wooden gunwale.

I passed a blanket across to him, and we sipped our drinks, our hands cupped around the reassuring warmth of the mugs, staring out in the darkness. I sensed, rather than saw him start to allow himself to relax. I shuffled lower in my seat, and a few minutes later, he did the same. The quiet between us was a comfort rather than another source of stress. There was nothing that Jack could say to make things better for me right now, but his solid, silent presence was exactly what I needed, a good friend sitting in solidarity with my pain.

I think it was the shriek of an owl which dragged me awake in the middle of the night. I'd not intended to fall asleep, wanting to keep all my senses alert for Hilda's return, but at some point, I must have drifted off, fatigue finally winning its battle against my hyper alert anxiety. I lay in the darkness, surrounded by warmth, gradually realising that its source was not the blanket, but the man I was now snuggled up against.

'Sorry,' I whispered into the night, mortified that I'd ended up in this position. What must Jack think of me, trapped as he was with my arms wrapped around his torso, as if he was a giant teddy bear I was clinging to. I loosened my grip, trying to shift steadily so I didn't disturb him, but as soon as I moved, he stirred beneath me.

'Is Hilda home?' he asked groggily.

'No.'

'Then let's go back to sleep,' he said, his steady breathing suggesting that he'd done exactly that almost immediately.

Left with a choice of waking Jack up again or accepting I was going to spend the rest of the night in his arms, I settled on the latter, telling myself it was the only polite thing to do. In truth, I wasn't awake long enough to continue justifying the choice to myself. I drifted off again nearly as quickly as Jack, my mind quietened by the comfort I felt being entwined with him.

# Chapter Thirty

That night curled up next to Jack was the last bit of peace that I got to experience for a while. Sunday, and then Monday, dawned with no sign of Hilda, and despite searching frantically, there was still no trace of her. She hadn't been handed in to any of the rescue centres, none of the vets within a thirty-mile radius of Oxford had even seen an Irish wolfhound in the last week, and despite Leo's police contact putting out the lost dog equivalent of an all points warning to his colleagues, there was no news on that front either.

I went through the motions of opening the shop, more because I didn't know what else to do, but after frightening off several customers with my haunted expression and my frantic questioning about whether they'd seen my dog, Jack quietly took over behind the counter, while I settled into torturing myself still further by scrolling through my social feeds hoping to receive a message about a sighting. Plenty of kind people had reposted and shared, making well-meaning suggestions and offering positive thoughts for Hilda's safe return, but of course there were a few cruel comments in response to Liam's video, and those were the ones I kept returning too, as I continued blaming myself for Hilda's disappearance.

'Stop reading them,' said Flick, her expression concerned during our FaceTime call. 'They're only going to make you feel worse.'

'But what if that means I miss something important?' I pointed out. 'Somebody must have seen something. She didn't just vanish into thin air.'

'Be that as it may, Flick's right. No good ever comes out of doom scrolling,' said Jack. 'You'll make yourself ill.'

'Seconded. It was irresponsible of Liam to post the video in the first place,' said Flick.

'He was trying to be helpful,' I said, although I wasn't sure I entirely believed my own assertion.

'Trying to get the views up on his channel more like,' muttered my best friend disapprovingly. 'As I know to my cost, Liam's only real love is his social media engagement. He could have framed it in a more sensitive manner. The sensationalist captions he's added were guaranteed to provoke a pile-on.'

'I'd endure all the pile-ons in the world if it brings her home,' I said. 'I'll take all the help I can get.'

Flick looked guilty and I hastened to reassure her.

'That's not a dig at you, lovely. You've done everything you can.'

As soon as Flick had heard the news, she'd written an article for the *Oxford Gazette*'s website. She claimed her editor had been happy to post it, but I suspected she'd had to pull a lot of strings to get him to agree to publication, the *Oxford Gazette* not normally being the kind of newspaper to feature lost dog stories on its pages, printed or otherwise.

'I'm sure there's more I can do. I'll skive off work and come back to help,' she said.

I sat up straight. 'You'll do no such thing. I'm not having you jeopardise your job.'

'I can find another job,' she said, determinedly. 'I feel utterly useless being stuck here in London, not being able to give you a hug.'

'You love being a journalist. And your virtual support is more than enough. Promise me you won't come back here until originally planned.'

She looked dubious.

'Felicity Summers, I mean it. You will make me be a whole lot more stressed if you turn up, because I'll feel responsible for you risking your career, and frankly that's an added pressure I could do without right now.'

'Fine, if you absolutely insist,' she said grudgingly. 'But you only have to say the word, and I'll be there in a flash.'

'I know you've got my back, don't worry.'

She only agreed to hang up after I suggested she try her contacts at the council to see if any of them had heard anything about an Irish wolfhound living wild in the city.

I sent Jack away too.

'The Jericho Wine Barge has barely been open since the official launch night. I know you're right next door, and I promise I'll call you if I need you. You've done more than enough. You can't put your life on hold just because I've made a mess of mine.'

'You haven't,' Jack started to argue back.

'You know what I mean. Somehow, I need to find a way of getting used to this new normal until Hilda returns. And the only way I can do that, is by myself.'

He didn't look convinced, but after extracting a promise I'd summon him the second I needed him, he eventually agreed to leave me to it.

The Oxford Bookship was a lonelier place once Jack had gone, but I told myself I had to get used to it. I was incapable of standing still for even just a second, throwing myself into work and starting conversations with every customer out of a desperate need to fill the silence. My usual ability to match people with their perfect reads seemed to have deserted me, and although I didn't sell any books, nobody left the barge without a Missing Dog poster pressed into their palms. My heart ached every time I saw Hilda's scruffy face staring up at me from them.

In the middle of the afternoon, my phone started ringing. I clicked answer with trembling fingers, not even pausing to check the name or number on the screen.

'What's this about Hilda being on the run?' asked Nana Rose, not bothering with the preliminaries.

'It's all my fault,' I said. I knew I should try to pretend everything was alright, but Nana had obviously heard what had happened, despite my efforts to protect her from my anxiety, and she knew me far too well for me to get away with dissembling.

'Nonsense. The reason I rang is that I might have a lead

for you. Eric's just taken a call from some holidaymakers lodging a complaint that it's unsafe for them to remain in the area because for the last hour there's been, and I quote, "an unearthly creature howling in the haunted boatshed". I mean I wonder how some people survive on the day to day. "Haunted boatshed"? Most unlikely. But perhaps they were on to something. Don't you think it could be Hilda they're hearing? What do you reckon, my darling?'

The moment Nana Rose had mentioned 'unearthly howling' my pulse had started accelerating with hope. Because that had been exactly the noise that Hilda was making when I first saw her in the rescue centre. It had been a heart-wrenching sound, one which had made me all the more determined to jump over whatever hurdles I had to in order to bring her home with me.

'That does sound like her. Did Eric manage to work out from them where the so-called haunted boatshed might be?'

Nana Rose sighed. 'It's obvious that these holidaymakers were not the most sensible sorts. But reading between the lines, it sounded awfully like the storage place belonging to your new neighbour.'

'Jack's boatshed? That can't be right.' If this had happened when I'd first encountered Jack, I would have immediately jumped to the conclusion that he had been involved in Hilda's disappearance. But now I knew without a shadow of a doubt that even if she did happen to be in his storage place, it wouldn't be because Jack had put her there. I trusted him completely. 'We checked around that area yesterday.'

'It sounds like the noise has only been happening for the

last hour or so,' said Nana Rose. 'Perhaps she wandered in when he was fetching something and he accidentally locked her in.'

I frowned. Accidentally? It would be pretty hard not to notice a dog the size of Hilda. My mind was racing. This was no accident. The more I thought about it, the more convinced I became: Hilda had been shut in there because somebody wanted to make Jack look guilty.

'I really hope she's there. Nana Rose, I love you dearly, but I'm going to hang up right now and go to check, if you don't mind.'

'My darling girl, I would expect nothing less. Let me know as soon as you find her. I will be sending all the positive vibes your way, as you young people like to say.'

I blew a kiss down the phone, and then hurried out of the Bookship, bumping straight into a guy standing on the well deck, wearing a tweedy suit completely incongruous for the weather.

'I'm really sorry but I've got to go. I think I might have found my lost dog. She's been missing since Saturday, and I've been tearing my hair out with worry.'

He blinked at me, unsurprisingly startled by the stranger who was oversharing with him. Then he beamed widely. 'That sounds like very good news,' he said. 'I guess I'll come back on another occasion.'

'Please do,' I said, already halfway across the gangplank by now.

The noise of my sudden exit brought Jack out on deck too.

'I might know where Hilda is,' I shouted across to him, then set off at a run along the towpath, heading for his boatshed.

Jack caught up with me.

'What about your customers?' I asked breathlessly.

'Your customer agreed to keep an eye on them for me,' he said, in a similar state of wheeziness. 'Matthias someone. I figured if he's a book person he's a decent sort. That's what you always say, anyway.'

'But he's not a regular. I've only just met him,' I said.

'I'll worry about that once we've found Hilda,' responded Jack.

I burst out laughing, teetering on the edge of hysteria with the high tension of the situation.

'Where are we heading?' asked Jack, continuing to match my pace.

'Eric had a tip-off about noise coming from your storage shed,' I said.

'*My* storage shed?' Jack stumbled in his tracks, and I reached out to stop him falling.

'You okay?' I asked.

'I'm fine. But Molly, I promise you, I haven't locked Hilda in my shed. I would never dream of doing such an awful thing.'

I briefly paused and faced him. His expression was a mix of total sincerity and complete horror. 'I know that,' I said. 'I have a theory about what's been going on, but do you mind if I share it with you once we've actually found her?'

We set off at a run again. As we neared the boatyard, I caught Jack's arm.

'Did you hear that?'

Before he could reply, another distinctive howl came over the breeze.

'That's definitely her,' I said joyfully. 'Hilda, we're nearly there,' I added in a yell.

There was an impatient ruff in response.

We rushed to the door of the storage shed, Jack pulling a key out of his pocket. He shoved it into the padlock and tried to turn it.

'It's not working,' he said in confusion, examining the lock more closely. 'This isn't the right lock. My padlock is brass whereas this one seems to be aluminium.'

I peered through a gap in the wooden wall and was rewarded by a waft of Hilda's pungent doggy breath from the other side, the most beautiful scent in the world right now.

'There's my girl,' I said. 'Someone must have broken in to leave her there.' I fished my phone out of my pocket. 'If they were able to break open your padlock, there must be a way of us doing the same. I'd look it up in a book, but in these circumstances, I reckon it's quicker to see if there's a video online teaching us how to do it.'

'Screw that,' said Jack. 'There's a quicker way still. Stand back, Hilda.'

And before I could say anything more, he raised his foot and kicked the door in a move which a kung fu fighter would have been impressed by.

The door shuddered under his attentions.

'Be careful, Jack,' I urged, before adding a kick of my own.

The wood shattered, the door bursting open, and I was nearly felled by a hairy whirlwind.

'My Hilda, my darling girl,' I cried as she frantically licked the tears off my face, a giant paw resting on each of my shoulders. 'You weigh a ton, old thing,' I said affectionately, wrapping my arms around her and enjoying every moment of this chaotic embrace.

She responded by throwing herself into zoomies, joyfully lapping the boatyard while Jack and I stood in the middle watching her and laughing.

'She looks in pretty good form to me,' he said.

'Maybe once she stops charging around, we can check her over,' I said, although I was in no hurry for her to do that. I'd been afraid I'd never see her running like this again, and I was soaking up every moment of it.

Eventually she calmed down a little and flopped at my feet, immediately rolling onto her back so I could administer belly rubs.

'That's my girl,' I said again, as she groaned appreciatively. I took the opportunity to feel around her torso, checking her over for any sign of injury, but thankfully there was no sign of harm. Judging by her full tummy, it certainly looked like she'd been eating well wherever she'd been for the last couple of days.

Jack bent down and gave her a pat too, before breaking away to inspect his shed.

'Come and take a look at this,' he called a second or two later.

Hilda shadowed me as I walked across to the building, but as soon as we approached the threshold, she hung back, refusing to move.

'Don't worry, I won't make you go back in there,' I promised. 'What have you found?' I called to Jack, reluctant to leave Hilda's side now that we'd been reunited at last.

He emerged from the building holding two dog bowls. 'One was empty, and this one had a small amount of water in it. Whoever left her in here didn't intend for her to go without basic sustenance at any rate.'

'But the very fact of locking her in a strange place was enough to cause her stress. Also, if it hadn't been for the tip-off from the holidaymakers, I would have had no idea she was here,' I pointed out.

'She looks pretty happy now, thank goodness,' said Jack.

'I still want us to take her to the vet to get checked over,' I said, then realised I was making a big assumption. 'Sorry, I meant, I'll take her to the vet. You don't have to come with me, unless you want to?'

'I'm more than happy to come along. It will put my mind at rest too. I haven't slept a wink either since she disappeared. Apart from when we slept together on the well deck, of course.' Jack's face suddenly blossomed with colour as he realised what he'd said. 'I meant when we were both asleep but in the same place,' he amended clumsily.

'I like it when you blush,' I said, without thinking.

Neither of us knew how to respond to that so we both

smiled at each other goofily for a moment, before I pulled myself together and dragged my mind back to the practicalities.

'Do you happen to have a piece of string or something on you?' I asked. 'I didn't stop for long enough to grab a lead on my way here to find her.'

Jack searched through his pockets. 'Afraid all I've got is a bottle opener which will do a fat lot of good. Perhaps you could use that?' He reached across and gently tugged at the ribbon I'd tied around my ponytail that morning in a vain attempt to boost my spirits.

'It's not very strong, but I reckon she'll be fine with it.'

'I'm prepared to bet she'll stick to your side like glue after your enforced separation,' he said.

Actually, Hilda seemed to welcome the ribbon being tied to her collar, pleased that there was something physically connecting the pair of us together.

'She's probably worried about you wandering off somewhere,' said Jack. 'She knows exactly where she's been for the last couple of days. As far as she's concerned, you're the one who's been missing in action.'

'If only she could talk and tell us what she's been up to.'

'Where do you think she might have been before she was locked in my shed?' asked Jack.

'That's the question, isn't it. I have an idea, but I'll worry about how to prove it once Hilda's got the all clear.'

As we waited in the reception of the vet's practice, I called Nana Rose to let her know the good news, then sent messages to Flick, Kat and all the other people who'd been kind enough to get involved in the search. And then I did a final scroll through Liam's socials before texting him a carefully phrased message.

> Have you heard anything about Hilda? It's been over 48 hours since the Bookship drifted and she disappeared…

I was lying by omission by not telling him that I'd found Hilda, but I wanted to test my theory. I'd not seen him since he'd filmed my desperate appeal for my missing pet. He'd said he was taking the *Lydia* for a spin, but while he'd continued to post about the hunt for Hilda, the videos were mostly rambling pieces to camera from nondescript parts of the riverbank, rather than any actual footage of a search in progress. The clips seemed more heavily edited than usual, and in none of them was he actually on board his boat.

'Hilda Bramble?' The vet interrupted my train of thought by calling us through into the consulting room.

I quickly told her as much as I knew.

'Goodness me, a case of dognapping in Oxford? That's very concerning. Let's take a look at you, poppet,' said the vet, slipping Hilda a treat, then setting to work examining her carefully.

Hilda was extremely patient, only letting out one little grumble of protest when the vet pressed the stethoscope against her chest.

'I'm sorry, that was cold, wasn't it?' the vet apologised. 'Well, she looks fighting fit to me. Perhaps an extra treat or two tonight to remind her she's safely back home.' Hilda thumped her tail against the wall in approval. 'Don't you gobble them down too quickly,' added the vet with a twinkle. 'I'll expect you'll sleep well tonight.'

That was addressed to Hilda still, but I noticed that Jack joined me in nodding in agreement.

# Chapter Thirty-One

As we emerged onto the street, I turned to Jack and spontaneously kissed his cheek, swept up in the emotion of the moment.

'Thank you. I don't know what I would have done without you over the last few days,' I said.

He put his hand up to the place I had kissed, as if he couldn't believe that it had really happened.

'It was what anyone would have done,' he said.

I shook my head. 'No. You went above and beyond that. Having you by my side was about the only thing that kept me going.'

Jack's expression softened, then he reached across and brushed a loose tendril of hair away from my face, carefully tucking it behind my ear. His gentle touch sent a quiver of awareness through my skin.

'I'm glad I could be there for you,' he said simply.

We started walking down the street together, heading back towards the canal. Our strides matched each other's exactly, Hilda lolloping happily between us, two tall people with a matching rangy dog. It felt so right, and I realised it wasn't just because Hilda was back where she belonged. A big part of this feeling of contentment was because of the man at my side, who had been a pillar of support through the darkest of days.

As we turned the corner into the little community garden by one of the footbridges over the canal, I paused.

'Jack there's something I really need to get off my chest.'

'You don't—' he started to say.

'I always tell people not to judge a book by its cover, but that's exactly what I did with you. I judged you on appearances, dismissing you as overprivileged and entitled, and my prejudice meant that I was all too willing to believe the worst of you when Liam was gossiping and putting his own spin on your joint history.' I cringed internally as I thought about how foolish I'd been. 'But despite me doing my best to act as the worst neighbour you could imagine, you were always straightforward in your dealings with me. I'm not going to lie; you gave as good as you got, being difficult and winding me up no end. And somewhere along the way, I started to enjoy our interactions, to look forward to them, infuriating as you can be at times. Basically, what I'm trying to say is that as it happens, despite a lot of my behaviour towards you suggesting the contrary, the truth is, I really like you, Jack Siddall.'

Jack chuckled. 'That was a speech worthy of Darcy's clumsy first proposal to Elizabeth,' he said.

I pulled a face. 'Sorry, was it that bad?'

His expression grew serious. 'I think we're both as inept

as each other when it comes to trying to convey what we really mean.'

'I'll try again.' Or at least, that was what I had intended to say, but the words didn't emerge properly because Jack had closed the distance between us, his mouth a mere breath away from mine.

'May I?' he asked.

I decided action rather than words was the best way of responding. I pressed my lips against his and rejoiced in the rightness of the sensation of his mouth joining with mine. Perhaps my heightened emotions were a result of the stress of Hilda's disappearance followed by the overwhelming relief of her return, but at that moment, I didn't care. The man had been discombobulating me for weeks, and now he was sending my senses awry in the best possible way. I pressed myself against him and shivered with delight as he cupped the back of my head, his fingers teasing their way through my hair, sending my curls into even wilder disarray than normal. I responded by tracing my hand down his spine towards his narrow hips trying to pull him closer still, until a cold wet nose shoved itself between us, forcing us apart.

Jack grinned ruefully. 'I think Hilda's objecting to being a third wheel. Perhaps we should head somewhere less public.'

There was nothing I wanted more at that moment.

He interlaced his fingers with mine and we continued our walk back towards the boats.

'Hang on a minute,' I said as a thought belatedly occurred to me. 'What made you think of Darcy's cringy proposal anyway? Have you been watching the film again?'

Jack gave a sharp intake of breath.

'How very dare you? I happen to have read the book now,' he said in a proud tone.

'You finally decided to see what all the fuss was about?' I teased him.

'You seemed so passionate about it, that I couldn't resist,' he responded, sending an instant glow through my veins. 'I can confirm I'll definitely be tapping you up for all my book recommendations in the future.'

'You do know the way to a girl's heart,' I said, immensely touched by his words. 'I shall take great delight in initiating you to the wonders of my book collection.' I giggled. 'That sounded a bit suggestive.'

'When it comes to you, I am very open to suggestions,' replied Jack.

---

'You certainly are,' I said a while later as I rested my head on Jack's chest. I'd always doubted whether the bed in my cabin would be comfortable enough for two people and I was delighted to have been proved wrong. Admittedly the logistics of two six-foot individuals fitting into the confined space had been a bit interesting to start with, but with a lot of laughter and some most enjoyable experiments we'd found we fitted together there just right.

'I am what?' he asked, idly sketching a pattern on my

inner wrist before lifting it to his mouth and pressing a kiss on its sensitive skin.

'Open to suggestions,' I said, responding with a teasing exploration of my own. It felt so right to be curled up together like this, prejudice and misunderstandings in the past, Hilda safely home, fed, watered and catching up on sleep in the bookshop cabin. There was no way of knowing what the future might hold for Jack and me, but I was excited to find out.

'Always happy to oblige, Ms Bramble,' he said, his voice rumbling against my ear. 'May I make one of my own?'

I propped myself up on one elbow and looked down at him, enjoying his expression of pleasure as my hair tumbled around his face, tickling his neck. 'I'm all ears.'

He responded by pulling me down for another kiss.

'I like this suggestion,' I whispered against his lips.

'Me too. I'm afraid what I was actually going to suggest was rather more prosaic,' he said.

'Intriguing. Fire away, Mr Siddall.'

'What I was wondering was whether I might make us some dinner, Ms Bramble? It's a long time since lunch, and a lot has happened since then.'

As if it had heard the suggestion, my stomach grumbled, and I laughed.

'That sounds like an offer I can't refuse. After all, it's important we keep our strength up for any future suggestions we might like to indulge in.'

In deference to any passing ducks, Jack pulled on some clothes before he left to start setting up a romantic dinner for two in the towpath garden. Remembering the sparse contents of his fridge, I suggested I take charge of the food after all, while he happily agreed to pick out a special bottle of something from the Jericho Wine Barge to toast Hilda's safe return. I put a couple of portions of the lasagne which had been intended for the Food and Fiction event into the oven, and while I waited for it to reheat, I gave Hilda her extra treats as recommended by the vet.

'Don't get too used to this, Hildy-girl,' I said, as she practically inhaled the food. 'You'll be back to normal rations tomorrow.' She thumped her tail happily, enjoying the moment in the way that dogs are so good at doing.

'Dinner is served,' I said, emerging from the Oxford Bookship a short while later, a plate of steaming lasagne in each hand. Hilda trailed me closely, no doubt hoping that I might be about to accidentally drop some of it. 'Oh Jack, that's beautiful.'

Twilight had fallen, but the table awaiting me was bathed in the warm buttery glow of a candle lantern. The soft scent of flowers from the small vase at the centre of the table filled the air, while two glass flutes stood ready by a silver bucket full of ice.

I set the plates down and stroked Hilda, as Jack gently eased the cork out of the bottle of Prosecco. The way he did it with such care so as not to startle my dog made me like him even more.

He poured the bubbling liquid into the glasses and then passed one across to me.

'Here's to Hilda's safe return,' he said as we clinked our glasses together.

'And here's to the best neighbour I could have hoped for.'

'I thought the best neighbour was no neighbour?' he said with a twinkle.

I took a sip of Prosecco, pretending to consider my answer. 'Well, you're here now. Better the devil you know, and all that. I guess I'd miss you if you went. Just maybe.' The warmth of the smile I gave him left him in no doubt that my feelings were stronger than my words would suggest.

'I shall endeavour to prove my worth still further,' he responded. 'Once we've eaten, of course.'

'I'll look forward to that,' I said.

We tucked into the meal, although I couldn't have told you what it tasted like because my attention was solely on the man sitting opposite me. At some point my phone pinged but I didn't bother to check the screen. I wanted to relish every moment with Jack. The morning would be soon enough to see if Liam had taken my bait.

And then once the final bite of achingly sweet baklava had been consumed, we retreated indoors, where Jack demonstrated that he was as good as his word.

## Chapter Thirty-Two

The next morning, I was setting up the sign for the Oxford Bookship on the towpath – slightly later than usual, having been delayed by saying goodbye to Jack before he headed off on a trip to the wine wholesaler – when Hilda suddenly started growling.

'Hey, girly, that's not like you. What's the matter?' I asked as she backed up.

Spotting Liam hurrying towards us, I rested my hand gently on Hilda's head to reassure her.

'You got my text then? You found her in Jack's shed?' said Liam, his phone already out ready to record my reaction. 'I couldn't believe it when I got the DM from a viewer saying they thought they'd heard her in there. I'm so happy she's back safe and sound.'

He tried to stroke Hilda, but she moved behind me, burying her head in the folds of my skirt, no doubt pretending to herself that if she couldn't see Liam, he wasn't actually there. I slid my mobile out of my pocket and surreptitiously pressed the record button before resting it on top of the shop sign. It wouldn't be a professional shot, but as long as it picked up what was said, that was what mattered.

'I did find her. Can you send me the viewer's DM? I'd really like to send them a personal thanks for letting us know where she was.'

Before he could respond, I plucked his phone out of his hands. 'Which platform was the message on?' I asked, as casually as I could manage, while my heart pounded with adrenalin. 'I can't see anything in your Insta DMs.' I clicked into a storage folder and started spooling through the raw footage in there. 'No, nothing on your TikTok either.'

'Maybe it was on YouTube. Actually, I might have accidentally deleted it,' said Liam. 'Can I have my phone back, please?'

I channelled my inner Miss Marple and prepared myself for the confrontation. 'No, I'm going to keep hold of it for now. There was no DM, was there?'

Liam gaped in horror at me. 'What are you talking about?'

'You didn't need a private message to say where Hilda was because you knew exactly where she was all along.'

'That's ridiculous,' he said. 'Of course I didn't know that.'

He even had the audacity to smile at me. He wouldn't be smiling for much longer.

'You knew because you put her there, after you stole her and kept her hostage on your boat first. There's proof here. I can't believe you had the audacity to film her on board there.' I turned the phone round so he could see it. 'Look, that's the upholstery on your bench. It's unmistakeable.'

Liam tried to snatch the phone back, but I neatly sidestepped him.

'That's from when we had that drink together,' he said.

I shook my head. 'You're going to have to try harder than that. I didn't bring Hilda with me then. And the footage has a date stamp of Saturday lunchtime.'

He was starting to look unsettled now.

'The date settings on my mobile keep playing up. I can explain, it's not what it looks like,' he said, lunging for the phone again. I held it out of his reach.

'I found her. And I was looking after her for you,' he tried again.

I shook my head. 'You should stop lying now, Liam. Every moment of the search for Hilda is etched into my memory. I'm not going to get over the trauma of it for a long time. And I know for a fact that the time on this date stamp is before I bumped into you on Saturday afternoon. I was on my way to search Castle Mill Stream, but you said you hadn't seen her. I needed to get back to tell the Food and Fiction guests the event was off so I foolishly believed you...' The words caught in my throat and I swallowed, steeling myself to get to the end of this confrontation '...I believed when you said you hadn't seen her, and I trusted your promise that you'd keep an eye out for her when you were travelling on the *Lydia*. But Hilda was actually on board your boat the whole time and you were trying to keep me away from Castle Mill Stream, because you knew if I went anywhere near, she would have barked to let me know where she was. You pretended to be my friend, but you stole my dog and cast my boat off to cover your traces.' Liam was shaking his head, but I pressed on. 'I'm naively hoping it was a spur of the moment thing after you happened to find the Bookship unlocked, but your later actions suggest there was something much more calculated going on. If you'd let her go after keeping her in your boat for a couple of days, I probably wouldn't have suspected you, but you broke into Jack's shed and locked her in there to make it look like he was the one responsible for her disappearance. And you only made up the bit about receiving a DM tip-off after I got in touch asking if you'd heard anything. How long were you going to leave her locked in there by herself?' With an effort, I lowered my voice. I refused to lose my dignity in front of this man. 'What were you hoping to achieve by setting Jack up? Did you imagine I was going to accuse him? I think you did this hoping that he would be publicly vilified, in some kind of misguided revenge for losing your job. Which was entirely your own fault, let's be quite clear about that. The whole thing is unforgivable. Can you imagine how frightened Hilda must have been?'

'I took good care of her the whole time. I never intended for her to stay in the shed for long. I left her with food and water,' Liam attempted to defend himself, finally recognising there was no point trying to deny it any longer.

'Oh well, that makes it all okay then,' I said sarcastically.

His shoulders relaxed a little.

'In case you're in any doubt, no, it bloody doesn't. It was totally irresponsible behaviour. What on earth possessed you? I don't know why I'm surprised though. Kidnapping Hilda wasn't the first time you'd tried something reckless as part of your mission to frame Jack, was it?' I was pacing up and down now, unable to contain my nervous energy. 'My stolen cable that you so kindly managed to find a like-for-like replacement for? What are the odds that if I compare the cable I'm using with the serial number on my original receipt, it will turn out to have been my own power cable that you oh-so-kindly "lent" back to me after you nicked it? If I push Eric, will he let slip it was you who instigated the complaint which led to the spot inspection? I'd be willing to bet my mooring I'm right.' I jabbed my finger towards him. 'There you were all the time, pretending to be the hero, creating situations to make Jack the scapegoat and drip-feeding me your insidious hatred of him. Did you plan for me to snap and accuse him of doing all these terrible things live on your channel, destroying his reputation for you? He tried to be your friend. Your nasty vendetta against him sickens me.'

I stared at the man who was shrinking before me, wondering why I'd ever considered him charming.

'I did it for you too,' he tried.

I actually snorted in disgust.

'What kind of warped logic is that? I'm at a complete loss as to understand why you would think stealing my dog and putting me through all kinds of stress would be something I would welcome.'

'I thought it would boost your online profile. And mine,' he added in a quieter voice.

His response nearly took my breath away. I shook my head.

'I'm sorry, I must have misheard you, because I thought you said part of your motivation was for social media likes, and no one in their right mind would think like that.'

'I figured creating an online buzz would help get you more customers. And get me more followers.' His tone suggested he still thought it was a perfectly reasonable course of action. 'You were grateful for the support I gave you. Nobody would have turned up to your stupid dating night if it wasn't for me,' he added.

I shook my head.

'No, you don't get away with saying that. There are at least three new couples who would argue the Blind Date with a Book night was anything but stupid. And you didn't think it was foolish when you were wringing it for content, did you? You promoted my events of your own accord. And there's a big difference between reposting an ad for a dating night and being cruel to a defenceless dog for clicks.'

Liam's face was ugly with anger. 'You've no idea what it's been like for me. I used to have a flat in Canary Wharf, and ever since I lost my job thanks to Jack bastard Siddall I've been stuck slumming it in a caravan on water. You don't know how tough it is trying to carve out a niche as an influencer. Sure, it's good to have fans, but the reality is that it's hustle hustle hustle all the time. Viewers are so fickle. Half of them don't even bother subscribing to the channel or watching my posts all the way through to the end, and all sponsors care about is the metrics.' He put on a silly voice. '"How many subscribers? How many views?"' Liam threw his arms up in the air. 'My numbers were falling until that video of you jumping onto the Wine Barge went viral. Then suddenly my channel was on the hot list again and the sponsors were chasing *me* for partnerships rather than the other way round. And then after that, my DMs were full of "How's that book girl doing?", "Has she saved any more boats?" Yadda yadda yadda. My viewers wanted drama, so that's what I had to provide for them. I had no choice but to do the things I did.'

'You always have a choice, Liam. The real issue is whether you're decent enough to make the right one.'

He shook his head, as if trying to block me out.

'I made choices that were the best for me *and* you, Molls. You can't argue with the fact that you've had more customers since I started featuring you and engineering decent storylines involving you.'

'There's so much to unpack here. For a start, I prefer to make my own choices, thank you very much, rather than having someone making decisions for me. As to "engineering decent storylines", this is my actual life we're talking about. I'm not some plaything to mess around with. I don't deserve your cruelty. And neither does Jack.'

'Oh poor little rich boy Jack Siddall,' he snapped. 'He had it in for me from the first day I started at that firm.'

I rested a reassuring hand on Hilda's head, gathering strength from her presence. 'On the contrary, from what I understand, he looked out for you and considered you to be his friend until you betrayed him. It's clear the only person you truly care for is yourself.'

'Yeah, well, good luck with proving I've done anything wrong,' said Liam.

I handed his phone back and picked mine off the shop sign, quickly checking the screen.

'Actually, I don't have to prove it. You are the architect of your own vulnerability. All this effort you've put into increasing your platform and dragging Jack and me along for the ride means there's so much more at stake for you nowadays. And I've recorded our entire conversation. What would your viewers think if I posted the video online? Do you imagine sponsors would be so keen to associate themselves with someone who has so much mud attached to them?'

The expression of sheer horror on Liam's face could almost have made me feel sorry for him, but one look at Hilda's still trembling haunches steeled my resolve.

'Please don't cancel me,' he said quietly.

'Why shouldn't I? From what Jack's told me, you were offered a second chance before when you were allowed to resign from your position as a trader rather than being fired as you deserved. You clearly didn't learn anything from that episode, so how do I know you won't move on to the next victim now that you've finished with your games here? Someone needs to stop your path of destruction.'

'I won't do anything like this again, I give you my word,' he said.

'As you know, I deal in words. And I'm afraid I put very little value on yours.'

'I'll leave the area. I promise, after today, you won't ever see me in Oxford again,' he offered, the desperation in his voice growing. 'Please don't destroy my reputation. I don't know how else to make a living.'

'You're the one who's doing the destroying. How about making a living like the rest of us try to? By being honest and straightforward in your dealings with other people. We had this conversation before. If you have to resort to trickery and deception to get what you want, then you're not meant to have it.' I took a breath and made my decision. 'Look, here's what I'm going to do. I promise that I won't release this recording'—I held up my hand to stop his prematurely delighted reaction—'on the condition you promise in turn that this is the last of your underhand behaviour. You'll leave the area, and you won't come back to Oxford. You'll stop harassing Jack, and you'll think about the consequences of your actions. And while you're at it, stop advertising those dodgy protein drinks. If I hear the slightest rumour of you being up to your old tricks, then I'll publish this video online. You should remember that the boating community is a close-knit one, my best friend is a journalist who you heartlessly and very short-sightedly ghosted, and I'm highly motivated to ensure that you stay on the straight and narrow.'

Liam pursed his lips as he considered his options. I think he was still hoping I would relent and all of the trouble he was in would magically go away.

'How about you look at it as an opportunity for a fresh start?' I suggested. 'I followed you before you started all these silly tricks, and I know I wasn't the only one. Why don't you build a platform based on decent behaviour and an honest relationship with your viewers? Surely that's going to have more value and longevity?'

I didn't want to have to use the video in the future. It didn't sit right with me having this kind of hold over a person, whatever they'd done, but on the other hand, if I didn't take action, what was to stop him moving on to the next victim? Somebody else might come off even worse in their dealings with him.

Liam's shoulders slumped. 'I guess that makes sense. I'm sorry.' For the first time, he did seem to have some sense of shame about what he'd done.

I nodded in acknowledgement of his words. 'Thank you. I'm glad you've had the decency to apologise. I hope your channel brings you greater happiness in the future.'

And then Hilda and I watched him walk down the towpath and out of our lives.

# Chapter Thirty-Three

'Was that the *Lydia* I saw steaming at great pace towards the Thames?' asked Jack as he arrived back at the boats a while later, towing a heavily laden trolley behind him. I noticed that along with the wine bottles and supplies for his bar, he had a bag of Hilda's favourite dog biscuits stowed in there as well as a box with Becki's Bakery branding on it which I suspected might contain a treat or two for us humans to share. He was a very thoughtful man. I only wished I'd noticed it sooner.

'Liam decided it was time to start making better choices,' I said. 'Take a look.'

Jack watched the video in silence. As the confrontation came to an end, he put his arms around my waist and pulled me closer.

'I'm sorry. I feel responsible for what he did. If I hadn't intervened when my dad wanted to fire him, Liam might have learnt his lesson then and not ended up causing so much trouble for you.'

I squeezed him back. 'There were a lot of ifs and mights in that statement. There's only one person responsible for Liam's poor choices, and that's Liam himself. You wanted him to have a second chance because you're a good person. I'm beginning to think it's best not to dwell too much on the might-have-beens. After all, there's a might-have-been scenario where we never met, and that would have been somewhat disappointing.'

I deliberately understated it, trying to play things cool, although I have no doubt that my face gave away how I really felt.

Jack laughed and took a step back, assessing me with an expression which made my skin tingle in glorious anticipation. 'Only somewhat? I think I need to work on persuading you to upgrade your vocabulary there.'

'I might be open to persuasion,' I said with a grin. 'Why don't you have a go now?' I took his hand and led him onto the Oxford Bookship, while Hilda generously stood guard over the trolley in the towpath garden.

---

Jack's powers of persuasion proved to be most effective. It was still early days, of course, but everything was brighter when he was around. The rest of July passed in a whirlwind, our days filled with books and dog walks and ice creams in the sun, and the nights with drinks under the stars and laughter and whispered conversations entwined together in the dark before the canal gently rocked us to sleep. Life would have been pretty much storybook perfect if it hadn't been for the uncertainty about the mooring fees which was still looming on the horizon. Despite enjoying my best few weeks of trading yet, helped in no small part by the Words and Wine nights Jack and I had started running jointly, I was still a thousand pounds short of the four and a half grand I needed to pay my mooring fees.

'Relax, we'll find a way,' said Jack, massaging my shoulders as I hunched up over my laptop going through my end-of-month accounts for July. I couldn't believe it was already August. It would pass in a flash I knew, and then what? I needed to start facing the very realistic possibility that I wouldn't make my target.

'*I'll* find a way,' I said.

'Yes, I know you will,' he corrected hastily. Our first and only disagreement since we'd got together had been caused by Jack's suggestion that he lend me the money to pay the mooring fees. It had been a generous offer, one which I knew he'd made with the best intentions, but the Oxford Bookship was my responsibility; additionally, I didn't want anything money-related to taint my burgeoning relationship with him. The only thing that I would allow Jack to pay for was the repainting of the Oxford Bookship, as he was the one who'd damaged it in the first place. I'd booked the repair work in for September, figuring I might as well fit it in during the brief lull between the end of the school holidays and the start of the university term.

Of course, if I didn't find the rest of the money for the mooring fees then the painting would coincide with the start of my new itinerant bookselling lifestyle. Because I was determined that whatever happened, I wasn't going to give up on my shop.

'But if I don't raise the money for the fees in time… No it's okay, hear me out.' I put my hand up to stop the reassurance I knew Jack was about to offer. 'It will be sad, but it won't be the end of my world. And I certainly won't let it be the end of my business. I've started to realise that there are so many different kinds of success. I spent far too long telling myself I was a failure because I don't have bits of paper with exam grades on, and I think differently from other people. But I'm okay with that now. I've started a business from nothing, and sure, it's had its challenges, but think about the people I've helped, the readers I've pointed in new and exciting directions, the couples who've found each other thanks to some gentle intervention from my Blind Date with a Book events. All those things are much more valuable indicators of success for me than numbers on a spreadsheet. Someone told me once that the advantage of living on a canal boat is that home is wherever you happen to moor up. And even if the Bookship and I have to travel further afield than Oxford for a while until I'm in a position to apply for a permanent mooring space here again, then that's what I'll do. Nana Rose knew when it was time for her to move on from the Oxford Canal, and I know she'll understand my situation and support me if I have to temporarily do the same. She's always had my back and she always will.' I shuffled round in my seat so I could take Jack's hands in mine. 'As for you and me, I'm not going to let a few miles of canal and river systems stand in our way. I know that what we have is stronger than any distance.'

He squeezed my hands and smiled at me. 'I know that too. I think you're amazing. You should be so proud of everything you've achieved.'

'I finally am,' I said, beaming back at him.

My phone buzzed, making Hilda leap up in excitement. 'Heck, is that the time? We'd better hurry. I have an author event to host.'

Jack started setting up the refreshments table while I concentrated on creating a display worthy of the *Worse Things Happen at Sea* book which I was helping to launch tonight. The publisher had issued special editions for independent bookshops, with beautifully sprayed edges with a wave motif which I made sure were on view.

'It looks good, but I think we're missing something,' I said as I stood back and took in the full effect. 'The display doesn't really convey the fact that it's a murder mystery book.'

Jack nodded. 'I would offer to spill some red wine on the ground to act like blood stains, but it would be a shame to waste it.'

'Agreed. But you've given me an idea. I might need your help for it though.'

'I'm at your service, as always,' he said cheerily.

'You may regret that,' I said with a laugh.

'You're right, I do regret it,' said Jack five minutes later as he lay on the towpath while I attempted to chalk around his body to create a mock murder victim outline. Hilda had taken Jack's position as an invitation to play and was doing her best to 'help' by licking his ears and trying to sit on him. As a consequence, my lines were turning out rather wobbly as the pair of us couldn't stop laughing.

'I hope that will wash away,' said a familiar voice.

I automatically straightened my shoulders and turned round ready to face further criticism. But the sight of Eric's companion instantly made me melt.

'Nana Rose, you came,' I said, rushing forward to give her a big hug.

'Try to stop me, my darling,' she said cheerily. 'The doc's got me on these new painkillers, and they've worked wonders. I feel almost as high as I did back in the '70s, now those were the days. I was practically running along the towpath to get here, wasn't I, Eric?'

'I could scarcely keep up,' he said in polite agreement, although I couldn't help noticing that Nana Rose was still holding tightly to his arm.

'Thanks for coming with her,' I said quietly to him.

'Don't rule me out yet, oh Molly mine. I'm the one keeping him upright, not the other way round,' said Nana Rose with a wink.

'Nothing gets past you, Nana,' I said. 'Long may it continue.'

'I'm not going anywhere, I promise you that,' she said. 'Now then, Eric, why don't we go and test out some of that wine I see over there and leave these young people to their chalk outlines.'

'The Oxford Boating Association regulations say—' started Eric, but Nana spoke over him.

'Never mind the regulations. It's only a bit of fun and it'll wash away, no problem. You should be celebrating the life these two are bringing to the canal. Even if it is in the form of outlines of dead bodies,' she joked.

Eric hesitated then shrugged his shoulders. 'You're not wrong there, Rose my dear. Now, what can I get you to drink?'

As the pair of them headed over to the refreshments table I leaned down and helped Jack to his feet. We stood back to survey my work.

'That looks suitable murderous, what do you reckon?'

He grinned. 'I'll try not to take it personally how distorted the victim's shape is. But nobody's going to be in any doubt about the genre of the book being launched tonight, that's for sure.'

I reached across and brushed away a bit of chalk which had somehow ended up on his cheek.

'I wouldn't want to chalk round anyone else's body,' I said, enjoying the way his expression softened in response.

'Erm, hello? I'm really sorry to interrupt. I hope I'm not too early.' A petite woman with a worried expression was coming towards us along the towpath from the direction of Isis Lock. She was accompanied by a tall man dressed in an outfit which made him look like he'd stepped straight out of an Evelyn Waugh novel. He seemed vaguely familiar, but I instantly recognised the woman from her photo in the flyleaf of the book we were about to sell.

'You must be Eva, thank you so much for having your launch here,' I said.

She smiled nervously. 'Thank you for agreeing to host it. It feels very strange having a whole night devoted to something that's been in my imagination for so long. I really hope some readers actually turn up. I have this horrid image that nobody's going to buy the book and everybody's going to hate it.'

The man at her side smiled and gave her a reassuring squeeze. 'As I keep trying to tell my sister those are completely contradictory fears. If nobody buys it, nobody can hate it.'

Eva pulled a face. 'Thanks for the underwhelming support there. This is my annoying big brother, Matthias,' she introduced him.

He reached out and firmly shook my hand, then Jack's.

'You're the guy who looked after the Jericho Wine Barge when we were running off to rescue my dog,' I said, the memory flooding back.

'Happy to be of assistance,' said Matthias. 'My sister had sent me along to scout out the place, although I'd been intending to check out the Oxford Bookship for myself anyway. Gran practically strong-armed her into having a launch. Eva's more the hide her light under a bushel sort.'

I laughed. 'I know what it's like to have a grandparent full of big ideas. I'm very glad you decided to go ahead with holding the event here. Let me get you set up by the signing table, Eva. I hope you're feeling strong, because we've had a lot of pre-orders.'

'See, I told you it would be alright,' said Matthias, nudging his sister.

In fact, the evening was more than alright. I sold all the copies I'd ordered of *Worse Things Happen at Sea*, and by the end of the night even Eva looked relaxed, posing for pictures in front of the Oxford Bookship sign and proudly clutching her book. I stepped away from the impromptu photoshoot and went below deck into the bookshop cabin to check what was happening in there. Matthias was the only customer still browsing, which meant I could fully take in the number of gaps on the bookshelves.

'Looks like it's been a successful night for all concerned,' said Matthias, gesturing at the display table which had been thoroughly picked over.

'That's what I like to see.'

'I'm glad I've caught you. I've been meaning to ask about your intriguing shelving system,' he said, gesturing at the 'Books to inspire bravery' label.

'Ah, that. I know it's a bit different from conventional bookshops, but then again, this is no conventional bookshop. I'm a reader motivated by emotion. I tend to choose books because they feel right in that moment. I can't always put my finger on why that's the case, but everything normally becomes clear as I get into the story. That's the kind of experience I want to create for my customers too.'

'That sense that the right book will find them at the right time?' asked Matthias. 'Yes, that's something I very much empathise with.'

He took a wallet out of the breast pocket of his jacket and extracted a business card from its folds.

'May I give you this? I'm hoping you might be able to help me with my new passion project.'

I examined the card which was designed to look like an old leatherbound book. Written on the book's cover in beautiful gold cursive was:

*Matthias Jennings*
*Book Sommelier*
*The Book Nook Guest House*

'What's a Book Sommelier?' I asked.

'An excellent question. Much like a conventional sommelier creates wine lists and recommends perfect food and drink pairings, I do something similar, but with books. I aim to match readers with the read they need at a particular point in their lives, exactly as you do here at the Oxford Bookship. Only I will be doing it in my hotel, the Book Nook Guest House in Holywell Street, which I'm opening this autumn. Each room will have a literary theme, and I'll curate individual reading menus for my guests so they can get the most out of their stay.'

I recalled running with Hilda a few weeks ago past a boarded-up building with the red book banner and the 'Coming Soon' poster.

'Ah, I think I know where you mean. How exciting, a book-themed hotel.'

'Yes, the renovation work is going well, but I have one fundamental problem I still have to resolve: I need a supplier for all the books, and I was very much hoping you might be able to help me.'

# Epilogue

As soon as the bank transfer had completed, Jack popped open the bubbly, accompanied by a joyful woof from Hilda.

I stared at the automated response which had already landed in my emails.

'I can't believe it's actually done. The mooring fees are paid. The Oxford Bookship is safe. I'm staying here. For the next year at least.'

Jack clinked his glass against mine.

'I would say you've got this mooring for as long as you want it, judging by the size of the order Matthias put in for his new hotel, plus the ever-growing waiting lists for your bookish events,' he said. 'You're definitely the best bookseller around.'

'You're not doing too badly yourself, Mr "Oxford's Hottest New Venue" as seen in *The Times* no less,' I teased, sketching the speech marks in the air. I'd framed the article and had it on display in the Oxford Bookship, ready to direct my customers next door, just as Jack did on the Jericho Wine Barge when people started browsing the new Blind Date with a Book trolley which he'd set up by the bar.

We moved to the well deck and settled down in a nest of blankets and cushions, Jack's arm around my shoulders and mine around his waist, enjoying the peace of our surroundings as the sun gradually sank towards the horizon, bathing the boat in a golden glow.

'If you had told me three months ago that we'd be sitting together like this, I'd have suspected you'd been drinking too much of your stock,' I said quietly.

Jack chuckled softly. 'Likewise. You terrified and enthralled me in equal measure. But as our Blind Date with a Book label said, "It's a truth universally acknowledged that first impressions shouldn't necessarily be trusted."'

I turned to face him. 'You remember my clue exactly,' I said.

'Of course,' he said simply. He reached forward and picked up the book he'd been reading earlier, opening it to reveal what he'd been using as his bookmark.

'That's my original label,' I said, touched beyond description that he'd kept it.

'It helped me find my place at your side. It seems right to continue using it as I move on to each new chapter.'

I opened my book to reveal its matching bookmark. I'd originally put it in the recycling after the first Blind Date with a Book event but fished it out when doing one of my regular searches for something to hold my place in my current read. My reason for keeping it hadn't been sentimental to start with, but now I wouldn't part with it for the world.

'I feel the same. I'm excited to see what our next chapter will bring,' I said.

I snuggled closer to him and smiled as somewhere in the distance a duck quaked cheerfully, while the water of the canal continued lapping gently against the hull of the Oxford Bookship.

# THANK YOU FOR READING
## *BLIND DATE WITH A BOOK*

IT WOULD MEAN SO MUCH IF YOU COULD LEAVE A REVIEW
ON ALL YOUR PREFERRED PLATFORMS AND SOCIAL MEDIA
TO HELP SPREAD THE WORD!

---

YOU CAN ALSO FOLLOW ME ON
INSTAGRAM OR FACEBOOK @EMILYKERRWRITES
AND CHECK OUT MY WEBSITE AT
WWW.EMILYKERRWRITES.COM
FOR ALL THE UPDATES ON MY LATEST WORKS.

# Acknowledgments

Thank you, lovely reader, for choosing Blind Date with a Book. It's been a sheer joy spending time on the Oxford Canal with Molly, Jack and Hilda, and I hope you've enjoyed it too. Oxford holds a very special place in my heart as I spent four years at university there. It's been wonderful walking its streets again in my imagination and I would highly recommend a visit to the city of dreaming spires if you get the chance. Many of the locations in Blind Date with a Book are real, but I've used some creative licence here and there.

The Oxford Bookship represents the amazing bookshops which can be found in every corner of the world staffed by passionate booksellers like Molly who love to match readers to their perfect book. I am so grateful to all you wonderful people who support my writing and recommend my books to your customers. You're the best!

Sticking with those at the top of their game, I'm indebted to my editor Jennie Rothwell and the rest of the hugely talented One More Chapter team for helping to bring this book into the world. It's a real privilege to work with you all. I'm also extremely lucky to be able to call Amanda Preston my agent. You are brilliant at what you do, always have my back and are just an incredibly lovely person!

Finally, love and thanks to my family, both of the two- and four-legged variety, you inspire me in everything I do. Thank you for always being there for me. (No, that doesn't mean you get extra dinner, sorry boys!)

*Romance might be closer than she thinks…*

Kat Fisher wishes her parents had thought harder before they chose her name. A self-confessed romantic, she dreams of finding a guy who can live up to her book boyfriends.

Former police officer Leo Taylor is trying to decide his next step following his departure from the force. His habit of spreading his belongings around the library where she works has been niggling at Kat for days, and his joke about her name is the final straw.

Kat and Leo might not seem like the perfect match, but romance might be closer than they think. If only they could read between the lines…

**AVAILABLE IN PAPERBACK AND EBOOK NOW!**

***One typo. Two complete strangers. Ten thousand miles between them…***

Amy and Cameron have never met. But when Amy receives an email meant for Cameron, their lives entwine in ways they could never have imagined.

Cameron lives a life of adventure as he navigates an expedition around Antarctica whilst Amy's life is firmly on solid ground in Edinburgh.

As their connection grows, Amy finds herself asking; is it possible to fall in love with someone you've never met?

**AVAILABLE IN PAPERBACK, EBOOK AND AUDIO NOW!**

***What happens on holiday doesn't always stay on holiday….***

When Lydia wakes up after a wild night out in Kefalonia with a tattoo saying 'Awesome Andreas', she's mortified. She doesn't remember meeting anyone called Andreas. And after all, she's an accountant with a five-year plan. She's definitely *not* a party girl. The sensible thing to do would be to research how to get the tattoo removed and move on. But she's had enough of being predictable.

Instead, Lydia decides to track down the mysterious Andreas, but the path to true love is never simple. Perhaps Lydia is looking in the wrong places, and the right man for her is just next door, if only she'd take a chance on him . . .

**AVAILABLE IN PAPERBACK AND EBOOK NOW!**

*Unable to afford their own homes, two friends decide to buy a renovation house together as a project. What could possibly go wrong…?*

Freya dreams of owning her own home.

Charlie is struggling to get a mortgage.

When the two old friends bump into each other on a night out, Charlie jokes that buying together would solve all their problems. He doesn't expect Freya to say yes, let alone yes to a less-than-perfect fixer upper.

Nobody said renovating their dream home would be easy, but will Charlie and Freya fall out of love with the house, or in love with each other…

**AVAILABLE IN PAPERBACK AND EBOOK NOW!**

*A laugh-out-loud, feel good romantic comedy
to curl up in bed with!*

Young lawyer Alexa Humphries's one true love is her precious duvet, yet she is torn from its comforting embrace every morning while the foxes are still scavenging the bins outside and doesn't get back until long after most normal people are already asleep. Worn down by the endless demands of her suspicious boss and her competitive, high-flying housemate and fellow lawyer, Zara, Alexa barely recognises herself anymore. This wasn't how life was supposed to be.

But today is different. Today, Alexa just cannot get out of bed to face the world. Everyone deserves a duvet day, don't they?

**AVAILABLE IN PAPERBACK AND EBOOK NOW!**

The author and One More Chapter would like to thank everyone who contributed to the publication of this story...

**Analytics**
Imogen Wolstencroft

**Audio**
Fionnuala Barrett
Ciara Briggs

**Design**
Lucy Bennett
Fiona Greenway
Liane Payne
Dean Russell

**Digital Sales**
Laura Daley
Lydia Grainge
Hannah Lismore

**eCommerce**
Laura Carpenter
Madeline ODonovan
Charlotte Stevens
Christina Storey
Rachel Ward

**Editorial**
Rosie Best
Kara Daniel
Charlotte Ledger
Federica Leonardis
Victoria Oundjian
Jennie Rothwell
Sofia Salazar Studer
Helen Williams

**Harper360**
Emily Gerbner
Ariana Juarez
Jean Marie Kelly
Kamrun Nesa
emma sullivan
Sophia Wilhelm

**International Sales**
Ruth Burrow
Bethan Moore
Colleen Simpson

**Inventory**
Sarah Callaghan
Kirsty Norman

**Marketing & Publicity**
Occy Carr
Chloe Cummings
Grace Edwards
Katie Sadler

**Operations**
Melissa Okusanya
Vanessa Coubrough

**Production**
Denis Manson
Simon Moore
Francesca Tuzzeo

**Rights**
Ashton Mucha
Alisah Saghir
Zoe Shine
Aisling Smyth

**Trade Marketing**
Ben Hurd
Eleanor Slater

**The HarperCollins
Contracts Team**

**The HarperCollins
Distribution Team**

**The HarperCollins
Finance & Royalties
Team**

**The HarperCollins
Legal Team**

**The HarperCollins
Technology Team**

**UK Sales**
Isabel Coburn
Jay Cochrane
Leah Woods

**And every other
essential link in the
chain from delivery
drivers to booksellers
to librarians and
beyond!**

One More Chapter is an award-winning global division of HarperCollins.

Subscribe to our newsletter to get our latest eBook deals and stay up to date with all our new releases!

signup.harpercollins.co.uk/
join/signup-omc

Meet the team at
www.onemorechapter.com

Follow us!

@onemorechapterhc

Do you write unputdownable fiction?
We love to hear from new voices.
Find out how to submit your novel at
www.onemorechapter.com/submissions